The Crispin Chronicles

The Crispin Chronicles

Dawn Knox

Best wishes

Dawn Knox

Chapeltown Books

British Library Cataloguing in Publication Data
A Record of this Publication is available from the British Library

ISBN 978-1-910542-87-3

This edition published 2022 by Chapeltown Books
Manchester, England

Contents

Her Ladyship's Garden

Mr Willetts pressed his ear to Her Ladyship's library door – his eyes screwed up tightly as he struggled to listen to the murmur of voices coming from within. His neck had become stiff from the strange position he'd assumed but he was determined to ignore the pain and to find out what his mistress and Mr Po Lin, her Gardener, were talking about. It was an affront to Mr Willetts' dignity that the lowly Gardener was allowed in for a discussion while he, Her Ladyship's butler, was excluded with no idea of the topic of conversation.

Such meetings took place frequently – usually after Her Ladyship had returned from a trip, but the wooden library door was so thick, all sounds coming from the enormous, book-lined room were muffled and indistinct. On one embarrassing occasion, he'd pushed his ear so hard against the door, the latch had given way and he'd stumbled sideways into the library and tripped over the cat. He didn't think Her Ladyship had believed he'd come over dizzy in the passage and had keeled over. She'd merely remarked he'd made a miraculous recovery in managing to leap to his feet and aim a kick at the cat.

Nothing more had been said by Her Ladyship about his dizzy spell and the subsequent sideways ingress into the library, since then, Mr Po Lin had always bowed politely with a serene, if inscrutable smile on his face whenever the two men met.

Too obsequious by far, Mr Willetts thought and reminded himself *he* was the butler of the Old Priory and therefore in charge of the house. Mr Po Lin was merely a Gardener. He tried not to dwell on the fact the Garden in question was actually an entire estate.

I am his senior, Mr Willetts reminded himself.

Nevertheless, he'd have been happier if he could find out what was going on and why he wasn't involved.

Her Ladyship could hear the scuffling of her butler's feet outside the door and knew when she left the library, she would see the mark of an ear on the polished wood. It amused her greatly that Mr Willetts was so desperate to learn what business she had with the Gardener, that he was now waiting outside the study, with his ear pressed to the door. Mr Po Lin also seemed to be aware the butler was eavesdropping and both he and Her Ladyship kept their voices low and just in case the butler's hearing was more acute than they realised, they were careful not to let slip any clues.

Finally, their business was concluded and as the Gardener was about to leave the library with the latest brown paper-wrapped parcel under his arm, Her Ladyship rang for Mr Willetts on the pretext of discussing her diary for the rest of the week, but actually to prevent him from snooping any further. Not surprisingly, it took the butler seconds to enter the door and he glared at the Gardener as he left.

Her Ladyship took an unnecessarily long time to open her diary and find the correct week, then to check and recheck dates and times. When she judged Mr Po Lin could no longer be seen from any of the windows of the Old Priory, she sent Mr Willetts to the kitchen to bring her tea and scones and crept down the stairs after him, to hear Cook explode.

"Scones?" Cook shrieked, "I haven't got any scones. It's Wednesday. Jam tart day. Monday's scone day. You'll have to take jam tarts up."

Mr Willetts grumbled and insisted it was his head on the block and that Cook ought to be better organised. It was scones or nothing.

"Then it's nothing!" There was the sound of pots being slammed down on the range.

Her Ladyship crept back upstairs to the study and sat at the desk. Shortly after, Mr Willetts knocked at the door and entered with a tray on which he'd placed an ornate teapot, matching sugar bowl, milk jug, cup and saucer. And jam tarts.

"Thank you, Willetts," she said, pretending not to notice the lack of scones, "please tell Cook I'll be down shortly for a kitchen inspection."

Her Ladyship smiled.

Mr Willetts smirked.

She knew he would enjoy delivering that message because there was nothing that enraged Cook more than a kitchen inspection. It was most diverting. And

Her Ladyship was often in need of distraction. For all the dates and times she'd discussed with Willetts, the truth was, she didn't have a great deal to do. She looked longingly out of the library window at her Garden. How wonderful it would have been to walk over the lawns and admire the flowers but severe allergies meant the closest she got to her Garden was to admire it from the windows of the Old Priory and to listen to Mr Po Lin's reports. But she remained involved in the running of the grounds by ensuring that whenever she went travelling in her ancient Morris Minor, she brought back a Garden Ornament carefully wrapped in brown paper. She never saw the final resting place of each piece because she left that to her Gardener, but it made her feel part of the process.

She tried to escape in the Morris Minor as often as possible – or as often as she could give Roger, the chauffeur, the slip. On each return, he made it perfectly clear it was *his* job to drive and that he didn't approve of Her Ladyship helping herself to the car, but she didn't take any notice. It was actually most diverting and worth stealing away in the Morris Minor just to watch Roger in the rear-view mirror waving his arms. She paid her staff twice the going rate so it seemed fair they provide her with a certain amount of entertainment periodically.

Mr Po Lin, would by now, have reached the Gazebo and would be unwrapping her latest acquisition. It was a sturdy Garden Gnome with his hands on his hips in a "Do as I say and do it now!" sort of attitude, and she knew the trusted Gardener would place it in the perfect position.

Mr Po Lin unwrapped the tough-looking Gnome and placed it in the shafts of afternoon light, on his table. He was certainly a handsome fellow with his rosy cheeks, twinkling eyes and no-nonsense attitude. The Gardener turned the figure around and surveyed him from all angles – he had a perfect position in mind for the Gnome who, he was sure, was going to leave his mark on the Garden and its Ornaments. But what should he be called?

Mr Po Lin tilted his head to one side and rubbed his chin. *Bartrum.* Yes, that would be his name. Having completed one of the most important parts of the procedure, Mr Po Lin drained the last of his tea and picked up the newly-named Gnome. Bartrum would be placed in the position the Gardener had selected and then he would return to his cottage and allow the magic to begin.

The following day, the Wooden Robin opened one wooden eye and peered at his clock. How, you may ask, does a wooden eyelid open and more interestingly, how does a wooden eye see? Well, obviously, it has something to do with the wooden eye being connected to a wooden brain – assuming the Wooden Robin has a brain, of course. Or it may possibly be because the Wooden Robin lives in Her Ladyship's Garden where the unbelievable is the norm.

The Wooden Robin doesn't lose sleep over complicated questions such as how he can see with wooden eyes, walk on wooden legs nor why his socks always slide down and gather around his wooden ankles. He always sleeps like a log and he usually dreams of soaring amongst the clouds on wooden wings. From high in the sky he looks down on Her Ladyship's mansion, surrounded by acres of Garden and he often spots Mr Po Lin, the Gardener, mowing the lawn. After a few aerobatic manoeuvres, he swoops downwards and skims over the top of the woods catching sight of his reflection in the lake. Spiralling ever closer to earth, he makes out the Gnomes, Elves, Animals and other assorted Ornaments who live together in the Garden. He calls out and they look up at him and wave because – by and large, they're a cheery bunch – and they're all his friends.

This is one of the Wooden Robin's recurring dreams. However, this particular dream will never come true because he can't fly – and that's probably a good thing because he also has a fear of heights.

The clattering of the alarm broke into his reverie and brought him back to earth with a bump. Today was the day he'd volunteered to deliver the post for

Deano, the Post Kangaroo, who wanted the day off to visit relatives. Clambering out of bed, the Wooden Robin selected a bib from his drawer which he tied around his neck, then checked the front doorstep for the postbag Deano said he'd leave there.

Over breakfast, the Wooden Robin looked through the letters he had to deliver. One of them puzzled him. It was addressed to someone called Bartrum. He didn't know a Garden Ornament with such a name but he wasn't perturbed – after all, new Ornaments appeared all the time and before long, it was as if they'd always been there.

Not far away, Bartrum awoke, yawned and stretched. He had the sense of having done the same thing before in this bed, yet the memory only seemed half-formed. With a start, he realised there was someone else in the bed with him and then immediately, he knew it was Mrs Bartrum, his wife. It was strange he had no recollection of being married, nor, indeed, anything beyond the previous evening; nonetheless, he seemed to have a history.

"Good morning, dear," said Mrs Bartrum. "Whose turn is it to make tea?"

"Mine, I think," Bartrum said although he couldn't remember ever having shared a pot of tea with her before.

Bartrum was amazed he knew the way to the kitchen and where everything was. He paused to consider while the water boiled, recalling the previous evening when realisation that not only was he in the grounds of a beautiful country estate but also that he was actually alive, had come instantly, as if someone had switched on a light. After that, he had made his way to the home he didn't know he owned and had gone to bed. He had no recollection of where he had originally come from, and was only aware that in the Garden he had an identity that was more of a blank canvas than an oil painting and instinctively, Bartrum knew it was up to him to paint something really quickly.

If the past seemed rather indistinct to Bartrum, the future and its possibilities appeared to be very clear. He was destined to be in charge. And no one would stand in his way. He stood with hands on hips as he watched the steam puff out of the kettle.

With a slice of toast between in his beak and Deano's postbag slung around his body the Wooden Robin hurried out of his house, stopping at the gate to pull up his socks. Without hesitation, he turned left towards the Bartrum residence. He couldn't quite remember who Bartrum and his wife, Mrs Bartrum, were, nor did he remember having been to their house before, but for some reason he had the idea they were important and he would deliver a letter to them first. When the Wooden Robin knocked on the door, a large, robust Gnome opened it and looked at him, echoing the surprise that he felt. If there were such a thing as déjà vu in reverse, this was it. Not that the Wooden Robin had ever heard of "déjà vu", he simply had the feeling that although initially, he had no recollection of Bartrum or his house, the more he thought about it, the more his memories came into being and appeared to have been there all along. How else could he have known that this was Bartrum and that he was important, nor where he lived?

Bartrum, too, was perplexed. This Wooden Robin with a green bib around its neck held out a letter to him and enquired about his wife and son.

Son?

So, he had a *son*?

Well, yes of course he did! Now he thought about it, memories of young Wilmslow flooded back and having been reminded of yet another aspect of his life, everything became much clearer.

And suddenly he realised he must also be acquainted with the Wooden Robin with his drooping socks and green bib. Instantly, he knew, as if he'd always known, that the Wooden Robin was a delightful, if rather simple, colour-blind bird who had once bought a job-lot of bibs, believing they were all red. Sadly, they weren't and occasionally he put the wrong one on. Bartrum remarked upon it and the Wooden Robin winced, realising he'd made an error, then with the last yank at his socks, he waved cheerio and set off to deliver the rest of the post.

How strange, thought Bartrum, the more he rummaged through the emptiness of his memory, the more crowded it seemed to become. He carried the letter into the kitchen and after he'd shared a pot of tea with his wife, he realised the canvas of his life had a few splodges on it and pictures were beginning to take shape. Bartrum knew it wouldn't be long before it was a beautiful painting. He would see to that.

The Letter from OFSGAR

By the time the final brushstroke had been applied to what had been the blank canvas of Bartrum's life and the resulting picture had been framed and hung on the wall, several other paintings had spontaneously begun and were in various stages of completion.

In an uncannily short time, Bartrum had taken over the Garden, launching Mrs Bartrum into the position of the First Lady Gnome of the Garden, making her very happy. Many of the other Garden Ornaments grumbled about the coup they hadn't foreseen nor noticed while it was taking place. But they only dared to moan in the privacy of their own homes or burrows, and no one dared challenge Bartrum in public.

However, his new position brought challenges as well as privileges. And he suspected he was holding one of those challenges in his hand now. It was in the shape of a letter which had been delivered by Deano, the Post Kangaroo. Bartrum already knew who it was from because he'd spotted the large letters on the front, proclaiming OFSGAR, Office of Standards in Gardens – and that could mean only one thing – Her Ladyship's garden was about to be inspected.

Bartrum remembered the previous inspection which had occurred shortly after he'd appointed himself Head Gnome. He hadn't foreseen the rigorous nature of the scrutiny, nor how much of a toll it would take on his marriage. Mrs Bartrum had been less than understanding during those dreaded two days and as his stress levels rose, she'd threatened to leave him if he ever got "snippy" with her like that again.

He must make sure this inspection ran more smoothly than the last or he'd have to think up some way of placating his wife. He could do as she'd begged during the previous inspection and simply resign but he liked being in charge of Her Ladyship's Garden. By rights, the position should have gone to one of the Marble Elves because everyone knew they were the most intelligent of the Garden Ornaments. Exactly *how* everyone knew was a mystery – it wasn't like there were exams to pass. And no one ever mentioned it but everyone knew that everyone knew.

Bartrum was clever, ambitious and ruthless in the extreme. He was also shrewd enough to recognise who were the bright sparks in the Garden and to enlist or even bully them into assisting him whenever his authority was under threat.

Today was going to be one of those days.

He held his breath as he began to slice open the envelope. There was no doubt there would be an inspection – the only uncertainty, was when it would be and how much time he would have to prepare. It didn't take a Marble Elf to know that if an inspector was to arrive that day, the Garden was likely to go into special measures and ultimately be closed down – even the Wooden Robin could have worked that out, if he were given a few clues and a prod with a sharp stick.

But what might happen if the Garden closed? Would they all be cleared away and thrown on the rubbish heap? Would Her Ladyship bring in new Garden Ornaments? Or would Mr Po Lin be fired and the Garden gradually turn into a wilderness. Bartrum shivered. He had no idea but it wasn't going to happen on his watch. He would call a meeting and insist that changes were made and the best person to supervise those changes, he knew, would be Crispin, the Marble Elf. Not that Crispin would relish the task. He was a gentle Elf who liked a quiet life. He already had a full-time job keeping Sylvester, his nephew – a grumbling, mumbling teenage Marble Elf – in check. But needs must. And Crispin would understand that unless the Garden Ornaments collectively pulled their socks up, life may never be the same again – quiet or not. And if for some reason, Crispin didn't grasp the importance of this inspection, then it was Bartrum's job to make him understand, by any means – fair, foul or otherwise.

A few hours later, Crispin was ready and waiting for his nephew, Sylvester. He clicked his tongue in disapproval.

"You're not going to Bartrum's meeting like that!"

"What? What?" said Sylvester, checking his reflection in the hall mirror. "I cleaned my teeth and combed my hair," adding "yesterday" under his breath.

Crispin's gaze travelled down Sylvester's figure and rested on his feet.

"What?" asked Sylvester again. And in that interesting way teenage boys have of not being able to spot the obvious when it comes to cleanliness and sensible clothes – he couldn't see it.

"Boots…" said Crispin, nudging Sylvester's right boot with his toe.

"It's clean!" snapped Sylvester.

"Yes, and that should help you work out what's wrong."

"I don't know what you're making such a fuss about. You usually complain when things *aren't* clean. Talk about making up the rules as you go along…"

"I'm not complaining because it's *clean.* I'm complaining because it's *mine*… and you're wearing it."

Sylvester looked down. On his right foot was a gleaming Elf boot with pristine, curled tip and on the left was his scuffed boot, with a tip that dangled limply.

"Oh… Well, where's my boot, then?"

"Wherever you left it."

Crispin decided it would be wiser to wait outside and not get involved in the door-slamming, drawer-slamming and frenzied swearing. He'd tidy up later, after the meeting. He looked at his watch. They'd have to leave in ten minutes whether Sylvester found his boot or not. Bartrum demanded punctuality and only death was an excuse for absence – and sometimes not even then.

Gnomes, Elves, Fairies and assorted animals waved and greeted Crispin as they passed his Toadstool on their way to Bartrum's meeting.

"Morning," trilled the Wooden Robin as he stopped to pull up his woollen socks. Crispin waved. "See you there," he called and checked his watch again.

Just four more minutes until they had to leave. Crispin closed his eyes and enjoyed the sun's warmth on his face. It was going to be a lovely day. But then as far as Crispin was concerned, every day was lovely in the Garden. Who could fail to be moved by the beauty of nature that was all around them?

Crispin checked his watch again. It was time.

"Sylvester!" he yelled.

The two Marble Elves made it to Bartrum's meeting with seconds to spare, although there was only room at the back, which suited Sylvester who was sulking.

Fluffy slippers with pom-poms are fine at home but if the laughter of a group of young Gnomes was anything to go by, they weren't likely to become must-have footwear any time soon in the Garden.

Although, as Crispin reflected, it's very hard to predict what might happen in the Garden and it wouldn't have surprised him to find Garden Ornaments out and about in fluffy slippers with pom-poms in the near future.

Nothing about the Garden ever came as a surprise to Crispin.

Well, it hadn't so far.

But Bartrum was about to change all that.

The Sweet Smell of Success

Gusty Bob arrived at the meeting and made for the small gap between the bottoms in the back row. There was no way he could fit into such a tiny space, even with the aid of the slimy mucous that covered his ample proportions but he'd noticed that in similar situations, space seemed to magically appear and on this particular occasion, he was confident the chaps would make room for him without any fuss.

At the right-hand side of the gap that was Gusty Bob's intended insertion point, Sylvester spotted the Stone Toad and went rigid. He shuffled to the left to fill the gap, then thought better of it as a long leg and webbed foot shot past his shoulder. He'd been too slow and the only option was to slide rapidly to the right – into Crispin.

"What are you doing?" Crispin yelped as he was shunted into the very large, very solid and very tattooed Gnome next to him.

Gusty Bob took advantage of the confusion and slipped into the tiny gap that had expanded when the frantic shuffling of bottoms, resulted in two people at the end of the row being forced off their Toadstools. There was now sufficient room for his width, including a buffering zone on either side. As he settled down, Crispin took in a lungful of air to compensate for being winded by Sylvester and simultaneously, the Stone Toad lived up to his moniker – Gusty Bob. Noxious gas was ejected from both ends of his slimy, amphibian body, filling the air with the fumes of decaying flies, worms and other rotting detritus.

Crispin coughed and spluttered. Others further away giggled and tittered, confident the evil cloud would have dissipated before it reached them.

"Order! Order!" Bartrum banged a rock with his gavel and scowled at the rows of assembled Garden Ornaments.

Gnomes, Elves and assorted animals and birds snapped to attention as Bartrum adjusted his glasses, placed his hands on his hips and scowled at them all.

"This sort of behaviour is typical of your lack of commitment to the aestheticalness of this Garden…"

" 'Ees what?" whispered Sylvester.

"He means the Garden is a shambles," replied Crispin.

Bartrum adjusted his hat and carried on.

"This cannot be allowed to continue. Rules will be enforced…"

Everyone groaned.

"And I will be closely watching the situation…"

"You and whose army?" muttered Sylvester.

"…assisted by my newly-appointed cohort of monitors…" continued Bartrum.

The audience sat up as one, eyes swivelling, looking for anyone who might be an informer.

"…who I will now appoint," finished Bartrum.

Suddenly, everyone seemed to find their feet completely fascinating. Everyone in the back row found Sylvester's pom-poms absolutely absorbing.

"You, you and you!" said Bartrum, pointing out two unfortunate Gnomes and the Wooden Robin. "And you and you!" he said, indicating Gusty Bob and Crispin. The Toad's sharp intake of breath eventually had to find release but by this time, Crispin was holding his nose.

The gap between Gusty Bob and the other "volunteers" increased imperceptibly until Bartrum, who was issuing orders, found he was having to turn his head from side to side to keep everyone in view.

"Stop moving!"

The gap stabilised.

"Correct Garden Uniforms must be worn. With immediate effect. So far today, I've seen Gnomes wearing raincoats, sombreros, flipflops. This will not do. Everyone needs to be in regulation uniform. And you!" he pointed at the Wooden Robin. "You're wearing odd socks."

The Wooden Robin blushed. "I'm s…so sorry, I got confused…"

"And as for that green bib…"

The Wooden Robin looked down at his chest in horror.

"Well, just do your best…" said Bartrum, faltering slightly when he saw a fat tear roll down the stricken robin's wooden beak.

He turned back to the others. "You will check that all equipment is in working order. Doggett's fishing rod no longer has a hook. What's the point of a Fishing Gnome who can't catch fish? And if Perkins thinks it's funny he's swapped his wheelbarrow for a toy tractor, then you need to convince him otherwise. Understood?"

The team of monitors nodded and Gusty Bob let loose a loud belch.

Bartrum winced and the gap widened once more between the Toad and the other monitors.

"You have until full moon to ensure this Garden is once more a place of aestheticalation."

"Ees what?" whispered the Wooden Robin.

"Clean and tidy," whispered Crispin.

Three days later, Bartrum assembled his monitors. "It appears the smartening up of this Garden is quite beyond you! I see very few improvements… and I'm not happy. I'm not happy at all. Why are there still Gnomes out of uniform? I'm thinking specifically of Jubbly."

Crispin took one step forward and three sideways, away from Gusty Bob. "Well, sir, I asked him to change back into uniform but he said he was having an identity crisis and that he had to find his inner self. Once he'd done that, he'd wear whatever was appropriate."

"I see, well that explains the curling tongs and can

of hairspray, I suppose. I have to say his feminine side seems to be winning. But that doesn't explain the sombrero..."

"He feels he may be a Mexican trapped in the body of a woman, trapped in the body of a Gnome..."

"Well, he, she or Gonzalez had better make up their mind very soon because OFSGAR inspectors are due by the end of the month and you know what happens if they put you in special measures..." he paused dramatically.

Everyone looked at him blankly.

"You obviously don't realise the OFSGAR inspectors have the powers to close us down!"

They all gasped in horror. Gusty Bob's breakfast of squashed earthworm and mouldy bread had been fermenting nicely within his batrachian intestines and the resulting methane had inflated them almost to breaking point, so a gulp of air had been most unwise. His internal gaseous pressure became critical. Something had to give... and it gave, resulting in a prolonged, thunderous blast that manifested itself as a green haze that floated upwards into the morning air. Everyone fled.

They reconvened at the bottom of the Garden after it had been ascertained the noxious cloud was floating away from them and towards the Old Priory.

"No need to prolong this meeting," said Bartrum, nervously eyeing Gusty Bob, "I have only one thing more to say. Since you seem incapable of enforcing the rules, I will bring in a trouble-shooter…"

Crispin's elation was short-lived. Rather than being dismissed as he'd hoped, he discovered he was now part of a disciplinary force, under the direct command of a newly-appointed leader.

"Who is the trouble-shooter?" Crispin asked nervously, hoping Bartrum wasn't going to promote one of them, and more specifically, not him.

Bartrum tucked his briefcase securely under his arm, glanced anxiously at Gusty Bob and rocked onto the balls of his feet as if about to take flight.

"Susan," he said and hurried away with a purposeful stride.

"Susan?" asked the small Gnome. "Who's Susan?"

A shiver ran down Crispin's spine as he realised who Bartrum meant.

The shock had been so great, it momentarily deprived him of his senses or he'd have followed Bartrum and escaped before Gusty Bob got wind of the trouble-shooter's identity and particularly before they all got wind of Gusty Bob.

Instead, he blurted out, "Oh no, Bartrum's put Spiteful Sue in charge!"

The Wooden Robin's knees gave way. "No!" he wailed, as he sank to the earth.

"What're we going to do?" asked the small Gnome.

“We’re not going to panic, that’s what we’re going to do,” said Crispin, ushering everyone away from the Toad, “although you know what Spiteful Sue did to Gusty Bob the last time she was here.”

Thankfully, Crispin, the two Gnomes and the Robin made it into the begonias before Gusty Bob realised what was going on.

“No!” he yelled. The green cloud floated up into the plum tree, searing the leaves in its path.

Crispin, the two Gnomes and the Wooden Robin met in secret that evening, by the pond. They didn’t deliberately exclude Gusty Bob but then again, they didn’t try too hard to find him either.

“It’s just as well Bob’s not here,” said Crispin. “He gets much too agitated when the subject of Spiteful Sue comes up. I know cats have a good sense of smell and I can see why Gusty Bob might annoy her but what she did with that cork was really quite unnecessary.”

“This is all going to end in tears,” said the Robin, who was fulfilling his own prophecy. He wiped his beak noisily. “As soon as Spiteful Sue turns up, Gusty Bob will be so nervous he won’t be able to control himself.”

“I hope she doesn’t arrive before that green gas cloud disappears or she might do what she threatened the last time she was here,” said the small Gnome.

“What was that?” asked the Robin.

"She said his aroma upset her feline sensibilities and if he couldn't control his emissions, she'd fit him with a catalytic converter."

"Feline sensibilities," said Crispin thoughtfully. "Hmm, I wonder…"

Later that evening, Crispin found Gusty Bob hiding under an upturned flowerpot. They talked far into the night and finally, Crispin handed the Toad a large bag. He took it, saluted gravely and shuffled off into the begonias.

"What d'you mean he's gone?" squeaked the small Gnome indignantly. "That's just great! As if it's not bad enough being ordered about by a Nazi Cat, we're now down to three men."

"Four," corrected the Wooden Robin.

"Three," said the small Gnome firmly. "No one in this Garden takes a Robin wearing odd socks seriously…"

"Enough!" said Crispin. "If my plan works, Spiteful Sue won't be needed, the task force can disband and the Garden can go back to normal."

"We're listening," said the small Gnome, elbowing the Robin out of the way.

Several days later, at another Garden meeting, Bartrum banged his gavel on a rock, dislodging a tiny snail that lost its grip and slithered back down its slime trail with a whimper.

"Congratulations," said Bartrum shaking his head in wonder. "I don't know how you did it, especially with Susan disgracefully deserting us." He beamed at everyone. "But, we are finally ready for any nit-picking OFSGAR inspectors. By the way, you all look resplendable!"

"Re what?" asked the Robin.

"He's saying we look nice," said Crispin.

All it had taken was a length of rubber tubing, a bottle of water and instructions to Gusty Bob "to infuse the water with his unique fragrance" and once he had done that, he was to go on a brief holiday. Crispin had liberally sprinkled drops from the bottle of noxious liquid around the Garden and shortly after, Spiteful Sue had complained bitterly and flounced off.

In a hastily-convened meeting, of all the Garden Ornaments except Bartrum, Crispin pointed out that observing the Head Gnome's strict rules – just for a day or two – would be advantageous. Thankfully, everyone cooperated and even Jubbly agreed that he could explore his Gnome persona for a few days and wear regulation Gnome clothes. After all, as he pointed out in a heavy Mexican accent, what he wore as underwear, was his own affair.

It had seemed a shame to waste what was left of the specially prepared liquid they'd used to repel Spiteful Sue, so despite a few complaints from some of the Ornaments, Crispin dripped some around the Garden and warned everyone, if asked by the inspectors, to blame the pig farm a few miles away. The inspection had been carried out with great haste and there was no time to probe deeply into the lace peeping out of the bottom of Jubbly's jerkin, nor of the pair of pom-pom slippers that were lying discarded beneath a hedge and had been missed during Bartrum's pre-inspection inspection.

Yes, a disaster had been averted and it was all thanks to Crispin. Now the whole Garden could relax. The early morning sun was barely peeping over the top of the hedge when Crispin opened one eye. Today would be a day of rest he decided and he turned over for another snooze. For the first time in ages, he could relax. Spiteful Sue had gone, Gusty Bob was back from his "holiday", the OFSGAR inspectors had awarded the Garden an outstanding report and Bartrum was off to stay with his cousin for a week. There was just the problem of the revolting smell that hung over the Garden but the weather forecast was looking promising. With relief, Crispin informed everyone that the wind would be blowing in a north-easterly direction, away from the Garden.

Crispin didn't allow himself to feel guilty, after all, it wasn't his fault the stink was heading towards the pig farm and anyway, he consoled himself, it wasn't like they'd notice anything amiss.

A Visit from Peggy the Pram

"Crispin? Are you awake?"

"No! Go away. I'm having a duvet day. I don't intend to wake up until the day's nearly over."

"Okay, but you'll want to get up for this! The Garden Syndicate's won the Lottery! We're rich!"

Crispin weighed up the chances that Sylvester had been misinformed.

"Really?" he finally managed.

"Yes, I saw Bartrum at the Post Office getting the winnings and it was a big pile of notes. We're rich, I tell you!"

Crispin got up. There'd be no peace until he let his nephew into the bedroom and anyway, now, he was curious. Sylvester was a good chap – although sadly, sometimes a few toadstools short of a fairy ring, but if he'd actually seen Bartrum with the winnings…

"Get dressed!" Sylvester shouted over his shoulder when Crispin finally opened the bedroom door.

Sylvester was flinging open cupboards and drawers, searching through the contents in a frenzy.

"What on earth…?" Crispin surveyed the chaos.

"I can't find my wallet," said Sylvester. "You haven't seen it, have you?"

"You know I have! You told me to hide it the last time you got into financial difficulties. Remember? You signed up for that exclusive gym. You know, the one that was due to be built in the Sunken Garden, and surprisingly, still isn't there. Remember the debt collection people made our lives hell until I paid your backdated fees?"

"Oh yes, I'd nearly forgotten."

"Well, I haven't. I've only just managed to grow my eyebrows back. And until you learn your lesson, your credit cards are confiscated."

Sylvester scowled, thrust his hands in his pockets and stomped off.

Crispin groaned. Sharing a Toadstool with Sylvester was like being a permanent babysitter. But at least the wallet was safely tucked away in Crispin's pants drawer – a place Sylvester would avoid at all cost.

As Crispin dressed, he noticed Gusty Bob outside in the Garden. The Toad waved and shouted, "Bartrum's called an extraordinary meeting. You need to be in the Sunken Garden in five minutes."

Crispin waved cheerily and closed the window as Gusty Bob hopped off to summon the rest of the Garden Ornaments. He wanted to ask why the meeting wasn't going to be held in the normal place and he let his imagination run riot as he pulled his socks on. The meeting must surely have been called to announce the syndicate's win and hopefully to hand out the winnings.

When Crispin arrived at the Sunken Garden, most of the Ornaments had already gathered. A smiling Bartrum was standing next to a large object draped in a blue cloth. He banged his gavel on a rock, calling the meeting to order. This had been an act of showmanship rather than to actually call for silence. Tongues had not been wagging, although a few were poking out of mouths to assist their owners do a hard sum. The equation in question appeared to be X, "The total winnings" divided by Y, or "The number of Garden Ornaments" which would give M, "My share of the winnings". But no amount of tongue protrusion could come up with the answer until Bartrum announced the value of X, how much the syndicate had won.

"I have the greatest pleasure in announcing…" began Bartrum.

Everyone stopped the mental arithmetic.

"If that's the pile of money under that cloth, we're rich beyond our wildest dreams," squeaked the Wooden Robin.

"…that our syndicate has won the Lottery…" Bartrum paused for dramatic effect.

Garden ornaments cheered, whistled and waved. Gusty Bob scuttled off into the begonias and emerged a few seconds later.

"Has Gusty Bob taken up the trumpet?" the Robin asked Crispin. But there was no time to reply because Bartrum had banged his gavel again and everyone fell silent waiting for the all-important X to be announced.

"…knowing how much we all love the Garden, I've taken it on myself to spend the money on your behalf on a beautiful water feature, to be installed here in the Sunken Garden." He grabbed the cloth and with a flick of his wrist, he unveiled it.

There was a collective gasp.

"No!" wailed Sylvester. "This is dreadful!"

"It's not that bad," remarked the Robin, peering at the enormous stone shell, in which stood a statue of a scantily clad woman with a large urn on her shoulder, from which water would presumably pour.

Growls of dissatisfaction erupted and banging the gavel again, Bartrum carried on, "There's just one more item on the agenda. The cesspit needs cleaning and over the next few days, I'll be looking for volunteers."

Suddenly, Bartrum was alone in the Sunken Garden with Venus in her shell. Somewhere in the begonias, there was a long drawn out fanfare, and a green cloud rose skyward.

"You'll be on cesspit duty for the rest of your life if you damage that fountain," said Crispin wagging his finger.

"If I don't get some money I'm going to be dead for the rest of my life," Sylvester wailed. "It's all the fault of that stupid fountain."

"Just sit down and tell me what's happened," said

Crispin trying to sound calm. "It can't be that bad…" and knowing Sylvester, it couldn't be that bad – it would be worse.

"Well, when I thought I'd won some money, I bought a widescreen telly. Seven whole inches of High Definition, 3D, poke-you-in-the-eye-with-jazzy-colours, viewing. And now I can't afford to pay for it."

"But you can't have bought anything," said Crispin, glancing at the pants drawer. "I've hidden your credit cards."

"I know, I got it on hire purchase. If Bartrum had handed over the cash, I'd have paid it off today."

"This is probably a good time to point out there's no electricity supply in the Garden at the moment while the workmen are doing something in the Old Priory," said Crispin.

"You mean…?"

"Yes, a telly won't work."

"Well, in that case, neither will that stupid fountain," said Sylvester triumphantly.

"The fountain doesn't run on electricity, it's gravity-fed. And before you ask, we have an endless supply of gravity in the Garden. Now, go and cancel the television."

"That might not be an option."

"Because?" Crispin asked with a sinking feeling.

"Because I bought it from Peggy the Pram."

For a moment, Crispin was speechless. He ran a finger along each eyebrow, remembering the last time Peggy the Pram's rent collection boys had paid Sylvester a visit. Foolishly, Crispin had tried to be the Voice of Reason but it turns out Dragons and Gargoyles can't differentiate between reconciliation and obstruction. A jet of flame had shown Crispin what the Dragon thought of his Voice of Reason and the two Gargoyles had pulled some extremely scary expressions in case Crispin hadn't got the message.

"Cancel it!" said Crispin through gritted teeth. "Grovel if necessary. And don't touch that fountain!"

"Well? How did you get on?" demanded Crispin several hours later.

Sylvester was grinning. He had a small paper bag tucked under his arm.

"Did you cancel it?" Crispin touched his eyebrows and peeped through the curtains to see if Sylvester had been followed.

"Well, not exactly…" Sylvester smiled sloppily.

"No one goes to bed until you tell me what happened," said Crispin sternly.

"I decided to go and graffiti the fountain or cut its gravity supply but Venus smacked me with her urn. Anyway, when I came round, I was lying on the grass on my back and as I looked up, I suddenly realised what a beautiful woman she was. And do you know what?"

"Enlighten me."

"Well, I fell in love. Right there and then. I tried to apologise but she socked me again, so I thought I'd go and get some flowers and try to make a good impression. It just so happened Peggy the Pram was outside the garden gate and when I told her about the lottery money, the fountain, and falling in love, she said she could help."

"And you *believed* her?" Crispin squeaked.

"Yes, look! She let me have these half price." He took three small bottles out of the paper bag. "They've got a money-back guarantee. And she'll give me a week to pay for the television. Apparently, she can't give refunds, it's against company policy."

Crispin was beyond rage. His knees were also knocking.

When a pedlar had appeared at the garden gate some months before, with a pram full of wares, Crispin had jumped to several conclusions. The green outfit had led him to believe the pedlar was a leprechaun and since leprechauns always seemed to be male and Irish, he thought them reasonable assumptions to make. He'd been right about the leprechaun part. But completely wrong about the gender and nationality. If he'd thought about it, he'd have known there have to be lady leprechauns somewhere and apparently, Peggy was one of them. And surprisingly, she wasn't Irish at all. She came from London. Peggy the Pram turned out to be a streetwise Cockney Leprechaun with a group of friends she referred to as "The Boys".

One encounter had been enough for Crispin and now, he was about to become entangled with her and her henchmen again, thanks to Sylvester.

He picked up the tiny, ornate bottles one by one and read the labels, "Essence of Dreams, Wish Tonic, Love Elixir," and removing the top of the Wish Tonic, he took a sniff. There was no scent at all and in all likelihood, it contained water.

"You realise you stand no more chance of paying her in a week's time than you do today, don't you?" Crispin asked. It would undoubtedly mean a visit from Peggy's Boys. He took his rucksack out of the cupboard. It was time he went to stay with his cousin for a few weeks – Sylvester was beyond hope.

Without permission from Bartrum, Crispin knew he'd be in trouble if he left the Garden. And with the cesspit beginning to reek, he knew what his punishment would be. But at first light, he'd beg for permission to leave and he'd advise Sylvester to do the same. It was quite likely they wouldn't have a Toadstool to come back to, once "The Boys" had visited but at least they'd both still be alive.

However, Sylvester stayed out all night and the only clue to his whereabouts was the empty bottle of Wish Tonic on the table. He'd been talking non-stop about Venus, and Crispin could imagine exactly what he was wishing.

That night, the chair Crispin had propped under

the door handle was no match for Peggy and her Boys. They carried out a systematic search of the Toadstool but Sylvester hadn't returned and they could find nothing of value. The pants drawer had proved a step too far, even for The Boys and it remained undisturbed.

Having learned to keep the Voice of Reason to himself, in desperation, Crispin tried the Voice of Dishonesty.

"Sylvester's in the Shed," he screamed, as a shaft of flame streaked across the top of his head.

"What happened?" Sylvester asked, peering at the singed furrow in Crispin's usually neat hairdo.

"It was done by a Dragon looking for you!" snapped Crispin.

"Has he gone?"

Crispin nodded.

Sylvester slid into a chair with a groan. "I wish I'd never got up this morning."

"Technically you didn't get up. You never went to bed," said Crispin.

"Don't remind me."

"I'm still alive, thank you for asking, and by the way, Peggy and The Boys won't be back." Crispin slammed a drawer shut.

"Sorry," said Sylvester, "I can see you've been through it but I've had such a bad night. Where are they, by the way?"

"I told them you were in the Shed."

"Not the Shed of No Return?"

Crispin nodded and allowed himself a smile.

"But no one who goes in the Shed, ever comes out," said Sylvester.

"Exactly!"

"Ah! I see! Very clever!" said Sylvester.

"So," said Crispin, "what happened to you?"

"Well, I tipped the Love Elixir into Venus' water and the Essence of Dreams for good measure and guess what?"

"She thumped you again?"

"No, she fell in love with me."

"Well, from where I'm standing, your life looks pretty rosy. Peggy's gone and Venus loves you. What's the problem?"

"We broke up. I couldn't turn the gravity off and she just gushes water the whole time. It was playing havoc with my bladder and I had to keep going off to the gents. And after standing in that water a while, I went all wrinkly. She's a lovely girl but it'd never have worked."

Nightly Disturbances

He didn't want to go out on such a night but since Bartrum had appointed him Law Officer, Crispin had no choice – well not until the fuss died down anyway.

The ridiculous sheriff's badge Bartrum had pinned to Crispin's chest and insisted was always worn, gleamed dully as he stepped out of the Toadstool onto the damp grass.

He turned up his collar against the drizzle.

"Where're we patrolling tonight, guv?" said a voice from behind an upturned flower pot.

Crispin winced.

"Don't call me that. And we are *not* patrolling anywhere. *I* am going for a walk," Crispin said, crossing his fingers. He didn't like lying but Bartrum expected results, and saddled with his two deputies, Crispin was doomed to failure. There was no doubt, deputising Sylvester and the Wooden Robin had been an act of sheer folly.

"Well, I'll walk with you," said Sylvester, emerging from behind the pot. He'd obviously been polishing his deputy's badge because it gleamed brightly on his puffed-out chest. "Us lawmen have got to stick together in our never-ending fight against the criminal underworld."

"All right, all right!" snapped Crispin, who knew there was no way he was going to shake off Sylvester.

"Just keep your voice down or the Wooden Robin'll hear."

"Hear what?" asked the Wooden Robin, hopping out from behind the pot. His deputy's badge shone brightly at the top but the bottom was splattered with mud. Pinned to his green bib, it was so large in comparison to his tiny body, it looked like a knight's shield. Every so often, the bottom point caught in his sock and sent him sprawling. Crispin had suggested, then ordered and finally begged the Robin to remove it for the sake of his neck and for the sake of Crispin's sanity but there was no way the Robin was going to take it off.

"It's my body armour," he trilled proudly.

"But you can barely walk."

"Yes, but when the shooting starts, I'll be safe."

"There's not going to be any shooting. This isn't Garden CSI."

"Well, you never know," trilled the Robin happily.

"C'mon," said Sylvester excitedly, "while you two are chatting, all sorts of crimes are being committed."

"They're not," said Crispin wearily. "Okay, follow me. But keep quiet!"

Sylvester was remarkably good at creeping along silently, although he needn't have bothered because the Robin's cries of "Wait for me!" echoed around the entire Garden. There could be no covert surveillance while the Robin kept tripping over his badge or stopping to pull up his socks.

At least it had stopped raining.

Despite the threat of being put on cesspit duty if he resigned, Crispin was seriously considering the possibility. If he couldn't solve the case of the Nightly Disturbances, he'd probably end up on cesspit duty for the rest of his life, anyway. He'd planned to hide somewhere near the Shed of No Return, although not too close because you just never knew if the odd person might find their way out and he was keen not to run into Peggy the Pram and her Boys.

The Shed was in the more disreputable part of the Garden although that was a rather unfair description. The only reason this part of the Garden could be described as "shady" was because of the giant oaks with their great canopies that cast a lot of shade. The presence of the Shed of No Return probably didn't help either. It was said the cries of those who'd entered could be heard at the dead of night but as no one ventured near after dark, it was hard to substantiate. The Garden Ornament who claimed to live closest, was Hercules, who'd never complained of noises but as he was a Stone Snail with a bad memory and he carried his home on his back he could actually have spent the night anywhere. He was also stone deaf.

The Ornament who lived the next closest and who'd made various complaints about nightly disturbances was Nina, a large lady Gnome, popularly known as Nina the Ninja. Larger than life and twice as colourful, Nina looked nothing like a Ninja but she'd earned the nickname because of her unerring ability of mysteriously appearing anywhere she wasn't wanted.

She was now waiting in her doorway, hands like sausage packs, resting on ample hips.

"About time!" she said with a sniff.

"What seems to be the problem, madam?" Crispin asked politely.

"Where do I start?" she started. "This part of the Garden is a den of iniquity, with robbers, muggers, smugglers, footpads, brigands, ne'er-do-wells…" she paused for breath, "and probably murderers."

Sylvester and the Robin each took one large step backwards.

"I see," said Crispin. "Have you been attacked?"

"No fear, I don't go out at night."

"Well, have you been robbed then?"

"Oh yes," Nina nodded her head vigorously. "They've been robbing me of my sleep since last Tuesday."

"As annoying as that may be, it's not actually against the law," Crispin pointed out. "Have there been any crimes committed?"

"Oh yes," she said, nodding vigorously again. "Robbing, mugging, smuggling, footpadding, briganding—"

"And don't tell me – ne'er-do-welling?" asked Crispin.

Nina nodded again. "Exactly! And probably murdering."

Sylvester and the Robin took another large step backwards.

"And," added Nina, looking left and right as if fearing someone might hear her booming voice, "there's been hauntings as well."

"H-h-hauntings?" stuttered the Robin. "I didn't realise there'd be ghosts involved."

Suddenly Crispin craved alcohol. Lots of alcohol.

"Perhaps we should come back tomorrow morning, guv. We wouldn't want to keep the lovely lady on her doorstep after dark," said Sylvester.

"You won't find ghosts tomorrow morning! They don't come a-hauntin' during the day!" scoffed Nina.

"Although," said Crispin, spotting a chance to rid himself of his deputies, "this could be a long job and I think it would be best if we worked in shifts. I'll take the first one and you both come back in the morning." He turned to see whether they'd agree but Sylvester and the Robin had already gone.

"Huh!" snorted Nina. "The first sign of trouble and I'm on my own. Typical!" she said and with that, she turned and slammed the door.

Crispin wasn't too upset, he didn't think he could take more of Nina and her colourful and archaic list of felons and felonies. He crouched down behind a fern, thankful the rain had finally stopped, and he waited.

And waited.

He checked his watch.

A whole ten minutes had passed.

It's amazing how ten minutes on your own in the dark carrying out surveillance can erode long-held beliefs about there being no such things as ghosts, Crispin decided.

"Where's mine?" Crispin asked Sylvester, the following morning.

"You don't like doughnuts and coffee," said Sylvester, licking jam from his fingers.

"It didn't occur to you to bring me tea and toast?" asked Crispin incredulously.

"Real lawmen don't eat tea and toast," said the Robin licking the jam off his badge.

Crispin couldn't be bothered to reply, he was too tired… and achy… and hungry… and grumpy.

"I'm going to bed," he growled.

"Don't worry, guv, you leave it all to us. We'll have the case cracked in no time," Sylvester said.

"It's okay—" began Crispin.

Sylvester held his hand up. "We have it under control, guv, you go off to bed."

"But—" said Crispin.

"No buts, leave it to us, eh, Robin?" said Sylvester.

"Sure thing, Batman!" said the Robin.

The deputies fell about laughing.

Crispin walked off. He was too tired, achy, hungry and grumpy for stupid jokes.

"Fine…" he muttered.

Well, he *had* tried to tell them he'd already solved the case.

It was noon by the time Crispin woke up.

Sylvester and the Robin were sitting outside the Toadstool in the sun.

"Hey, guv, we've solved the crime!" said Sylvester.

"There hasn't been a crime!"

"I wouldn't be too sure about that. Look, we've got evidence," said Sylvester, pulling a sock out of his pocket. "See, here's the murder weapon."

"Death by sock!" trilled the Robin happily.

"That sock belongs to Bartrum's son. Go and give it back please," said Crispin.

"Wilmslow?"

"That's the one."

"Well, how did it get down by the ditch?"

"Never mind," said Crispin. "It's lost property. Go and return it!"

"But we still haven't sorted out the haunting. And we'd better do that, or Nina won't be happy," said Sylvester.

"You're absolutely right!" said Nina suddenly materialising behind them.

Sylvester clutched his heart theatrically.

"Typical!" said Nina. "Don't mind me and my problem. You're conveying socks about the Garden under armed guard—"

"Not at all, madam," said Crispin politely. "I'm pleased to report there won't be any further night disturbances. Although the haunting might prove slightly trickier to stop—"

"You saw the ghost?" squeaked the Robin.

"It wasn't a ghost at all," said Crispin.

"'Ere, you calling me a liar?" said Nina. "I saw him, robes and everything."

"Yes, he has robes but he's no ghost. He's very much alive."

"Who is it, guv?"

"The Hermit who lives behind the rockery"

"What, that unfriendly bloke who never talks to anyone?"

"He's a Hermit. He's not supposed to talk to anyone," said Crispin.

"Well, he does a lot of moaning and the like, while he's out haunting," said Nina.

"Apparently, he sleepwalks," explained Crispin. "I've been to see him and he's very embarrassed, so with any luck, he'll keep his door locked in the future."

"Well, I hope you're right," said Nina tartly, "or I shall be lodging a complaint against you all." And with that, she was gone.

"You know, guv, I don't think I'm cut out to be a lawman. Any chance I can resign?"

"Me too," said the Robin.

"Leave it to me," said Crispin.

"And?" demanded Bartrum.

"The nightly disturbances won't happen again and I've solved the case of the haunting," said Crispin.

"That's wonderful news! I must say, you've definitely exceeded my expectations."

Crispin unpinned his badge.

"Not so fast," said Bartrum. "You've done such a good job, I'm going to make your post permanent."

Crispin sighed. "Well, in that case, I need to make a full report—"

"There's no need," said Bartrum.

"Yes," insisted Crispin, "there is. I discovered the nightly disturbances were being caused by a group of young Gnomes meeting by the ditch at the end of the Garden. There were alcopops involved and gambling."

"Preposterous! I hope you dealt most harshly with the delinquents! We want none of their sort in our Garden—"

"Indeed. Here's the list of miscreants, just so you're aware who's involved..." Crispin took a folded sheet of paper from his pocket, laid it on Bartrum's desk and smoothed it out.

Bartrum was about to brush it aside when his eyes caught the name at the top of the list.

"My son, Wilmslow?" he gasped and sagged into his chair. "Who else knows this?" he whispered.

"The deputies and me."

"I see. Well, I think it might be timely to remind you of the need for confidentiality. We have a duty of care to each of those young Gnomes and we wouldn't want to stigmatise them, would we? Young people need to push the boundaries occasionally. No harm done. There wasn't much money involved, was there?" he asked fearfully.

"Oh no—"

"There, you see. No harm done. An innocent game of gin rummy, I expect."

"No," said Crispin, "it was poker."

"But no money was involved?"

Crispin shook his head and Bartrum smiled with relief. "Were they playing for matchsticks?"

"No – clothes."

"Clothes? They paid with clothes?"

"Well, I wouldn't say 'paid', more 'removed'."

Bartrum sank further into his chair and held his head in his hands. "Strip poker! Oh, the shame. Crispin, it just occurred to me that perhaps you and the deputies would like to retire from Law Enforcement. You've done an excellent job and no one can keep up the pace indefinitely…"

Crispin unclipped his badge and taking the deputies' badges from his pocket, he placed them on top of the list. "Yes, we'd love to retire," he said.

As he left, Bartrum swept the list and badges into the desk drawer and turned the key.

Just Desserts

Why does he always pick me?

"I expect you're wondering why I always pick you, Crispin," Bartrum said with alarming perception. "It's because I can rely on you."

Crispin sighed and took the list Bartrum held out. He considered volunteering for cesspit duty instead of accepting this assignment but there were glooping sounds coming from the putrid water, and Gusty Bob, who was currently on duty, had complained about the stench and the enormous bubbles that rose to the surface with alarming frequency. If Gusty Bob complained about a smell – well, it didn't bear thinking about.

Crispin sighed again. He knew he was beaten.

"Good, that's settled then," said Bartrum, smiling delightedly. "The French Chef arrives today, so you only need kitchen helpers, waiters, security and a band for tomorrow."

"Tomorrow?"

"Indeed," said Bartrum dismissing Crispin with a wave of his hand.

"It's imperative Lord and Lady Arscott, Sir Edmond Fairweather and the Honourable Mrs Shaydser-Grey enjoy themselves. Nothing must go wrong. Do you understand? Nothing! You'll be held personally responsible should any of our esteemed guests have cause for complaint."

* * *

"Band?" No, I don't know any bands," said Sylvester, "but if you like, I'll DJ for you. I'm wicked at mixing and scratching—"

"Thank you, but no. Somehow, I don't think Bartrum's guests are into Hippedy Hoppity or whatever it is you call that music. But I'd appreciate it if you could wait at the table."

Sylvester got up and stood next to the table. "What am I waiting for?"

"I haven't got time for this!" snapped Crispin. "I've got the dinner of the century to organise."

"Dinner? Why didn't you say? I'll round up a few of the chaps to be waiters, Gusty Bob can play any tune you like. If we put him in the begonias and are mindful of prevailing winds, the guests should be safe. And that new Troll pulls some pretty scary faces. He'll make a good bouncer."

Crispin collapsed backwards into a chair, his mouth open.

"Sometimes Sylvester, you amaze me. That's brilliant—"

"But if you change your mind about the DJ," Sylvester said, swivelling his hat round so it was back to front. "I'm your Elf."

Against all odds, everything was going smoothly. Sylvester's friends appeared, suitably attired in black, and once Crispin demonstrated that cutlery needed to be carefully positioned and not dumped in a heap, things started to pick up. Nina the Ninja, insisted on wearing the French maid's outfit she'd worn to a fancy-dress party. It was similar, although admittedly shorter, skimpier and altogether racier than a waitress's uniform but she was so keen and she arranged the flowers so beautifully, Crispin said she could stay, hoping he could restrict her to the kitchen once the guests arrived.

There was a deafening crash from the kitchen, rapidly followed by a stream of French invective. Crispin didn't speak French but judging by the tone and volume, the language had nothing to do with culinary arts and a lot to do with temper.

When he arrived in the kitchen, the chef was standing on a chair, brandishing a meat cleaver.

"Monsieur!" he shouted when he spotted Crispin. "I cannot work in conditions such as zeeze, I need 'elp zat is 'elpful. Not zeeze numpties. Zay are not 'elpful at all." He waved the cleaver at the startled kitchen aids.

A large Gnome rolled up his sleeves. "I'll give you 'numpty'! You jumped up little—"

"See! You are a numpty" the irate chef shouted, leaping from the chair. "I am not jumped up, I am jumped down. And I queet!" He flounced out of the kitchen, thumbing his nose in a Gallic insult that was lost on the kitchen aids.

"Oooh—" said Sylvester.

"Stop!" said Crispin. "If you're thinking of adding 'La La' to that 'Oooh', it won't be funny,"

Several of the younger Gnomes tittered.

Crispin wailed and held his fists to his temples.

"Don't worry," said Sylvester, "we've got another cook."

"We have?"

"Frank used to be a cook."

"Frank?" asked Crispin weakly, wanting Sylvester's solution to be a real solution and not the craziness he suspected it might be.

"Yes, Frank Fowle, the Troll. He used to be a cook."

Having seen the unsavoury character guarding the door, Crispin didn't doubt Frank Fowle knew how to use a knife, but could he handle a fork or spoon?

Fortunately, before the French Chef had flounced, he'd left lobster bisque gently bubbling on the Aga, a peacock that was browning nicely and a splendid chocolate gateau, decorated with enormous whirls of cream which were still wobbling gently after the flamboyant and vigorous exit of the chef.

"What you gawpin' at?" Frank Fowle asked the kitchen aids with a sniff. He wiped his nose up his sleeve – the entire length of his sleeve.

The kitchen aids were mesmerised.

"What yer bleedin' waitin' for? C'mon, we got work to do," he said and seized a wooden spoon by the bowl.

Crispin couldn't decide which was most excruciating, watching Frank stir the bisque with the handle of the wooden spoon, the bowl clutched tightly in his ham-sized fist, or Bartrum fawning over the guests. The self-appointed Head Gnome was sporting a rather fine pair of red, velvet trousers and a lacy shirt. Mrs Bartrum was resplendent in orange satin, her hair piled high on her head and she'd even shaved her face for the prestigious occasion.

The guests were equally as colourful and grand, and were happily scoring points, establishing their position in the social pecking order. The Gazebo which had been set up as the dining room sparkled with fairy lights and from somewhere in the begonias, music drifted on the breeze – thankfully, away from the Gazebo. A satisfied Crispin headed back to the kitchen. To his surprise, waiters were loading trays with steaming lobster bisque, ready to take into the dining room. Against all odds, it was all going perfectly. There was only one thing that bothered him. He wished Frank would stop putting his finger up his nose.

Crispin checked his watch. Everything seemed to be going surprisingly well and when he realised he was getting in the way, he hid in the pantry watching the coming and going of the waiters and of Nina, the French maid-waitress, as plates charged high with food left the kitchen and empty dishes returned. It was amazing how fast Frank could organise the courses and staff. Crispin wasn't sure he actually knew what he was serving, especially when he told the waiters the "lobster beaks" were ready but it all went to the table in the right order and from the laughter in the Gazebo, a good time was being had by all.

It was difficult to see the furthest end of the kitchen from his hiding place in the pantry, but as that was where Frank was working, Crispin was happy with his restricted view. The sight of the Troll with his finger up his nose whilst dolloping food onto plates was more than Crispin could bear. He could, however, see the pile of dirty dishes grow ever taller and he suspected that later, it would be his job to wash them. Frank didn't seem too concerned about cleanliness. Still, mused Crispin, Frank *had* saved the dinner.

It was going brilliantly although Crispin couldn't imagine why Mrs Bartrum was shouting so loudly but since the other guests were laughing and cheering, it was all right. Wasn't it?

Apparently, it wasn't. Well, not from Nina's point of view. She burst into the kitchen hotly pursued by Bartrum wielding a feather duster. The same French maid's feather duster that Crispin had banned from the dinner. Luckily for Nina, whose stiletto shoes were hampering her escape, Frank was a messy cook. If Bartrum hadn't been so intent on tickling Nina, he might have avoided the blob of chocolate cake on the floor and he wouldn't have aquaplaned across the flagstones on a thin film of cream. Crispin watched aghast as Bartrum collided with the Aga, collapsing in a red velvet and lace heap.

"Blimey! Just like a sack o' spuds," remarked Frank as he kicked the rest of the cake under the table. "There, that's better. Can't have people slipping over, can we?"

Crispin rushed to Bartrum's aid but just as he was wondering at the wisdom of slapping him, there was a piercing scream from the Gazebo. Mrs Bartrum ran into the kitchen. "Murder!" she screamed. "Murder most foul!"

"Fowle? That's me an' I ain't done no murder! It's all a frogging lie!" said Frank.

"Sylvester, look after Bartrum," Crispin said. "I'll find out what's happened."

The Honourable Mrs Shaydser-Grey was lying spread-eagled on the floor, her fuchsia pink evening gown smeared with chocolate cake. Lady Arscott crawled out from under the table, fanning herself with a table-mat, Lord Arscott was snoring, his head on the table and Sir Edmond was staggering about the room. "Ah, Crispy, my dear fellow, Mrs Shaydser-Grey seems to be dead. Either that or she's still in character from Charades." He stumbled against the table, waking Lord Arscott.

"Fore!" shouted Lord Arscott before slumping into his dessert.

"What happened?" Crispin whispered, not really sure he wanted to know.

"She went down like a sack of Maris Pipers. Or possibly King Edwards. Crispy, dear chap, is there any more of that divine chocolate cake? I'd kill for a slice..." said tiny Sir Edmond, as his knees buckled. Crispin rushed forward just in time to catch his diminutive body.

Just like a sack of Jersey Royals, thought Crispin.

At first light, the Garden was unnaturally quiet. However, Crispin, who'd been up all night, had sorted everything, and everyone out.

Mrs Bartrum's cries of "Leave my husband alone, you hussy!" had drawn Crispin to the edge of the cesspit and he'd patiently explained to the Head Lady Gnome, who fortunately had only gone in as far as her knees, the glooping sounds were coming from goodness knew where under the surface of the cesspit – and not Nina and Bartrum enjoying a passionate fling. He led her back to her husband, who'd finally regained consciousness and with one hand holding a pack of frozen peas to his forehead and the other pinching his nose, he shepherded his stinking wife home.

When Lord Arscott's driver arrived, he stoically tucked his employer under one arm, Lady Arscott under the other and carried them to the coach.

"Over-exuberance," Crispin said, by way of explanation for their dishevelled appearance. *I hope,* he thought, fearing Frank Fowle had inadvertently poisoned everyone.

"Whatever," said the driver.

Tiny Sir Edmond had wandered off and was later

found half a mile away in the graveyard, by his driver, who took him home.

And to Crispin's relief, the guest who'd given most cause for concern, Mrs Shaydser-Grey wasn't dead, just dead drunk and he'd gratefully handed her over to *her* driver, to take home.

Although everyone had survived and had eventually made it home, the evening had been an unmitigated disaster. It wasn't his fault Frank had poisoned everyone but Crispin doubted that even Bartrum would dare put Frank on cesspit duty, so Crispin would bear the brunt of the punishment and it would probably involve soap, a toothbrush and the cesspit.

He hurried the black sack to the bins and was surprised how much rubbish was already there. Mrs Bartrum's orange gown was stained brown, possibly with chocolate cake or possibly not, but obviously now unwearable. A French maid's outfit and feather duster had also been discarded and to Crispin's amazement, a mountain of empty drink bottles, six of which he noted, had once contained finest French cognac.

It was Sylvester who explained what had happened, once he'd woken up and had two paracetamol tablets. Frank had apparently added a bottle of cognac to the "lobster beaks" and all the guests had asked for seconds and then thirds. The roast peacock had been served with a delicious cognac sauce which took a further two bottles and the chocolate gateau had been liberally laced with…

"Cognac," said Crispin sighing. "And I suppose you and the other staff ate the leftovers."

Sylvester nodded and then winced.

Bartrum summoned a dejected Crispin to his office.

"Excellent evening, Crispin, my dear chap. An absolute triumph," he said to Crispin's amazement. "Everyone had a wonderful time and have asked when the next dinner will be, so, I'd like to book you for next Tuesday…"

A Little Girl at Large

Crispin tapped on Sylvester's bedroom door. "It's Monday. Garden Inspection. Get up!"

Sylvester swore.

"I don't know where you've picked up all this bad language from but you can take it back and leave it. It's not my fault it's Monday and Garden Inspection. Don't take it out on me!"

Sylvester's bed creaked and Crispin knew he'd pulled the duvet back over his head.

He tried another tack. Opening the front door, he said loudly, "Yes, Bartrum, I'll make sure Sylvester is there at Garden Insp—" before he could finish, Sylvester was halfway to the bathroom.

Crispin waved to the Wooden Robin, who was walking past the Toadstool.

"Did you say something?" he trilled.

Crispin knew better than to explain he was only trying to frighten Sylvester into getting up.

"No, just admiring the day," Crispin said and waved again.

"Stop sulking," said Crispin over breakfast. "I fooled you for your own good. As soon as Garden Inspection's over, you can do what you like, even go back to bed. But you know what happens when a Garden Ornament is missing at inspection time. Big Po leaves no stone unturned until they're found and you know how long that can take. The last time Jubbly had an episode, we all had to stand in the sun for hours."

Despite his grumpiness, Sylvester smiled at the memory. It was one of those days when Jubbly had woken up feeling more female – and Mexican – than usual. It was also Monday and Garden Inspection Day. Jubbly had arrived at his position on time and waited for Mr Po Lin to tick him off his list as he progressed throughout the Garden. But the Gardener's memory of the Gnome with his thumbs tucked into his braces, definitely didn't match what he was now seeing, standing next to the birdbath. Jubbly had surpassed himself. His long red skirt with braid decoration and white frilly blouse were set off with red and white flowers in his hair and a matching fan.

Mr Po Lin grabbed Jubbly round the middle and stabbing the air with his finger, he shouted in the direction of the Old Priory, "So, Mr Wirrets, you think you can replace one of my Ornaments with a cheap copy?" He'd deposited Jubbly in the rubbish bin, soiling his outfit and convincing him that in future, he definitely wouldn't be female or Mexican on any Monday when Mr Po Lin carried out his inspection. It was hours before Mr Po Lin gave up looking for the "real" Jubbly. He'd been convinced that Mr Willets, who'd been to Spain the previous week had taken Jubbly and replaced him with a travesty of a Gnome, as a joke. He was certain that, one day soon, a postcard would arrive from Torremolinos, supposedly from Jubbly.

Of course, a postcard never appeared. Crispin, whose position was next to the drystone wall, had to stand in the sun for three hours and almost passed out before Mr Po Lin had given up searching, abandoned Garden Inspection and gone to mow the large lawn.

At the following Garden Inspection, Jubbly was there by the birdbath, thumbs tucked into his braces and Mr Po Lin gave a triumphant glance at the Old Priory and a grunt of satisfaction as he ticked him off the list.

The inspection had gone well although now, the Garden Ornaments were on high alert after Bartrum's post-Garden Inspection meeting. Not only was there a compulsory health check that afternoon but more immediate and worrying was the news that a little girl had gone missing.

"Big Po placed her by the maze," said Bartrum, "but when I went to inform her of this meeting, she wasn't there. I can only assume she's wandered off. We must find her immediately. She's just a young girl and she's probably terrified."

"You promised I could go back to bed!" grumbled Sylvester as he and Crispin scoured the area near the Shed of No Return.

"Stop being such a… a *teenager*!" snapped Crispin. "There's a little girl somewhere in the Garden, lost and afraid. Stop thinking of yourself and go and check over there."

With hunched shoulders and hands deep in pockets, Sylvester stomped to the bushes. He was wondering whether Crispin would notice if he slipped back to the Toadstool, when a voice from the bush brought him back to reality with a start.

"Hello! Would you like a dab of my sherbet? I've got a Mint Humbug if you'd pwefer…"

Sylvester leapt backwards and swore.

"Ooh!" said the Little Girl crawling out from her hiding place under the bushes. "You shouldn't thay that. That'th a thwear word. I know all the thwear wordth and that'th a bad one. You're very naughty."

"Have you had any luck?" shouted Crispin from the boating lake.

"Yes," shouted Sylvester. "I've had some luck and it's all bad luck. I've found her."

Crispin arrived out of breath. "Oh, thank goodness, I was beginning to wonder if we'd have to dredge the lake. You must be…" he paused, trying to remember if Bartrum had told them her name.

"She's the girl with the scruples," Sylvester said caustically.

"Are they like gob thtopperth?" she asked, her enormous, violet eyes gazing adoringly at Sylvester.

Crispin was tempted to ask what they were talking about and then thought better of it.

"My name'th Wendy Wuthell," she said. "Who are you?"

While Crispin introduced Sylvester and himself, she continued to stare admiringly at Sylvester, who was quite oblivious to the adoration.

There was something completely surreal about a little girl who was twice as tall but half the age of Sylvester, and Crispin couldn't help adding, "For a little girl, you're rather… big."

"Yeth," she agreed quite happily, her chestnut curls bobbing around her heart-shaped face.

"Shall I show you how good I am at curttheying?"

"Curtseying?" Crispin asked, certain he'd misheard.

"Yeth," she said, "I'm really good at it. I'll show you."

"No," said Sylvester.

"Yes, please," said Crispin as her bottom lip began to quiver. He jabbed Sylvester in the ribs with his elbow and mouthed *Be nice.*

Wendy took hold of the bottom of her dress with chubby hands, put one ballet-shoe-clad foot forward and bending the knee of the other leg, she sank into a deep curtsey and looked through her lashes to see if Sylvester was impressed.

He wasn't.

"I know," she said, "I'll teach you both how to do it."

"No," said Sylvester, moving out of range of Crispin's elbow.

"Well," said Crispin, "that's very kind of you but we need to let Bartrum know you're safe."

"Bartwum?"

"Yes. Bartrum's in charge, so we really need to go and find him…"

"Ooh! You mean like a king?" asked Wendy, her face lighting up. "Well then, you thimply have to learn how to curtthey."

"Well, not so much a 'king', more a sort of leader—"

"Pleathe! You'll like it, really you will!" Her eyes filled with tears. "Pleathe!"

"What on earth…?" said Bartrum as he entered the clearing in the woods followed by a group of young Gnomes.

"Ah, Bartrum…" said Crispin leaping up from his curtsey.

"Your Majethty!" said Wendy sinking more deeply into hers.

Sylvester groaned with embarrassment and collapsing sideways from his curtsey, he lay there pretending to be dead.

Even Bartrum was sitting upright watching Nurse Bludgett warily. He'd given Gusty Bob special permission to wait near the begonias until everyone else had been seen. This was more for the other Garden Ornaments' benefit than the nurse's. With her face mask and strong, medical smell, Nurse Bludgett always seemed impervious to Gusty Bob's signature odour.

"You are an absolute disgrace!" the nurse bellowed at the Garden Ornaments, tapping the palm of her hand with the nurse's stick. "You are flabby and unfit and I am placing you all on a strict diet."

Not one Garden Ornament dared groan or disagree, although there was a sound that could have meant anything, which came from the begonias.

"Now, line up! I will see you all individually. You!" she yelled, indicating Jubbly with her nurse's stick. "Here! Now!"

Jubbly gulped and stepped forward.

"What'th she going to do?" Wendy whispered to Crispin.

"She does tests and gives jabs."

"Jabth?" said Wendy. "I'm up to date with my jabth."

"It doesn't make any difference. If you slouch, sniff or breathe at the wrong time, she'll jab you anyway."

As if to prove the point, Nurse Bludgett jabbed Jubbly with the end of her nurse's stick. "Stop blubbing," she said. "Behave like a man."

"I don't want to go to the nurthe," objected Wendy but Sylvester had pushed her forward.

"Name?" asked Nurse Bludgett.

"Wendy Wuthell, but I don't want any jabth—"

"Well Miss Russell, no one is interested in what you want—"

"Wuthell, my name's Wuthell, not Wuthell," said Wendy indignantly. "You thpell it W, U, T, H, E, L, L."

"Silence!" Nurse Bludgett jabbed Wendy with her nurse's stick. She shook her thermometer vigorously. "Open wide."

Wendy opened her mouth to reveal a well-sucked pear drop and a red tongue.

"Spit that out!" shrieked Nurse Bludgett. "Don't you know sweets rot your teeth?"

"I will not!" cried Wendy with equal passion. "I haven't got any more!"

Nurse Bludgett jabbed her again and held a bowl in front of her face to catch the pear drop.

Wendy opened her mouth but rather than ejecting the sweet, she let rip with a scream so loud it shook the windows in the Old Priory and set off the burglar alarm.

For a second, no one moved, then hands clapped over ears as everyone, including Nurse Bludgett, was almost knocked backwards by the force of the shock wave.

A sharp jab with the nurse's stick only served to increase the volume of the scream and fearing for her eardrums, Nurse Bludgett hastily gathered her equipment and fled.

By the time Wendy stopped for breath, Nurse Bludgett was halfway down the tree-lined avenue, vowing never to return to the Garden of the Old Priory.

"We've escaped!" said Sylvester gleefully. "And it's all thanks to Wendy."

"Me?" asked Wendy, not quite understanding what had happened but delighted Sylvester was smiling at her. She blushed and looked down at her ballet shoes then back at Sylvester with unconcealed devotion.

"Ooh, I've got an idea! Play hide and theek with me!"

Sylvester was about to say "No," when he had a "light bulb" moment. "Yes, let's," he said.

"Weally?" Wendy squealed, clapping her hands together.

"Oh, yes. You go and hide and I'll count to a hundred. One, two—"

Wendy squealed again and ran off to the woods.

"Sylvester, you should be ashamed!" said Crispin.

"Three, four—" said Sylvester sauntering off with his hands in his pockets, away from the woods and towards the Toadstool.

"She might go into the Shed of No Return, she might drown in the lake…" said Crispin but Sylvester had already gone.

Crispin groaned and headed towards the woods.

It hadn't been hard to spot Wendy hiding in the

tree, with her bright pink dress, although Crispin couldn't imagine how she'd got up there.

It proved harder to get her down, as her petticoat had caught on a twig and despite not liking heights, Crispin had to climb up to free her.

"Quick, we need to hide. Thylvethter will be coming any minute."

Crispin explained Sylvester might not be coming after all.

"A headache? Poor Thylvethter, he'll be weally dithappointed. I hope it goeth thoon."

"Yes, I'm sure it will. He'll sleep it off and be as right as rain tomorrow." Crispin had his fingers crossed behind his back.

"Okay. Well, what shall we do now, Cwithpin? Shall we play with my dolly?"

The Halloween Party

There had been no intention to overthrow Jubbly from his newly-appointed position as Garden Party Committee Chairman.

It had just happened.

Although anyone who'd listened to an irate Jubbly after the event could have imagined plots, espionage and even weapons had been involved.

But they hadn't.

In fact, the committee members were happy with Jubbly as chairman and as an important party was coming up, they were more than content their necks weren't on Bartrum's block. For once, Crispin had managed to escape being selected for one of the Head Gnome's so-called "top jobs". He'd been suffering from gastroenteritis when Bartrum had called the meeting to select the party committee, although it was unlikely that would have been sufficient to stop Bartrum from selecting him. It had been Sylvester who'd saved Crispin's bacon although arguably it had been Sylvester who'd caused the food poisoning in the first place by cooking out-of-date bacon. When Bartrum had asked for Crispin to step forward as chairman of the committee, Sylvester had announced he was indisposed and suffering from gangrene.

Bartrum, who was rather squeamish, felt the need to sit down, and while he was erasing from his mind visions of a mutilated Crispin with body parts dropping off, Jubbly had volunteered.

Bartrum picked four others to assist Jubbly, informed them their first event would be a Halloween Party in a week's time and closed the meeting. The less he thought about Halloween, the better. Blood and guts were definitely not his thing.

Jubbly had obviously given a great deal of thought to the party, judging by his suggestions.

"Well, what d'you think?" he'd asked, surprised at the silence which met his ideas.

Klaus, the Bavarian Gnome, looped his thumbs behind the braces of his lederhosen and stood up slowly. "Speaking for myself, I'm wondering whether people might be confused by having a Mexican theme for a Halloween Party—"

"What's a Mariachi band anyway?" trilled the Wooden Robin.

Nina the Ninja was too busy to reply. She was sliding her chair away from Doggett, the Fishing Gnome, who kept pressing his leg up close to hers.

"But a themed party is so much fun," said Jubbly amazed at the lack of support.

"Yes, indeed," said Klaus, "but doesn't a Mexican Halloween Party include two themes? Isn't that slightly unnecessary?"

"We'll have a show of hands," declared Jubbly who wasn't ready to give up. "All those in favour of a Mexican Halloween Party, raise your hands—" He raised both of his.

Klaus's hands still gripped his braces, the Wooden Robin didn't have any hands to raise and Nina's hands were on top of Doggett's, prising them off her knee.

"Stabbed in the back by my own committee!" said Jubbly, picking up his sombrero. He jammed it on his head and stalked off muttering under his breath about mutiny and revolution.

For a second, no one spoke.

"Oh dear, I didn't mean to upset him," said Klaus, as all eyes looked to him to chair the meeting.

And so, the committee led by Klaus, organised the Halloween Party, with the usual crab-apple bobbing, chocolate fountain filled with strawberry jam to look like blood and all the other gruesome things one associates with a horror-packed evening.

The popularity of a movie that had been shown on the outdoor screen in the Sunken Garden a few weeks before, ensured that zombie outfits were the costume of choice on the night. Both Crispin and Sylvester had both chosen a zombie theme and once they'd discovered this, they'd both tried to outdo each other with makeup and latex rubber glue which when applied thinly, passed for flaky, wrinkly skin. There was no doubt that of all the zombies at the party, Sylvester and Crispin were the most zombied-up and were widely predicted to win the Best

Costume Prize which would be awarded by Bartrum at the end of the evening.

Jubbly had registered his protest by arriving as a Mexican zombie and he spent the evening canvassing for votes. If he were to win the best costume, it would be one in the eye for Uber-Kommandant Klaus Bossy Boots and his plain and boring party. But he had strong competition in Crispin and Sylvester, whose latex glue seemed to flake off on demand and there was plenty of demand to see the Elf-Zombies shed sheets of skin.

Bartrum, as Count Dracula, and Mrs Bartrum, as Mrs Dracula, mingled with the guests, while Bartrum congratulated himself on having had the foresight to delegate the organisation of the party. He was counting the minutes until it was over. The sight of blood, even if it was strawberry jam, was so distasteful he'd quite lost his appetite and he avoided the melon ball "eyeballs", the jelly "worms" and the very popular witch's brew.

He was one of the very few who didn't sample the delights of the Wooden Robin's witch's brew punch and in fact, would never sample its delights, because, after the party, the Wooden Robin was very hazy about the recipe. He had vague memories of pouring in wine and rum and of having the idea of adding a dash of vodka but he didn't remember much after that. This was possibly due to the trauma of what happened next. Whilst adding a drop of vodka, he'd slipped and by the time he'd surfaced and swum to the edge of the bowl, the vodka bottle was empty. Getting out of the bowl had been tricky and he kept slipping back into the punch, hampered by his sodden, woollen socks. Fearing for his life, he gave one super-avian thrust, propelling himself up and out of the punch bowl – and out of his socks, which sank to the depths, along with several wooden feathers.

Once he'd got his breath back, he tasted the punch. It was nuclear strength, but he wasn't too worried, he could fix that. He hopped barefoot to the Kitchen Garden and dug up a few potatoes. If raw potato slices were capable of absorbing excess salt from soup, several raw potatoes in the punch would soak up excess vodka easily. It occurred to him later he ought to have washed and possibly peeled the potatoes first but by that time it was too late.

Klaus hadn't sought the position of Garden Party Committee Chairman after Jubbly had flounced out of the meeting, but having had the responsibility thrust upon him, he was going to do the best he could. He wasn't a Bavarian Gnome for nothing. Organisation and efficiency were in his DNA. And so far, the party was going exactly as planned. Although it occurred to him that it might actually be going a bit better than planned. People weren't having a good time – they were having a *fabulous* time and the events weren't going well, they were going *brilliantly* – one could almost say *riotously*.

As a dedicated beer drinker, Klaus hadn't sampled the punch and by the time he got anywhere near it, he had more pressing matters to deal with. One young Zombie Gnome had a vampire Elf in a headlock and was demanding he returned the potato. As far as Klaus knew, there hadn't been any potato dishes at the party but before he could break up the fight, shrieks from the "blood" fountain called him away. Another fight had broken out but this time, it was a food fight and it appeared to have been initiated by Jubbly. Scooping up handfuls of strawberry jam, he pelted Crispin, who was shrieking with laughter and rather than ducking, he was deliberately blocking the sticky missiles with his body, amidst cries of encouragement from onlookers.

Klaus wasn't sure what to do. No one was getting hurt and other than Jubbly's pride, which was definitely hurting, everyone seemed to be having a great time. Garden Ornaments clapped him on the back and congratulated him on such a splendid event and a few asked if there was more punch as it seemed to have run out and if there wasn't any, were there any more of those potatoes, which Doggett explained, packed quite a punch on their own. Nina the Ninja, who'd been dancing with Doggett, thought this was hilarious and only stopped laughing when a bout of hiccups threatened to choke her.

This is madness, thought Klaus, it's as if everyone is wildly drunk but they can't possibly be.

Bartrum, who also hadn't sampled the Wooden Robin's witch's brew punch, was stunned at the success of the party. He checked his watch, wishing the whole thing was over. Blood and guts were all very well in the right place which according to Bartrum, was inside a body and completely out of sight. He was also very surprised to find everyone including Mrs Bartrum, in a very excitable state. Even the usually steady and reliable Crispin was behaving in a most unseemly manner and to make things worse, Bartrum was almost certain Crispin was going to win the Best Costume Award. And it would be Bartrum's job to shake his hand and pin the winner's badge to his chest, all of which sent shudders of revulsion up his spine. If Crispin hadn't been so lively and loud, Bartrum would have been convinced he was still suffering from gangrene as there seemed to be a lot of dead skin hanging from his body and what's more, it looked as though gangrene was contagious, because that dizzy Elf, Sylvester, seemed to have caught it from him, judging by the sheets of skin hanging from his body.

At 10.55 pm, Bartrum blew his whistle. Enough was enough. And Bartrum had decidedly had enough. He found Klaus, the only other Garden Ornament at the party who wasn't behaving like a turbo-charged teenager, and was informed, as suspected, that Crispin had won the Best Costume Award. Bartrum was surprised to see how disturbed Klaus was about the liveliness of the guests and he kept apologising. Perhaps Bavarians were less excitable than Gnomes of other nationalities. He would ask Klaus tomorrow when all this tomfoolery was over. In the meantime, he had a badge to pin on a Zombie's chest and a gangrenous hand to shake.

His stomach looped the loop.

"Poor Bartwum," said Wendy sympathetically as she helped Sylvester and Crispin home. With her witch's hat on, she loomed even larger than normal over the two Elves, who were giggling hysterically.

"Weally!" she said crossly. "You two are dithgwatheful!" which sent the Elves into paroxysms of laughter.

"Although," she added with a smile, "it was funny when Bartwum pinned that badge to your shirt."

Crispin was doubled over, holding his stomach and Sylvester was now on his back with his legs waving in the air, as they remembered what had happened.

With a look of extreme distaste, Bartrum had shaken Crispin's fingertips, then quickly wiped the flaky, fake skin off his hand on his cloak and once he'd stopped gagging, he reached forward to take a piece of Crispin's tattered shirt. Crispin had zombied it up so much, there was more tatter than shirt and Bartrum was struggling to find enough fabric to pin the badge to, without touching the sloughing, bloody expanse that was Crispin's chest. Finding a scrap of material large enough, he inserted his fingers behind it and in so doing, revealed a large lump of strawberry jam from the earlier "blood" fountain fight.

"Ooh, look!" Jubbly had cried. "That strawberry looks just like a heart!"

Bartrum had pulled his hand away so sharply, he disturbed the last remaining threads of adhesion between Crispin's chest and the latex rubber zombie skin.

"Ooh, look, his chest's fallen off," squeaked the Wooden Robin, as the fake skin came away in a large sheet, "and his heart's fallen out," he added as the strawberry fell with a plop onto Bartrum's foot. There was a rapturous round of applause but Bartrum was unaware of the noise.

He'd fainted.

"Mind your stomach doesn't fall out!" shrieked Sylvester as Crispin collapsed next to him, barely able to breathe for the laughter.

"You two are now being very thilly. I'm going home. It'th after my bedtime," said Wendy stamping her foot.

Crispin hadn't realised it was possible to laugh any louder or harder. But apparently, it was. So, he did.

After some time, their muscles could take no more and they managed to stand up and stagger along, arm in arm.

"I think we're losht," said Crispin as they crossed the Ornamental Bridge for the third time.

"Yesh," agreed Sylvester. "How about a shwim?" he said pushing Crispin off the bridge, forgetting their arms were still linked.

"Noooo!" said Crispin as they both sailed through the air.

The cold water sobered them up quickly and the remnants of the latex glue floated off to be found by Mr Po Lin on his next Garden Inspection. The Gardener decided to keep it to himself that on Halloween, not only had he heard unworldly sounds coming from the Garden but that he'd found evidence that an enormous beast had shed its skin. He dared not imagine what it was nor what it had metamorphosed into.

"We'd better get home to bed," said Crispin, whose teeth were chattering with cold. The hilarity was rapidly being replaced by a thumping headache and hypothermia. Sylvester agreed. He was similarly subdued and cold.

Suddenly, from the undergrowth, there was a noise so terrible, that both Elves froze in horror.

"Run!" shouted Sylvester.

"What is it?"

"It must be the Beast. I saw it in a film and it sounded just like that! It's half-wolf, half-bear, half-puma and half-raccoon—" gasped Sylvester.

Both Elves fled in terror.

Crispin was fumbling with the front door handle by the time he had a chance to think. Such a beast would indeed be loud, scary and enormous but it was also a mathematical impossibility.

And so, the reputation of the terrifying Halloween Beast, prowling in the woods, roaring ferociously as it shed its skin and metamorphosed into something even worse, was born and grew exponentially.

Not everyone was dismayed by the appearance of such a horrifying chimaera. In his capacity as Guardian of the Garden, Bartrum expressed his reluctance at cancelling next year's Halloween Party and imposing a curfew but as he told everyone, "Needs must." With such a dreadful creature on the loose, he couldn't take any chances. He then resisted the urge to click his heels in the air. Yes, Bartrum was very pleased.

Jubbly was also very pleased when he learned that next year, Bartrum wanted him to organise a daytime Mexican Fiesta just after Halloween to make up for the lack of celebration.

The Garden Ornaments were pleased at the thought of a celebration and Doggett offered to hypnotise the Wooden Robin to see if he could remember the recipe of his wonderful punch as he thought that with a splash of Tequila, it might be considered very Mexican.

Wendy was also pleased. Not because of the prospect of a fiesta the following year but simply because her new, black cat, Trilby had come home. It was a shame he hadn't been able to accompany her to the party as the witch's black cat but he was home now. And a cat is for life, not just for Halloween.

Probably the Garden Ornament who was the most pleased was Trilby. He'd had a dreadful few days and had stared into the jaws of death. It had all started with that piece of bacon he'd found near where those dreadful Elves lived. He was beginning to wonder if they'd poisoned it deliberately. The stomach cramps had been so severe, he'd been unable to leave his secret hideaway in the hollow near the Ornamental Bridge. Trilby was a very polite cat and had been upset that the natural acoustics of the hollow, amplified his moans and the sounds of his body's attempts at evacuating the dodgy bacon but he was certain no one would have heard him over the sounds of the party. But then those two evil Elves had come by, wailing, shrieking and scaring him witless. Still, he was well now, although he'd neither forgiven nor forgotten those two miscreants and he had a long memory, which was lucky as he still had eight and a half lives left.

A Glimmer of an Idea

The highly acclaimed Halloween Party *hadn't* been organised by Jubbly.

Whether the Mexican Fiesta that Jubbly would organise next year would be successful was likely – but not a certainty.

So, Jubbly knew people considered his organisational capabilities to be an unknown quantity and were still to be tested. Logically speaking there was no reason for Jubbly to feel so confident in them. But there had never been anything logical about Jubbly.

"A Glimmer of an Idea" was always enough to launch him on a new course in life, without taking the time to have "The Complete Idea" or to worry about the details which would propel "The Glimmer of an Idea" into a sensible scheme. So, no one was surprised when he announced his talents were wasted on pushing a wheelbarrow around the Garden and that he was going into business.

"The Glimmer of an Idea" had trickled into his consciousness one morning. Having selected a cream trouser suit and silky, red blouse with matching accessories, Jubbly turned this way and that, as he admired the softly draping, but rather figure-hugging, ensemble, in the mirror. And then he spotted it. He gasped in horror but there was no mistake. VPL. Visible Panty Line.

Yes, the outline of his knickers could be seen quite clearly through the cream fabric of his trousers and the more he rearranged his underwear, the worse it got. He rummaged through his drawers for different knickers but every pair he pulled out was the same – grey and heavily elasticated around waist and legs. Under a flouncy Mexican skirt, they could not be detected but the cream trouser suit was unforgiving and the elasticated lines just above his knees were quite unacceptable. Reluctantly he changed into a calf-length sweater dress which was thick enough not to show his VPL.

Something must be done, he thought. And the "Glimmer of an Idea" was conceived.

Jubbly's ideas were as varied as they were frequent and thus far, had never come to fruition, so no one was expecting much of this current "Glimmer of an Idea". However, when boxes addressed to Jubbly began arriving by post, there was mild speculation. When each Garden Ornament received an invitation to Jubbly's opening event, there was frenzied excitement.

The post-round of Deano, the Post Kangaroo, usually didn't take long. In fact, normally there was very little post at all. But he'd just made a delivery to every single Garden Ornament, including the Hermit, who was most indignant at the thought of his privacy being invaded by a letter.

"All right! If you don't want it, throw it away! Don't

get your knickers in a twist!" Deano said, which under the circumstances was rather amusing, although the significance of his comment didn't become apparent to the Hermit until curiosity drove him to open his letter.

Deano prided himself on being a kangaroo who didn't jump to conclusions but by the time he'd finished the unusual day's delivery, it occurred to him that since all the envelopes were the same shade of pink and the handwriting on each was identical, they may have all been sent by the same person. The fact that on each envelope, "GARDEN" was misspelt as "GRADEN", added weight to his theory. One thing Deano was sure of, was that so much mail from one person constituted spam, and the pink envelopes only added to his belief.

Crispin placed Sylvester's letter in his cereal bowl so he wouldn't miss it, then he carefully opened his own. Inside was a pink card, on which was written:

Jubbly & Sons International Ltd.
cordially invites you to the launch of Nundies,
on Saturday at 2.00 pm
in the Gazebo.
Nundies, for all your underwear needs.
From the scantiest of undies to undergarments for the
more chunky-bodied
Nibbles provided.
Ban VPL forever!
RSVP

"You keep up with all the modern trends, don't you? What does VPL stand for?" Crispin asked Sylvester when he finally appeared for breakfast, after having been called six times.

"Dunno," Sylvester grunted as he poured milk into his bowl on top of his letter.

Jubbly had been unable to persuade any of the Garden Ornaments except Nina the Ninja and a few of the Fairies who lived at the end of the Garden, to model the undergarments for him, but Bartrum had put his foot down. Ever since he'd drunkenly chased Nina with a feather duster at a dinner party, Mrs Bartrum had been most unreasonable when it came to anything to do with Nina the Ninja.

"Perhaps Mrs Bartrum might consider modelling a few of the items," suggested Jubbly.

"No," said Bartrum and there was no arguing with that.

In the end, Jubbly made a rather tasteful display of most of his wares by draping them over flower pots. He placed a large bowl of nachos and a dip nearby and waited for the masses whose lives were about to be greatly enhanced. Yes, his name would go down in history as the eradicator of the VPL.

But things didn't unfold as Jubbly had envisaged. True, there had been an excellent turnout. Most of the Garden Ornaments had accepted his invitation although predictably, the Hermit had declined. But, even so, Jubbly thought he saw a robe-clad figure hiding behind the lupins. However, sales at the launch had been extremely disappointing.

His post-launch analysis offered him a slight hope though. First, he hadn't realised that people didn't understand the undesirability of the VPL – in fact, most people didn't know about it at all. Now he'd pointed it out, everyone would be keen to avoid it and they would eventually come to him to buy. Second, there had been so much demand for mail-order forms, he'd run out.

If Jubbly's business didn't appear to have taken off, Deano's post business certainly had. Garden Ornaments were now queuing up to buy stamps from Deano and letters poured out of the Garden. He tucked them in his pouch, hopped to the Post Office in the village and handed them to the postmistress. The following day, there was a pile of letters to be delivered to the Garden. A pile very much like the ones he'd taken to the Post Office the previous day.

"It's going to take hours to deliver all of these," he remarked to the postmistress.

"I don't think so," she'd replied. And she'd been right. It didn't take any time at all because they were all for Jubbly.

The following day, a very weary and flustered Jubbly was first in the queue to buy stamps for a huge pile of parcels.

"Word got around quickly about Nundies," he said to Deano, "although I'm a bit disappointed by the lack of support from my so-called friends in the Garden."

It took several days for Deano to work out what was going on and he decided to ask the postmistress for her advice, after all, if he pointed out to Jubbly that all his mail-order customers were, in fact, Garden Ornaments who were having their goods delivered to PO boxes in the Post Office, both he and the postmistress stood to lose a lot of business. Demand for stamps had bordered on the hysterical and the postmistress had only met the demand for PO boxes, by using a pile of shoe boxes.

"No one would thank you," observed the postmistress. "People are paying for privacy. And you can't put a price on that. They're all embarrassed to let their friends know they're buying Nundies."

"Nundies?" queried Deano, who didn't live in the Garden and therefore hadn't been at Jubbly's launch. "What are these Nundies I keep hearing about?"

"Undies for the discerning," said the postmistress.

"Undies for Numpties!" said Deano scornfully.

"Don't be so quick to mock," said the postmistress eyeing Deano's VPL and smoothing her hand over her VPL-less bottom. "They do what they say on the packet," she added, sliding a Nundies catalogue over the counter to Deano.

"Really?" he asked, tucking it in his pocket.

"I see you took my advice," the postmistress said, scrutinising Deano's VPL-less uniform several days later.

"Yes, I'd no idea what a difference it could make! And I love those little lacy thingies with the feathers and ribbons…"

"I don't need to know that," said the postmistress quickly.

Jubbly's lack of business acumen rapidly became apparent a few weeks after the launch of Nundies. If the returned customer satisfaction forms could be believed, his customers, whoever they were, seemed to be completely satisfied with their new purchases, and yet, sales had stopped. Why?

"What's up?" Crispin asked a worried-looking Jubbly when he bumped into him.

Jubbly explained.

"Ah, I see. Well, remember, they're such good quality garments, your customers aren't going to need to buy more for some time," Crispin explained, smoothing his hand over his VPL-less bottom.

"But if everyone is so satisfied, why aren't they spreading the word?"

"I think you'll find people are happy to lose their VPL but are embarrassed to tell their friends how they did it."

Crispin was right, people were pleased with their sleek silhouettes. However, they now had more pressing matters that needed attention. The initial delight at VPL-less reflections in the mirror had given way to dismay when it became clear that Lycra-clad bottoms were at best lumpy and at worst, definitely bulging.

If people were too embarrassed to admit to buying Nundies, they were certainly not going to reveal how much greater their body mass index was than they'd realised, so it might have appeared to be a bizarre coincidence that all the Garden Ornaments had suddenly taken up jogging around the Garden.

"Nurse Bludgett's warning about everyone being unfit must finally have made an impression," said Bartrum between gasps for air as he staggered along the woodland path. Mrs Bartrum could only wheeze as she stopped to bend double and catch her breath.

The newest resident in the Garden was Boggy, a rather zealous Eco-Gnome. Strictly speaking, he wasn't a Garden Ornament as he'd never been purchased by Her Ladyship, nor placed in position by Mr Po Lin. He'd crept into the Garden and set up base camp in a tree, from which he intended to educate everyone in how to rethink, reduce, reuse, recycle, renew and any other useful word beginning with "re".

Today, Boggy would begin his demonstration with banners and speeches and everyone would join him to save the planet. He'd chosen the location where he would spearhead his campaign carefully. After all, if you had to warn people about the dangers of greenhouse gases, where better to start than in a place with several large greenhouses? People needed to know they were at imminent risk of exposure to… well, he was a bit hazy on the actual details of what greenhouse gases did that was so dangerous, but you couldn't argue with science, could you? However, if his message fell on deaf ears… well, he'd just stay in the tree and make a nuisance of himself until they saw sense. It was for everyone's good. But he wasn't looking forward to it. Of a nervous disposition, Boggy hated confrontation. Nevertheless, the survival of the planet depended on him and he was sure he was up to the task.

He'd painted "Save the Planet" on a bedsheet and step one in his campaign was to dangle it from the bough on which he was sitting. Unfortunately, he unfurled his banner at the same moment that Mrs Bartrum had recovered her breath and stood up straight. She'd run headlong into the sheet, tearing it from the bough, becoming increasingly tangled the more she struggled. Muffled cries of "Bartrum! Save me!" rang out through the woods.

Fortunately for Mrs Bartrum, most of the Garden Ornaments were seconds behind her on their morning jog and in no time, there was quite a gathering under the tree to untangle her.

Unfortunately for Boggy, by the time the wailing

jogger had been freed, his banner was lying trampled underfoot and no one knew he was an Eco-Gnome who was going to save the planet. He looked down at the angry, Lycra-clad mob who were shouting at him, waving their fists – and his courage failed.

A pack of people dressed in similar clothes who seemed to have violent tendencies could only mean one thing – a gang. He'd inadvertently wandered into a gangland ghetto. He had to admit, they didn't look like the traditional idea of a gang but the chance of so many people being in one place at one time in a Garden was unlikely unless it had something to do with organised crime. As his legs gave way, he plummeted to earth.

Even more unfortunate for Boggy, his braces caught on a branch as he fell, leaving him dangling slightly above the heads of the dreadful, colourful gangsters. A large little girl, who was taller than most of the Garden Ornaments managed to grab his foot, but by wriggling wildly, he slipped from her grasp. The force of her pull against the elasticated braces sent him hurtling through the air in a graceful arc. On the trajectory he was following, he would have landed in a pile of leaves – if it hadn't been for the Shed of No Return. As it was, Boggy slammed into the front of the shed, striking the door with such force, it smashed to pieces. There was a shocked silence, broken only by a cheery "'Ello, mate!"

A pram emerged from the shed, followed by a green-clad figure. "Am I glad to see you! You got any food? I'm 'Ank Marvin*."

At the sound of Peggy the Pram's Cockney lilt, Sylvester and Crispin looked at each other in horror and sidled into the bushes.

"No, we can't play hide and seek, Wendy, we've already explained we can't be seen in public while Peggy the Pram's around," said Crispin with as much patience as he could muster. It was several days after Boggy had smashed open the Shed of No Return and it had been kind of Wendy to take them in and hide them in the Wendy House, but the prospect of another day of colouring, dressing up and I-Spy was more than he could bear. Perhaps it would be better to face Peggy and her Boys.

"But I told you, Peggy'th gone."

"You didn't tell us anything of the sort!" said Sylvester.

"Oh thorry. I thought I'd told you."

"Aaargh!" said Sylvester, jamming his fist in his mouth in frustration.

"But I like having you two thtaying with me."

"Where've you two been?" Jubbly asked as he jogged past Crispin's Toadstool. "Peggy left a few days ago. Bartrum wants to see you both. You know he doesn't

---

* Cockney Rhyming Slang. Hank Marvin = Starving

like it when anyone leaves the Garden without permission…"

"We didn't leave the Garden, we've been staying with Wendy," said Crispin.

"Ouch," said Jubbly sympathetically, "you probably both need a holiday. If I'd known where you were, I'd have come and let you know. Peggy seems to have lost her memory while she was in the shed, so it looks like you two are off the hook. And even better, she bought out Nundies! She bought all my stock and is going to London to set up a shop."

"That's wonderful news!" said Crispin. "Let's celebrate!"

"Great idea! All back to my place for crispbread and cottage cheese," said Jubbly, running his hand over his much reduced and VPL-less bottom.

Doggett Sees the Light

Doggett the Fishing Gnome hadn't caught a fish for over a week.

It was unprecedented, inexplicable and exasperating.

Doggett was desperate.

Not only had his fishing expertise been called into question but his pursuit of Nina the Ninja had ground to a halt. True, his progress was almost at a standstill anyway, so a bit of deceleration wasn't noticeable, but that wasn't the point. He'd tried everything to rekindle the spark that had been ignited at the Halloween Party but the only time she showed him anything less than disdain, was when he gave her a fish. At any rate, she opened the door to take whatever fishy offering he had. If he had nothing, she merely peeped through the letterbox and told him to go away. Over the last few days, she hadn't even bothered to look through the letterbox.

He needed a fish and he needed it now. But despite having been perched on his rock all morning, the float on his fishing rod barely moved on the still surface of the pond.

"Afternoon," said Crispin, who was out for a stroll. "Caught anything?"

Crispin didn't know much about fishing but he was fairly sure that stamping of feet and loud swearing wouldn't do much to attract a bite.

"I was only asking…" he said indignantly when Doggett paused for breath.

"Sorry," mumbled Doggett, "it's a sore point."

Crispin shrugged and turned to walk off.

"I heard that, Doggett!" said Wendy, who'd arrived silently from the bushes. "You should be ashamed. You thaid naughty wordth to Cwithpin, I'm going to wite your name down in my book. And I'm going to fine you. That'll be five penthe." She held out her hand. "It gave me thuch a shock, I thwallowed my barley sugar."

Doggett dug deep in his pocket and handed her five pence.

"Now," she said, taking a pencil and notebook from her pocket, "what'th your name?"

Once Wendy and Crispin had gone, Doggett sat down again and stared at the unmoving float, willing a fish to nibble his hook. A fly landed on his ear and he brushed it away irritably. It circled his head and settled on the same spot. He batted it away again. The fly established a pattern of alighting on his ear, taking off with split-second precision, nanometres ahead of Doggett's death blow, and performing two triumphant laps of his head before settling daintily once more on his ear.

Finally, Doggett could stand no more. He pulled his hat down over both ears, reeled in his fishing line and stomped home, muttering to himself. He took the long route, so he could pass Nina's Toadstool but without a fish, he knew it was pointless knocking.

And anyway, the sky was steely grey and if it didn't rain before he got home and drench him, he'd be very surprised.

In fact, the elements did surprise him. It didn't rain.

It hailed. And the hailstones were the size of marbles.

Lightning streaked across the sky, and thunder boomed overhead, shaking the leaves of the tree under which he was sheltering. Someone had once said it wasn't wise to stand under a tree, in case of lightning strike. So, what should he do? He vaguely remembered being told he should be out in the open. But there was more to it than that… Ah yes! Now he recalled… he should be out in the open, crouching down with his bottom in the air, so there were no pointy bits, like his hat, to attract lightning.

Crispin peered out of the window at the leaden sky. Day seemed to have turned to night. He winced as hailstones as large as Wendy's gobstoppers hammered against the glass, threatening to crack it. With alarming frequency, lightning streaked across the Garden, throwing everything into stark relief, including the strange object in the middle of the lawn.

"What's that?" Crispin asked but there was no reply because Sylvester was cowering behind the sofa, pulling a cushion over his head more tightly with each thunderclap. Crispin cleared a circle in the condensation on the window with his finger, and screwed up his eyes trying to identify the strange object. It was the same size and shape as Elliot the tortoise but when the lightning flashed, Crispin could see this tortoise – if indeed it was a tortoise – was bright red.

Elliot was brown.

He was also a technophobe, unlike this red tortoise, who had an aerial.

A large, red, remote-controlled tortoise? Crispin wondered.

A ragged, jagged streak of lightning sliced through the darkness, crackling with electricity. It sought the fastest route to earth and Crispin watched in horror as it snaked its way towards the tortoise's antenna until it made contact. Blue light pulsed down the aerial to the tortoiseshell, emitting tiny flares as it progressed. As the figure cartwheeled across the Garden, Crispin realised with shock, the remote-controlled tortoise was actually a Gnome gripping a fishing rod, with tongues of blue flame licking at his body. Grabbing his raincoat and with a colander on his head for protection against the hailstones, Crispin dashed into the storm. Running on smooth, slippery hailstones was challenging, but Crispin managed to remain upright. That is, until he reached the top of the steps to the Sunken Garden where his feet desperately tried to find purchase – and failed. With Elf boots scrabbling, Crispin's body pitched forward, resulting in a rather ungainly swallow dive. He landed in a heap at the bottom of the steps, thankful he'd only twisted an ankle and not broken his neck.

He hobbled painfully towards Doggett, who was leaning against the sundial, with a dazed look but a beatific smile on his face. Blue sparks continued to crackle from his skin and clothes, making him glow with an ethereal, blue light. His hair, beard and eyebrows were singed black and they steamed gently in the cool air.

Crispin wasn't sure whether it was wise to touch him but he definitely couldn't leave him there in such a sorry state, discharging electric sparks into the air. Gritting his teeth, Crispin seized Doggett and pulled him to his feet.

"Ow!" gasped Crispin as electric currents coursed up his arms, sending his muscles into griping spasms. If he'd been capable, he'd have let go, but his fingers had locked and were no longer under his control.

"Oooh!" said Crispin, as the pain subsided, to leave interesting tingles travelling up and down his body.

"Mmm!" he sighed as the tingles increased in intensity and became surprisingly pleasurable. So pleasurable, he nearly dropped Doggett while he enjoyed the sensations. He also noticed that his ankle which had been too painful to support his weight, no longer hurt.

Crispin settled Doggett on the sofa in his Toadstool and went to find Nina. Other than calling for Nurse

Bludgett – something he was reluctant to do – the only person Crispin could think of to help Doggett, was Nina. Not that she was medically qualified – or even trained, but Crispin knew she'd once been to a fancy-dress party as a nurse and she still had the costume. He left Sylvester in charge and forbade him to touch Doggett.

As soon as Crispin had left, Sylvester investigated the steaming guest.

"Ow!" Sylvester said when electricity sparked between his finger and Doggett's shoulder. Just as he'd begun to wish he'd heeded Crispin's instructions, the muscle spasms gave way to interesting tingles. "Oooh!" he said, and finally, "Mmm!" as rather pleasing vibrations rippled up and down his body. He was still quivering with pleasure when Wendy knocked at the door. She had a laptop under her arm and feeling unusually mellow, Sylvester smiled at her and invited her in.

Bending slightly to get in through the door, she followed the beaming Sylvester into the living room.

"Don't touch Doggett," Sylvester said.

"Okay, Thylvethter." Her horrified expression suggested she had no desire to touch the charred Gnome.

"Why are there blue thparkth coming off him?"

"It's a long story..." said Sylvester, who had no idea. "Anyway, what can I do for you?"

"You know you told me how clever you are with

technology? Well, I thought you might be able to mend thith…" Wendy smiled coyly at him, unable to conceal her adoration.

"What seems to be the problem?" asked Sylvester, taking the laptop and trying to lift the lid.

"I think it openth on the other thide…"

"I'm just testing the hinges… Yes, they seem to be okay…"

He turned the laptop around, opened the lid and stared at the black screen. "Yes, it's definitely broken."

"Aren't you going to turn it on?" Wendy asked, leaning over to press the On button.

"Of course! I was just carrying out visual checks first…"

"Oooh, Thylvethter, you're tho clever!"

The screen was still black.

"It might take me a while to fix, so if you'd like to come back later…" Sylvester said. Crispin would be back any time soon and he'd probably know how to repair it.

"But I'd love to watch you… Pleathe…"

"No, I can't work with an audience."

"Shall I come back in ten minuteth?" she asked, her face alight with hope.

"Make it half an hour."

"Okay… If you're sure…" she said ducking to get through the door on her way out.

"I am," said Sylvester following her to make sure

she left. As he passed the sofa, he couldn't resist touching Doggett again.

"Ow!" Sylvester gasped.

"What'th the matter?" Wendy's face was full of concern as she rushed back into the room.

"Nothing," said Sylvester through gritted teeth. "Oooh!" he added.

"Thylvethter, you're glowing…"

"Mmm!" sighed Sylvester.

"Are you all right? You've got blue thparkth in your hair…"

"I'm fine," said Sylvester, "but perhaps you'd better bring this back tomorrow. I'm a bit busy looking after Doggett at the moment."

As he handed her the laptop, it sprang to life. The screen lit up, music blared and it vibrated.

"Oh, Thylvethter! You're tho clever!" Wendy squealed and clapped her hands. "How did you do that?"

Sylvester was so surprised, he almost dropped the laptop but he was enjoying the tingles too much to reply. He merely shrugged and gave himself up to the sensations, hoping Wendy would let herself out.

"No," said Nina, "absolutely not."

"Please," begged Crispin, "he's really poorly."

"I'll come on one condition…"

"Name it."

"Get him to stop bringing me fish and I'll

consider it." Nina crossed her arms over her ample chest.

"But I thought you liked his fish…"

"No, I loathe them but if I don't take them off him, he posts them through the letterbox and they slime up my doormat. I've been swapping them with Wendy, for barley sugars. Her cat likes fresh fish. But there are only so many sweets a girl can eat in one day and I'm getting a bit sick of barley sugars."

"I'll tell him to stop giving you fish. Now will you come?"

"Okay, just give me a few moments to find my nurse's uniform."

"I told you not to touch Doggett!" said Crispin crossly. "And don't deny it, I can see your hair standing on end and sparking."

"Is this the patient?" asked Nina rather unnecessarily. She seized Doggett with her sausage-pack hands and hoisted him over her shoulder before Crispin could stop her.

"Ow!" she shrieked. "Oooh!" and finally, "Mmm!"

As she carried Doggett back to her Toadstool, she had a very broad grin on her face.

"Someone's knocking at the door!" shouted Sylvester from the living room.

"Well answer it!" shouted Crispin, who was washing up in the kitchen.

The rapping continued and grew in intensity.

"They're still there!" shouted Sylvester who was curled up on the sofa.

Crispin rushed past with suds dripping from his rubber gloves. "You could've opened it," he grumbled.

"Who, me?" mumbled Sylvester.

Crispin had barely turned the latch when the door burst open and Bartrum barged in.

"You two! I'm deputising you, follow me! Well, come on! What're you waiting for?"

Sylvester leapt from the sofa, stood to attention and looked at Crispin for guidance.

"Err, what do you want us to do, Bartrum?" asked Crispin.

"I've been threatened and I need bodyguards – and that's you two!"

"But wouldn't Frank Fowle be a better bodyguard than us?" Crispin asked.

"I can't find him."

Sylvester shrank backwards. "I need the bathroom."

"No time for that! We… You need to nip this in the bud," Bartrum said.

"Err… and if we don't want to?" asked Crispin. "Will it mean cess pit duty?"

"Definitely! Starting immediately."

Crispin sighed and said to Sylvester, "Fetch your wellies and a nose clip. We're off to the cesspit for cleaning duties."

"I don't think so," said Bartrum, grabbing the two Elves and frogmarching them into the Garden. "When I say I need bodyguards, I mean it."

When they approached Nina's, Bartrum had each Elf by the ear. He pulled them both down behind a bush.

"Ow!" yelled Sylvester. "That hurt!"

"Shh, he'll hear you," said Bartrum. "We need the element of surprise when you attack. Look, there he is and… Oh no! He's armed with a light sabre!"

"What!" squealed Crispin.

"Lemme go!" screamed Sylvester as Bartrum propelled them both towards the light-sabre wielding figure.

"Hello, where did you two come from?" Doggett asked the two Elves who lay sprawled at his feet.

"Watch out for his light sabre!" yelled Bartrum from behind the bush.

"What's going on?" Doggett asked as he leaned his broom against the wall. The handle glowed with a blue light and electricity crackled from it until Doggett let it go, then it reverted to a normal yard broom.

"Well, how was I to know it was just a broom?" said Bartrum crossly. "It glowed and hummed like a light sabre."

"Tea?" asked Doggett.

"Don't you try and change the subject!" said Bartrum. "We need to sort a few things out!"

"We do?"

"Don't try acting all innocent. What about your challenge to my authority?"

"Did you challenge Bartrum?" Nina asked, appearing as if from nowhere.

"Not that I know of." Doggett scratched his head.

"You must have," insisted Bartrum. "All I keep hearing about are your superpowers and how you can heal people and mend things…"

"Oh that," said Doggett airily.

"Come on Man! Be a Gnome! If you're going to challenge me for control of the Garden, well… get on with it. But I warn you, I fight dirty and I have minders."

He grabbed Sylvester and Crispin who'd been creeping away and dragged them back.

"Challenge?" asked Doggett scratching his head and sending sparks flying. "Well, I ought to be sweeping up really, but I suppose I could spare an hour for a quick game of Scrabble if you like… We could play for matchsticks…?

"So," said Bartrum warily as the two Gnomes faced each other across the Scrabble board, "let me get this straight, Doggett, you definitely don't want to be in charge of the Garden?"

"*Me?* In charge of the Garden? No thank you. Whatever gave you that idea?"

A long searching look at Doggett's face assured Bartrum the denial was sincere.

"Very wise indeed," said Bartrum, smiling with satisfaction as he looked down at his Scrabble tiles. "Ah! Checkmate. I win."

"Checkmate? I thought you had those in Chess," said Sylvester.

"I've made the word 'Checkmate', you idiot," said Bartrum. "Look." He pointed to the word "CHEKMATE".

"Don't you spell 'Check' with a… Ow!" said Sylvester as Crispin elbowed him in the ribs.

"Now, tell me about these tingles I've been hearing so much about, Doggett," said Bartrum.

"Not much to tell really. When I come into contact with anyone, they get the tingles. People seem to like them. Especially Nina." He smiled at her shyly and she blushed.

"And is it true these tingles actually cure things?" asked Bartrum.

"Yep. Apparently."

"How about bunions?"

"I'd be happy to give it a go."

Doggett reached out and touched Bartrum's arm.

"Ow!" yelled Bartrum, his mouth falling open in surprise. Then, when the shock had passed, he added, "Oooh!" and finally, "Mmm!"

Doggett's Blues

"What the…!" Sylvester squeezed the brakes with all his strength.

Crispin, who was behind him on the tandem bicycle, nearly flew over his shoulder. "I told you not to brake sharply," he said and then spotted what Sylvester had seen.

"Just like traffic lights," said Sylvester, and Crispin poked him in the ribs.

"Remember what I told you about being tactful, Sylvester?"

Sylvester nodded. "Look a person in the eye and lie, lie, lie."

"I don't remember putting it quite like that," said Crispin. "Anyway, in this instance, leave the talking to me. Keep your mouth closed and just nod."

"Just nod," said Sylvester, "I've got it. But can I laugh?"

"No. Definitely no laughter."

"In that case, can't we turn around and pretend we haven't seen her?"

"Seen who?" asked Nina, who'd suddenly appeared next to them.

"Err… Wendy," lied Sylvester. Then remembering he should have left the talking to Crispin, he started to nod.

"Is he all right?" Nina asked Crispin, frowning as she watched the nodding Elf.

Crispin nodded.

"Well," Nina said eventually, "what d'you boys think of my new look?" She patted her hair.

Sylvester nodded harder, his chin bouncing up and down off his chest.

"It's very… err… red," said Crispin.

"Yes, but do you like it?" Nina patted it again.

"Oh yes, it's very… err… lovely."

"D'you really think so?" she asked.

"Oh, yes," said Crispin, "and it goes so well with your outfit."

"Like traffic lights," said Sylvester who couldn't help himself.

"What he means," said Crispin quickly, "is that a green skirt, orange blouse and red hair are just like traffic lights because they are… um, they are so striking, they'd stop traffic." He mopped his brow.

"Striking, eh? How wonderful! So, d'you think Doggett will like it?"

Crispin and Sylvester nodded so hard, their eyes seemed to rattle in their sockets.

"Definitely," said Crispin uncrossing his fingers. After all, Doggett was besotted with Nina and would find her attractive if she'd just crawled out of the cesspit wearing a sack.

Doggett peered into the pond. His glowing, blue reflection stared back at him balefully and beneath the surface of the water, fish lined up to bite his hook and experience the tingles that passed from his body, down his fishing rod and into the hook.

If fish had been able to speak, they would have been saying "Ow!", "Oooh!", "Mmm!", as they nibbled his bait and were hoisted to land. He was catching so many fish, he'd taken to throwing them back, where they joined the end of the queue, jostling to get a bite of his hook once more.

I've got everything I ever wanted – more fish than I know what to do with. I'm popular with everyone and Nina says she loves me, thought Doggett gloomily. *What more could a Gnome ask?*

It was all getting him down.

And to make matters worse, Crispin and Sylvester had just pulled up on their tandem bicycle next to the pond.

"Need a hand?" asked Sylvester leaping from the bike. Doggett knew what was coming next and didn't bother to say "No."

Sylvester would find any excuse to shake his hand or clap him on the back, to get a dose of the tingles.

"Ow!", "Oooh!", "Mmm!" said Sylvester, wandering off into the woods with a soppy smile on his face.

"Everything all right?" asked Crispin, who'd noticed Doggett's despondent expression. "You look like you're a bit under the weather."

Doggett sighed and shook his head.

"Why don't you go and see the doctor?" suggested Crispin.

"Nah. He doesn't like me. He said I'm putting him out of business because I keep healing people with my superpowers."

"Well, what about the Hermit? He knows about herbs and stuff. P'raps he can help… that is, if you can get an appointment. He's a bit reclusive."

"What seems to be the problem, my son?" the Hermit asked.

"Well, I… that is, I… um…"

Where to begin? thought Doggett. *How can I tell him I'm afraid people only want me for my superpowers and so they can get a dose of the tingles? Suppose they wear off? What then?*

"Take your time, my son."

"Well, Father, it all started the night of the storm…"

"What started, my son?"

"Well, I… that is, I… um…"

"Is it the flies that are bothering you, my son?"

"Flies?"

"Yes, the flies buzzing around your head."

"Well, I suppose they're a bit of a nuisance. They've been doing that all day but the frogs have been eating them."

"Frogs?" asked the Hermit, his eyes opening wider. "Have you seen many?"

"Quite a few. They live down by the pond."

"How about crickets?"

"What about them?"

"Have you seen many, my son?"

"I saw one this morning. Why?"

"Oh dear, oh dear," said the Hermit, wringing his hands. "I fear you have a terrible curse on you, my son."

"A curse?" wailed Doggett. Panic welled up in his chest.

"I fear you may be a One-Gnome-Plague-Incident."

Doggett was beginning to wish he'd never come. What had started as a mild case of the blues had escalated to something of gigantic – one might even say, *biblical* proportions.

"Now, you must look out, my son, for the other plagues…"

"*Other plagues?* You mean it's going to get worse?" The panic in Doggett's chest was squeezing his heart.

"I fear so, my son. There are ten in all."

Doggett fainted.

"Slow down!" said Crispin later when Doggett appeared at his door. "Take a deep breath, I can't understand a word you're saying!"

Crispin wanted to pat Doggett on his shoulder to comfort him but it didn't feel quite right to self-administer a dose of the tingles. He hovered, waving his hands in what he hoped was a sympathetic way.

"I'm doomed. *We're* doomed and it's all my fault," wailed Doggett.

It took three cups of tea, two currant buns and lashings of sympathy before Crispin managed to get anything sensible out of Doggett. As he was a bit hazy on the details of the ten plagues, he consulted the dusty encyclopaedia that was used as a doorstop.

"But Doggett, most of these things occur naturally anyway. You find flies, gnats and frogs in gardens everywhere. They're nothing to do with plagues," said Crispin adopting the Voice of Reason. He batted away a fly that was hovering over Doggett's head.

"But what about the thunder and hail?"

"It's called 'weather'. It happens everywhere."

"Locusts?"

"Well, technically, one cricket isn't a plague of locusts."

"Sick livestock?"

"We don't have any livestock."

"Trilby's got a cold, I heard him sneezing…"

"He's a cat and that doesn't count," said Crispin firmly.

"Boils?"

"No one in the Garden has boils."

"Gusty Bob's got warts."

"Not the same."

"Darkness?"

"The sun's shining. It won't get dark until later. But that hardly counts as a plague. It's called 'night'."

"Well, what about the blood?"

"Blood? What blood?" Crispin's voice shot up an octave.

"There was blood coming out of the tap this morning."

"You're sure?"

"Well, I didn't see it coming out of the tap exactly but there was blood in the sink, so where else would it have come from?"

Crispin was silent while he took this in.

"And the only thing that hasn't happened is the death of a firstborn… yet…"

"No," said Crispin, "there'll be some explanation for the blood. And no one is going to die."

Doggett wrung his hands and looked about wildly.

"I've thought hard and the only firstborn I can think of is Po Lin Jnr…"

"No," said Crispin whose Voice of Reason was turning into the Voice of Panic. He was about to add there were plenty of firstborns in the Garden beside the Gardener's son. Wilmslow was Bartrum's firstborn son, for example, but he thought better of it. He didn't want to stoke Doggett's fears.

"More tea?" asked Crispin. He needed a plan, and more tea would give him time to think. He hurried into the kitchen.

"Have you got any more buns?" Doggett called after him.

Doggett regretted leaving Crispin without saying goodbye but it was probably for the best. He could have done with another cup of tea and a couple of buns but he was a disaster zone and he needed to do something before someone got hurt – or worse.

But what to do?

He swatted the flies circling his head. The frog on his shoulder shot out his tongue and snatched one of them from its orbit.

Doggett sighed.

There was nothing he could do about flies, frogs and the other things that had already happened, but he could prevent anything happening to Po Lin Jnr – if he could find him.

He was out of breath by the time he'd searched the Alpine Garden but finally, he spotted Po Lin Jnr behind a large boulder, strumming his guitar.

"I hate this Garden. I hate it, hate it, hate it and everything in it. La, la, la," sang Po Lin Jnr in a tuneless voice.

Doggett didn't know what to do. The boy seemed to be all right but just as he was about to creep away, Po Lin Jnr started to cough.

"Oh no!" gasped Doggett, breaking into a run. "He's choking and it's all my fault."

Mr Po Lin had asked his son to weed the Alpine Garden but Po Lin Jnr was bored. He'd decided to take a break and hope his father didn't spot him.

There was simply nothing to do in this Garden. Well, actually there was plenty his dad wanted him to do but nothing he felt like doing.

He'd thrown rocks at one of the Garden Gnomes for a while until he'd broken a nail. *It's going to be hard to play the guitar properly now,* he thought crossly.

Stupid Garden Gnome. He hated them all with their smug, little faces, always cheery, always getting in his way.

When I'm a rich and famous rock star, I'll buy this Garden and smash every one of them.

He closed his eyes and imagined himself performing to his adoring fans. Girls would fling themselves at him and he'd invite them to parties and… well he didn't know what might happen then, as his imagination didn't stretch that far. But once when he was in the Post Office in the village, he'd managed to read most of a rock magazine, and the life of a rock star was definitely what he wanted. There'd be lots of alcohol and he'd finally find out what it tasted like and why everyone seemed to like it. It was a mystery, but one day, he'd know. The other thing that puzzled him was why rock stars liked weeds. He hated them. His dad didn't like them and made him pull them up. He'd risked asking Mr Willetts, the butler, why rock stars like weeds but he'd got a slap round the head for his pains. He later overheard Mr Willetts telling Cook that no good would come of the Gardener's son and that he wouldn't be surprised if the boy was smoking weed, even now, behind the garage.

Po Lin Jnr had gone to the back of the garage to see what was so special about it and to find out if there was anyone else there smoking weeds but other than a few old tyres and a rusty bucket, it was deserted.

It suddenly occurred to him that now was a perfect opportunity to find out about weeds. He had plenty he'd just dug up and he knew there was a bonfire where he could get a light. What was he waiting for?

He'd watched Mr Willetts outside the Old Priory when he thought he was unobserved and had a rough idea what it was all about, although the rolled-up weeds looked nothing like what Mr Willetts had been smoking. And in fact, they tasted pretty disgusting.

When Doggett arrived behind the boulder, Po Lin Jnr had finished coughing and was lying on his back, staring up at the sky.

"Oh no! I'm too late!" Doggett wailed. He slapped Po Lin Jnr's face to try to bring him round but there was very little response. Climbing on top of the boulder, he cupped his hands around his mouth and yelled "Help!" at the top of his voice.

Something was very wrong, Po Lin Jnr decided.

He'd somehow inhaled a piece of leaf that had lodged in his throat, triggering a paroxysm of choking. Unfortunately, while he was coughing, he'd struck his head against the boulder and knocked himself unconscious.

But now, he was coming round. He opened his eyes and tried to orientate himself. Obviously, he was lying on his back because straight ahead of him was sky. Fluffy clouds sailed from one side of his vision to the other, accompanied by a steady drumbeat. He moved slightly and realised the drumbeat was actually throbbing, coming from the back of his skull. He groaned and that was when the world went mad.

Or perhaps he'd passed out again and was dreaming.

A small face came into his field of view. Blue sparks crackled from its head, giving the appearance of a halo.

Is it an Angel? Am I dead?

But the hammering in his head suggested he wasn't, unless of course, pain accompanied you when you died.

He closed his eyes. He didn't want to see that small, halo-encircled face. If he ignored it, it might leave him alone.

Something thumped him repeatedly on the cheek.

"Is he dead?" asked a tiny voice.

"I don't know. Quick, you do chest compressions and I'll see if there's any reaction in his eyes."

Tiny fingers tried to prise his eyelids apart but he held them firmly closed. Then, something pummelled him on the chest.

Enough was enough. Po Lin Jnr sat up despite the pounding in his head. He felt sick but he was going home before the small Angels took him.

"Hey! You've done it! Well done!" squeaked the small Angel with the blue halo to the other one.

By now, Po Lin Jnr was on his feet and was staggering away.

"Should we follow him?" asked Doggett. "He doesn't look very steady."

"No," said Crispin, "you're not responsible for him."

"But the plagues..."

"There's no such thing. Honestly, all the things that have happened have been quite natural."

"But what about the water turning into blood."

"There's a logical explanation for that."

"There is?"

"Nina has a new hairdo and I think you'll find what you saw in the sink was hair dye, not blood..."

"Really? So, I'm not cursed? And Po Lin Jnr is safe?"

"You're not cursed and Po Lin Jnr is fine."

Doggett hugged Crispin.

"Ow! Oooh! Mmm!" said Crispin with a soppy smile on his face.

When Po Lin Jnr grew up, he was going to ban all adults. They were completely irrational. When his dad realised he hadn't finished weeding the Alpine Garden, predictably he'd ranted and raved, using those well-used adult words, "lazy", "ungrateful" and "ne'er-do-well". Junior had played the sympathy card and explained he'd knocked himself out but this only prompted those other well-used adult words "lies", "dishonesty" and "ne'er-do-well". He judged that further explanation as to exactly how the accident had occurred would be unwise and would likely result in the use of words such as "disgrace", "idiot" and "ne'er-do-well". As soon as he could, he escaped to the village. He'd saved up enough to buy a rock magazine in the Post Office so he could do some research. The sooner he became a star and ran his own life, the better.

Nina gently lifted the sleeping Doggett's hat. There was nothing inside it except his head and she breathed a sigh of relief. Tomorrow, she'd remove it and wash away the fish slime but, in the meantime, why wake him unnecessarily, even if the stink of fish was still rather strong? She set the hat back in place and patted his head fondly. Doggett snored, his mouth sagging open. It was lucky the flies had gone, and the frogs. She lifted the bedclothes to check they had, indeed, disappeared.

Thank goodness for Crispin, she thought although she still didn't understand what he and Doggett had been talking about. But it had been Crispin who'd spotted the fish that Doggett had forgotten he'd stored under his hat earlier in the day while he'd been fishing. And it had been Crispin who'd thrown it away. The flies had followed the fish into the bin in the Garden and the frogs had followed the flies. She'd been delighted to rid the Toadstool of the source of the fishy stink but nowhere near as delighted as Doggett, who'd danced about, giving Crispin high fives and almost sending him delirious with the tingles. There had been a lot of talk about "natural causes" and "coincidences" although inexplicably, when either of them mentioned "plague", they both fell about laughing.

Oh well, she thought, *boys will be boys*. And Doggett had been very appreciative of her new hairdo although she wished he hadn't kept telling Crispin she'd cheated a little with her new look. She'd have liked to have kept the actual details of how she'd achieved such a beautiful colour to herself. Exactly why dying one's hair was so funny, she had no idea but she'd ask Doggett about the joke in the morning. Nina gently pushed his bottom jaw up to meet the top, cutting off the raucous snoring.

"Ow! Oooh! Mmm!" she murmured as she snuggled down beside Doggett.

Also tucked up in bed, but still wide awake, was Po Lin Jnr Every time he closed his eyes, he relived his near-death experience and felt those tiny fingers clawing at his eyelids and tiny feet bouncing up and down on his chest. He was wondering if what he'd first thought of as tiny Angels were actually small Demons. Sleep was impossible. And if he was honest, the rock magazine hadn't helped a lot. There was so much in there he didn't understand. But at least rock stars seemed to be accident-prone, just like him. The fact that a rock had knocked him out seemed a strangely good omen. If the magazine was to be believed, rock stars crashed into other people's pads – whatever they were – and regularly tripped over acid. Yes, decided Po Lin Jnr, one day in the very near future, he was going to fit in perfectly.

A Genie out of the Bottle

Crispin and Sylvester hurried through the grey, dawn light to the Gazebo. Frost glittered like rhinestones in the grass and they shivered, despite their woolly hats, scarves and mittens.

"It could be worse," said Crispin trying to cheer up the grumpy Sylvester, "Bartrum could have called the meeting in the Sunken Garden and then we'd all freeze to death."

Sylvester muttered something under his breath – and under the circumstances, Crispin didn't challenge him.

By the time they arrived, Garden Ornaments had already started to assemble and were huddling together for warmth. Bartrum stood at the front, gavel in hand, waiting to begin.

"As it's rather chilly this morning, I'll keep it brief. We need to discuss the arrangements for Christmas. There are decorations and lights to be hung and a pantomime to be organised, followed by a party. Lord and Lady Arscott will be spending Christmas with Mrs Bartrum and myself and I can't impress upon you enough the importance of making sure they have an enjoyable time."

Crispin bent his knees slightly so he was completely hidden behind the rather stout Gnome in front. Surely Bartrum wouldn't choose him for any of the tasks. He didn't mind helping to hang the decorations but he didn't want to be in charge of anything. Especially not the pantomime…

"So, I've decided Crispin – where are you, Crispin? Show yourself, please. Ah! There you are," he said as the stout Gnome in front of Crispin bent over to tie up his bootlace. "You're in charge of the pantomime. I expect everyone to pitch in and help. Is that clear?" Heads nodded and faces reflected a mixture of sympathy for Crispin and relief at not being chosen themselves.

"Jubbly, you're in charge of the party and Klaus, you're in charge of lights and decorations. Any questions? No? Good. Time for a nice, hot cuppa," he said and banged his gavel, dislodging a tiny icicle from the bottom of the rock which hit the ground with a tinkle. The meeting was closed.

"It could be worse," said Sylvester mimicking Crispin. "We could have had the meeting in the Sunken Garden and then we'd have frozen to death…"

Crispin muttered something under his breath and stomped home.

For several weeks, Trilby had been looking for an opportunity to strike back at the Elves. He was convinced they'd deliberately poisoned him. When Crispin had insisted Sylvester help with the chores, he hadn't realised the younger Elf had no idea about food hygiene. It had all worked out well for Sylvester, whose stomach had been able to cope with "past-its-best" bacon and who'd subsequently been banned from cooking duties for the rest of his life. It hadn't worked out well for Crispin whose stomach had objected to the bacteria that had been incubating in the meat, nor for Trilby who'd come across the bacon in the bin and had also been violently ill.

And now Trilby wanted revenge.

He'd observed Crispin with a mop and bucket, washing the doorstep.

"Sylvester!" Crispin shouted. "You need to hurry up or we'll be late."

There was no reply and Crispin jumped over the wet step and shouted again from inside the Toadstool.

Trilby took his chance. He ran straight into the bucket, spilling sudsy water all over the hall. He wasn't fast enough to avoid drenching himself and as he fled – dripping wet – through the freezing Garden, dark thoughts about the horrible Elves filled his mind.

Revenge had not been sweet. It had merely been soapy, cold and wet.

How did other people settle scores? He would do some research.

"Oh no!" wailed Crispin as he surveyed the flood in the hall. "And it would have to happen now! I've got auditions in fifteen minutes but I need to clear up this mess! Sylvester!" he yelled.

"What? What? Oh! Why did you do that?"

"I didn't!" snapped Crispin. "This is going to take ages to clear up. You don't think you could delay the auditions for a while, do you?"

"I could start them for you if you like," said Sylvester.

"Oh, that would be wonderful. You'd do that for me?"

"Of course," said Sylvester, tiptoeing through the flood. "I'll see you in the Gazebo when you've finished. Don't rush," he added as he made his way down the path, whistling tunelessly.

Ah, bless him, he must finally be growing up, Crispin thought fondly.

It probably made sense for Sylvester to start the auditions, anyway. He'd volunteered to get a suitable script but whenever Crispin had asked to look at it, Sylvester had claimed he was still reading it.

He must know it inside out, thought Crispin, who still hadn't set eyes on it. Well, never mind. Everyone knows the story of *Aladdin*. Hopefully, the panto will direct itself.

Crispin arrived at the Gazebo just as the auditions were finishing.

"Great script!" called Doggett, "and great casting."

"Have you got a part?" Crispin asked.

"Oh yes, I'm SuperTingle. And I get to fly. Well, suspended on a wire, of course."

"Fly?" asked Crispin weakly. Well, he'd soon remove

that bit from the script – he didn't want the responsibility of people dangling from wires. He'd told Sylvester to find a script for the simplest *Aladdin* production he could. Who was "SuperTingle" anyway?

"Where's Sylvester?" he asked.

"Oh, you mean Harry Hunter!" said Nina. "He's just talking Wendy through her part."

"Please tell me she's not going to fly!" said Crispin. "She'll bring the Gazebo roof down."

"Oh no, although she might have a few stunts…"

Alarm bells started to ring in Crispin's head.

"But everyone loves the script!" said Sylvester crossly. "And you did say I could do the auditions."

"Yes, but for *Aladdin*, not *Harry and the Zombies*."

"*Harry Hunter and the Apocalypse*," corrected Sylvester.

"Whatever!" said Crispin crossly. "It's not a pantomime! Bartrum will be livid."

"He'll love it," said Sylvester with the confidence of youth.

"But I wanted a script for *Aladdin*. Where did you get this?" he waved Sylvester's script.

"I wrote it myself," he said proudly. "Don't you think Harry Hunter is a cool name?"

Crispin shook his head in disbelief.

Like a pantomime genie, once *Harry Hunter and the Apocalypse* had materialised in front of the Garden Ornaments, there was no stuffing it back in the bottle.

Crispin had begged everyone to change the production to *Aladdin* but no one wanted to give up their part and anyway, the tickets had already sold out. As yet, Bartrum had no idea he wasn't going to show Lord and Lady Arscott a *No-it-isn't-yes-it-is* sort of pantomime. Crispin's insistence there was no "flying" on wires, no climbing and definitely, no stunts, was not looked on favourably by Sylvester and the cast. In the end, rather than distress Crispin further, Sylvester held secret rehearsals. After all, Crispin would thank everyone when Bartrum and his guests pronounced *Harry Hunter and the Apocalypse* a success.

Crispin, meanwhile, had other problems on his mind. The Toadstool had become jinxed. It had started with the flood in the hall and now, the whole place smelled of rotting food. Crispin couldn't understand how decaying cabbage leaves and tomatoes kept appearing in the strangest of places – Sylvester's pants' drawer, the airing cupboard, on top of the wardrobe, up the chimney, in the umbrella stand – it was all very odd. Even Sylvester had complained about the stench. The only clue had been tiny, muddy paw prints on the white table cloth.

But the Elves didn't have a pet.

"Mice?" suggested Sylvester.

It was a mystery.

The day of the pantomime arrived and it was now too late for Crispin to do anything about *Harry*

Hunter and the Apocalypse. Klaus had done a wonderful job with the Christmas tree and decorations in the Gazebo and Bartrum had congratulated him on his efforts. Crispin knew he would just have to suffer whatever retribution Bartrum deemed necessary, in order to pay for his failure. Jubbly had assured everyone the post-pantomime celebrations would be the event of the year, so perhaps Lord and Lady Arscott would forget the pantomime once the party started.

Crispin was just one Elf and after all the misfortunes that had dogged him recently, he couldn't be expected to singlehandedly produce a pantomime and deodorise his Toadstool and the surrounding area. He'd done his best to find and remove the decomposing vegetables that had been appearing daily, but they'd been overwhelming – both in number and smell.

Well, thought Crispin, this is it.

Somewhere in the begonias, Gusty Bob began to tune-up. Crispin had tugged on the long piece of string which was tied to his leg – the signal that he should begin to play. It was a very, very long piece of string so the Toad was well out of sniffing range.

Just as well, thought Crispin, what with the lingering, rancid stink that was following him around and Gusty Bob's signature pong, Lord and Lady Arscott were in danger of serious olfactory overload. From his position in the wings, Crispin took the whole scene in. The curtains parted, Gusty Bob was putting heart, soul and plenty of oomph into his melody, Sylvester was poised to leap onto the stage from the other wing, while Bartrum and guests were sitting at the front of a large, spellbound audience.

Crispin was so nervous, his knees gave way.

By the end of the first act, Crispin's knees had regained some strength. Against all odds, *Harry Hunter and the Apocalypse* seemed to be quite popular. The audience stamped and cheered when Sylvester, as Harry Hunter, managed to outwit the wicked step-uncle, who had stolen the Kraptonite needed to give SuperTingle back his superpowers. McTavish, the Marble Cherub, with his notorious scowl, was the wicked step-uncle. It had been perfect casting, Crispin thought.

"Oh, no it isn't!" shouted Jubbly, as Widow Twerky.

"Oh, yes, it is!" replied the audience to the parody of a woman who teetered up and down the stage on stiletto heels, batting his enormous, false eyelashes and winking outrageously.

The only time Bartrum hid his eyes was during the battle, but as his son, Wilmslow, was chief of the zombies, he managed to overcome his dislike of all things to do with horror, long enough to peep through his fingers.

Harry Hunter seized the Kraptonite from McTavish, the wicked step-uncle, and with his Fairy

Godmother, played by the Wooden Robin, and Fairy Goddaughter, played by Wendy, he defeated the zombies in a climactic finish to the first half. Crispin tugged twice on Gusty Bob's string, to tell him to stop playing and the curtains closed to wild applause.

Scenery and costumes were changed and actors rushed to their places, ready for the second act which was announced by music from the begonias and the raising of the curtains.

"Here he is! Here's SuperTingle!" cried Harry Hunter to the Fairy Godmother and Goddaughter, pointing upwards.

The audience gasped as Doggett, in tights, vest and cloak, with sparks crackling from his body, swung onto the stage suspended on a wire.

Doggett did indeed look as though he was flying. Crispin was so engrossed, he didn't notice Trilby sneak up behind him with a mouldy Brussels Sprout held delicately in his mouth, intending to deposit it in Crispin's pocket – that is, until one of the scenery hands rushed past, treading on the cat's tail. Trilby screeched in pain and spat out the furry vegetable.

Crispin ducked to avoid it and fell over backwards, tugging with such force on Gusty Bob's string that he dragged him out of the begonias towards the Gazebo. Trilby, realising he'd been caught in the act, shot up the Christmas tree, rattling baubles and dislodging tinsel.

And that might have been the extent of the

trouble if Wendy hadn't spotted Trilby peering out of the branches at the top of the tree.

"Twilby! Come down!" she squealed.

Harry Hunter, who'd had his back to the tree and was unaware of what had happened, was wondering why the music had suddenly grown louder but he carried on regardless.

"I'm coming Twilby!" screamed Wendy starting to climb the tree.

The Wooden Robin hopped from foot to foot, pulling up his woollen socks, unsure what to do.

"Help!" screamed Wendy, whose dress had snagged on a branch.

The Gnome operating the wire dashed forward to see what was happening and as he let go, SuperTingle plummeted to the stage, amidst screams from the audience. Luckily, Doggett landed on his feet and he darted towards the tree to the cheers of the audience. He wasn't *playing* the part of SuperTingle, in his mind, he *was* SuperTingle – he was a real superhero – and somehow, his sparks seemed to flare more intensely than usual, crackling like tiny lightning bolts all around him.

"Nooo!" screamed Crispin, who was the only person to have correctly worked out what would be the result of Doggett coming into contact with the tree.

SuperTingle leapt into the branches, sparks crackling from his body, and it wasn't long before the decorations and pine needles were burning fiercely. He raced to the top, centimetres ahead of the blaze, freed Wendy, tucked her under one arm and scooped up Trilby. Harry Hunter grabbed the dangling wire and hurled it at Doggett, who caught it and leapt from the flames, which were now licking at his heels. In a graceful arc, he swung across the stage and landed next to the Wooden Robin, who was completely overcome and fell into the audience.

And that might have been the end of the disaster except that the wind had changed direction and with Gusty Bob so close to the Gazebo, a cloud of green, noxious, inflammable gas drifted gently towards the inferno.

The explosion blew Crispin backwards, temporarily deafening him, so he didn't hear the roar from the audience, the cheers, the whistling and the stamping of feet.

The fire had been so intense, it had consumed everything flammable and rapidly burnt itself out.

"This way to the party," Widow Twerky yelled, "follow me!" and putting up his lacy parasol, he twerked towards the party area, in his high heels.

"Hooray!" cheered the audience.

To Crispin, whose senses had been battered by the blast, it seemed as if everything was happening in slow motion. Through bleary eyes, he saw Lady Arscott approaching like an enraged bear; her arms outstretched. She was shouting, but Crispin's eardrums had been stretched to their limits and now, whatever the pitch, sounds were being transmitted to his brain as a low growl. Before the great, rumbling, bear-like figure of Lady Arscott reached him, Crispin fainted.

His hearing didn't return until the following day but Sylvester was eager to fill him in on what had happened.

"And if you hadn't fainted like a wimp..." Sylvester said.

"For your information, I passed out with the pain..."

"Whatever. Well, if you hadn't fainted like a wimp, you'd have heard how much Lady Arscott loved the panto..."

"Really?"

"Yeah, she said it was inspired."

"Really?"

"Yeah, and Lord Arscott said it was a triumph."

"Really?"

"Oh, and one other thing..."

"Bartrum?" asked Crispin weakly, fearing the worst.

"Oh no. He thought it was good too. No, what I was going to say was that Wendy said we could borrow her cat until you're well. She thought he'd cheer you up."

Sylvester left the room and returned a few

seconds later carrying a pink cushion on which sat Trilby, wearing a pink ribbon around his neck.

"Oh look," said Sylvester tickling him under the chin, "I think he likes me. He's smiling."

Stupid Elves, thought Trilby, fighting back the urge to bite Sylvester's finger. *But I will be avenged tonight when you both go to bed.* He'd carried out some research and found an interesting idea in a film and he was going to recreate a rather scary scene. True, he didn't have access to any horses' heads but he did have two particularly mature fish heads and they would do nicely.

The Christmas Beast

Crispin leapt out of bed and skipped to the window. It was so cold he was sure it must have snowed. But it hadn't, despite the short odds McTavish, the Marble Cherub, had been offering on a White Christmas. Not that Crispin was disappointed as he gazed out at the deep frost which coated the Garden. The sparkling, white crystals had turned everything into a winter wonderland and he knew that the chilly weather would ensure the presents he'd wrapped last night would be warmly welcomed by his friends. He'd been knitting for the last few weeks and an enormous pile of wrapped scarves waited under the Christmas tree, to be delivered as soon as Sylvester got up. There were some smaller parcels too because scarves weren't suitable for all of his friends.

Crispin had worried that when the Wooden Robin stopped to pull up his socks, he'd trip over a scarf. Instead, he'd found some fine, purple wool and using toothpicks, he'd knitted a pair of socks so skinny, they would hug the Wooden Robin's legs and not slip down. Well, at least he *thought* they'd fit, but he'd had to stop trying to judge the size by eye, when the Wooden Robin had complained that Crispin kept staring at his legs.

"They look like veins," Sylvester had remarked when Crispin held the socks up for inspection. Crispin wasn't sure whether that was a good thing or not.

Guessing what size to make Gusty Bob's bobble hat had also been a problem but in the end, it seemed to have turned out quite well. He'd decided against a scarf because of Gusty Bob's lack of neck and as the Toad's eyes were on the top of his head, a large hat would have been out of the question. But Crispin visualised the small bobble hat that he'd made, perched on the top of Gusty Bob's head, between his eyes, just like a crown. Well, Toads didn't need hats for warmth; they were, after all, cold-blooded animals.

Rustling of paper in the living room broke into Crispin's thoughts, "Sylvester!" he yelled. "Leave the presents alone!"

Wendy had invited the Elves for Christmas lunch and Crispin was grateful he didn't have to worry about cooking and could concentrate on visiting his friends to deliver the gifts he'd made. Sylvester had complained he wanted a "proper" Christmas lunch and not the bizarre meal he suspected Wendy might serve up. Crispin was relieved that for once, he didn't have to spend hours in the kitchen and was tempted to tell Sylvester that if he wanted a home-cooked meal, he could cook it himself but after the bacon fiasco, he decided it wisest to say nothing.

"Well, if I've got to eat jam sandwiches for lunch, can't we at least open our presents now?" Sylvester asked.

Crispin didn't need much persuading and while he made toast, Sylvester went to get the parcels. He staggered into the kitchen carrying an enormous armful of presents. Actually, the pile consisted of several small parcels and one huge one which he placed in front of Crispin.

"This is from me," he said proudly.

Sylvester had unwrapped his scarf, matching mittens and bobble hat before Crispin managed to find a square centimetre of paper on his parcel that wasn't covered in sticky tape.

"Come on!" said Sylvester, as he ripped the paper from his last present. "Ooh! A spy kit! I've always wanted one of those. Thank you!" He beamed at Crispin, who was scratching in vain at the parcel, trying to find a way in.

Sylvester had tried out all the false moustaches in his spy kit before Crispin finally managed to unwrap his present.

"What is it?" Crispin asked, gingerly poking one of the many hoses that coiled around the strange-looking contraption.

"It's a coffee machine. And I got you a jar of coffee too. D'you like them? I got them from Peggy the Pram."

Crispin's knees gave way.

"It's all right," Sylvester added, looking pained, "I've paid for them."

Crispin wasn't quite sure whether to believe him

after the previous encounters he'd had with Peggy, but it was Christmas, after all. A time to remember the good things. Still, the nagging thought that Peggy's Boys were on their way was worrying indeed.

"Look, you put the water in here and the coffee in there," said Sylvester pointing to different openings, "…I think… Oh no, perhaps you put the coffee in here…" He lifted flaps and wiggled knobs. "If you pour water in here, then the coffee must go here," he said, tipping granules from the jar into the funnel, "and perhaps here. Then you put the coal here and light it… just there."

Reluctantly, the machine juddered to life. Wheels and cogs turned, driving chains which operated pulleys and fans, all accompanied by the rumble of moving parts and the murmur of simmering water. Puffs of steam drifted out of the vents and from anywhere else that Sylvester had loosened when he'd been turning knobs, as the water in the boiler bubbled and gurgled so vigorously, the machine trembled.

"What do the instructions say we do now?" Crispin shouted, attempting to be heard above the rising whistle of the steam.

"What instructions?"

"Quick!" shrieked Crispin, grabbing a mug from the draining board and thrusting it under the nozzle from which steam and drops of water were hissing and spitting. He was just in time, as coffee erupted with volcanic ferocity into the mug and hitting the bottom with such force, it splashed out onto the worktop.

The Elves jumped backwards away from the scalding liquid and hid behind a chair while the machine continued to grumble and wheeze.

"Has it finished?" asked Crispin although he suspected Sylvester had less idea than he did. The growling and shrieking went on for some time after the delivery of coffee until the machine finally belched and was silent.

Crispin crept out from behind the chair and surveyed the puddle of coffee and scorch marks on the worktop. Raising the mug, Sylvester sniffed the contents.

"Mmm, I love the smell of fresh coffee. Milk or cream?" he asked.

Crispin, who wasn't very keen on coffee, was tempted to tip it into the sink but it wasn't often Sylvester made him a drink and he looked so proud of himself.

"Milk, please." Hopefully, it would dilute the coffee.

However, even when the small amount of coffee that remained in the mug, had been topped up with milk, it was still very strong and Crispin fought the urge to grimace.

"Mmm, lovely," he said and threw the rest down the sink while Sylvester was inspecting a hose that had become detached.

“Wow, it’s a beast of a machine, isn’t it? Shall we make some more?” asked Sylvester.

“Well, let’s wait until we’ve adjusted the machine slightly.” Crispin had no idea which part they would adjust nor how they would do it, but his nerves couldn’t stand another cup. “Anyway, we’ve got presents to deliver before Christmas dinner…”

Thankfully, Sylvester was easily distracted and ran to get his new scarf, mittens and bobble hat.

Crispin mopped up the mess and wondered which part of the machine was crucial and whether it could easily be removed and hidden, rendering it inoperable.

“Come on! I’ve packed everything up, let’s go!” called Sylvester from the hall.

“I love them!” chirped the Wooden Robin excitedly. “I’ve never seen knitted ones before!”

“But you’re wearing some,” said Crispin in surprise.

“What? French beans?” chirped the Wooden Robin.

“They’re not beans, they’re veins,” said Sylvester.

“Veins? But they’re green. You don’t get green veins,” said the Wooden Robin.

“They’re not green, they’re purple,” said Crispin and before Sylvester could say anything, he added, “and they’re socks, not beans or veins.”

“Ooh!” trilled the Wooden Robin, “how marvellous!”

"You can try them on if you like," said Crispin.

The Wooden Robin stopped hopping from foot to foot. "Um... if it's all right with you, I'll put them on when you've gone."

"But I'd love to see if they fit..." said Crispin.

"I'm sure you would!" said the Wooden Robin in a knowing voice. "Don't think I haven't noticed you eyeing up my legs when you think I'm not watching..."

"What? I wasn't eyeing up your legs!" gasped Crispin. "I was trying to work out how long the socks needed to be."

"Really?" asked the Wooden Robin.

"Don't be ridiculous!" said Sylvester scornfully. "Of course he wouldn't be looking at your legs. Who'd want to look at your skinny, little, twig-like..."

The Wooden Robin's eyes filled with tears.

"What Sylvester means," said Crispin quickly, "is that I was merely checking the length of your legs to see how skinny I needed to make the socks and how similar your legs are to fine, strong twigs..."

"Are you sure you haven't got a leg fetish?" asked the Wooden Robin doubtfully.

"No!" said Crispin firmly, "I haven't."

Gusty Bob, however, tried his present on as soon as he'd unwrapped it, although it became clear he couldn't move without the tiny, red bobble hat falling off.

"Perhaps it needs two ribbons sewn to it, to tie under your chin?" suggested Crispin.

"What chin?" asked Sylvester. "He hasn't got one."

"Since you so kindly pointed that out," said Crispin tartly, "you can help solve the problem."

"I can?"

"Yes," said Crispin, taking the spy kit box from his bag. "You can give Gusty Bob some of the double-sided tape you've got for sticking the false moustaches on."

"I can?"

"Yes, in fact, I think it's the least you can do. Perhaps you'd like to throw in a false moustache too…"

Crispin took the roll of tape and a rather fine bushy, ginger moustache out of the box before Sylvester could object and stuck a large strip of tape to the bobble hat before placing it on Gusty Bob's head.

"There, that should hold it until I can make something more permanent," said Crispin, holding a small mirror for Gusty Bob to admire his new hat and moustache.

"That was really unfair," grumbled Sylvester as they walked through the Garden to deliver the other presents. "You gave one of my moustaches away."

"It's Christmas," said Crispin, "a time of good

cheer and being nice to people, not commenting on people's thin legs or lack of chin. Anyway, I thought you wanted to be like a spy. You have to be smooth, suave and dashing, not critical and obnoxious. Spies don't upset people."

"I bet it would upset *you* if a spy killed you. Anyway, I can be smooth, suave and dashing…"

"Well, perhaps you could practise while we deliver the rest of the presents…" said Crispin and then hastily added, "I mean being smooth, suave and dashing. Not killing people."

Their last stop before getting to the Wendy House was Nina the Ninja's Toadstool. Crispin's bag was no lighter than it had been when he'd left home, as each time they'd stopped to deliver parcels, they'd also received presents. So far, everyone had loved their scarves. Each one had been specially customised, either with the recipient's name or some other feature. For example, Jubbly's scarf had the Mexican flag at one end and a pretty fringe at the other, so it would suit all occasions and personas. Crispin had knitted Nina's scarf in red, orange and green to go with her hair and favourite outfit and he'd warned Sylvester not to mention traffic lights. For Doggett, Crispin had used fire-retardant wool to knit a black scarf with blue lightning flashes.

"How thoughtful," said Doggett, wrapping it tightly around his neck. "This one won't go up in flames."

"My scarf matches my hair," said Nina, trying it on and admiring herself in the mirror over the mantelpiece.

"Yes, it's…" said Sylvester.

Don't mention traffic lights, Crispin mouthed at Sylvester.

"Don't mention what?" asked Sylvester out loud.

Nina swung round and looked at Sylvester, who was looking at Crispin.

"Did I miss something?" she asked.

"No," said Crispin. "Gosh, is that the time? We'd best be off…"

"Ow! Oooh! Mmm!" said Sylvester, quickly patting Doggett's arm, afraid he'd be dragged out before he got a dose of Christmas tingles.

Crispin grabbed him by the arm and pulled him to the door.

"What's the matter?" Sylvester asked.

"When I mouth something to you, it's because I want to send you a secret message. What you *don't* do, is to ask me to repeat it out loud because then everyone knows I've just tried to say something to you without them knowing. You'll never make a spy if you can't master that! Honestly!"

Sylvester was still sulking by the time they reached the Wendy House.

He'd put on a pair of sunglasses, a Fedora hat which he pulled low over one eye and stuck a large handlebar moustache on his upper lip.

"I'm sure Wendy will love your outfit," said Crispin in an attempt to stop the sulk.

"She might. But if she's made jam sandwiches for lunch I'm going to…"

"Don't be so ungrateful," said Crispin losing patience, "it was nice of her to ask us."

"Not if she gives us jam sandwiches," said Sylvester. "I'm starving."

"It could be worse, she might give us a bag of barley sugars and a gobstopper."

"You might be right," said Sylvester gloomily.

"I was only joking," said Crispin, "although it is a distinct possibility," he added anxiously.

Wendy opened the door, wearing a paper hat and carrying an armful of Christmas crackers.

"Oh! Thylvethter, aren't you handthome!"

"How did you know it was me?"

"Only you and Cwithpin are coming. It couldn't be anyone elthe. Oooh! I love Chrithmath, don't you?"

"I love Christmas dinner," said Sylvester.

Don't be so rude! Crispin mouthed at Sylvester.

"Don't what?" Sylvester said out loud.

Wendy peered at them. "Are you playing a Chrithmath game?"

"Yes, said Crispin, with his fingers crossed behind his back.

"Oooh, how wonderful! You can teach me how to play it after dinner."

She led them into the dining room, where the doll's table was set for lunch.

"When you've taken off that mouthtache, Thylvethter, I'll give you a kith under the mithletoe."

Sylvester pressed the moustache firmly in place.

"It's a real moustache," he lied.

Crispin sighed. This Christmas Day had the makings of a disaster. Thankfully, it improved significantly when Wendy poured the Elves a glass of sloe gin.

"Thit down and I'll bring dinner." After placing a cracker by each place setting, Wendy went into the kitchen. As Sylvester drank, the sloe gin dissolved the adhesive on the sticky tape attaching the moustache to his upper lip and it slithered into the glass. Once he'd fished it out of his drink, it appeared more like a dead caterpillar than facial hair, so he tucked it in his pocket, then quickly grabbed a handful of moustaches from his spy kit, stuck one to his face and put the rest in his other pocket. It wouldn't do to be caught without a moustache while there was mistletoe around. And there appeared to be rather a lot of it.

Sylvester sat at the table and groaned. "It's worse than I thought. She's gonna play 'Doll's Tea Party'."

"What's that?"

"It's where she pours imaginary tea into a doll's cup and then you have to pretend to drink it with your pinkie like this," Sylvester held his little finger up in an exaggerated curve. "And then she serves imaginary cakes and you have to describe them and say how delicious they are. I don't think I can bear it…"

"You seem to know a lot about playing 'Doll's Tea Party'."

"The last time I came over, she wouldn't let me go until I'd served all the dolls… She's got a lot of dolls," he added indignantly.

Wendy reappeared with a tray piled high with plates, dishes and a large, steaming roast turkey.

"Could one of you fetch the vegetableth and the thtuffing, pleathe?"

Sylvester nearly knocked her over as he rushed past her to get the rest of the food.

"This is wonderful, Wendy! I didn't realise you could cook," said Crispin as they tucked into turkey and all the trimmings.

"Oh, I can't," she said.

"But?" Crispin held up his loaded fork and gestured towards it.

"My chum Fwank Fowle cooked it for me."

Crispin froze. His fork remained in the air as he eyed it with suspicion, remembering Frank with his finger up his nose, cooking at Bartrum's dinner party.

"Don't worry, I know exthactly what you're thinking…"

"You do?"

"Yeth, but it'th okay."

Crispin's fork still hovered in front of his mouth.

"It is?"

"Oh, yeth, I thorted him out."

"You did?" Crispin asked, wondering how she'd persuaded the Troll to keep his finger out of his nostril. He placed the fork in his mouth and started chewing.

"Yeth, I showed him the pwoper way to hold a wooden thpoon. He thaid he pweferred to hold it by the bowl but he'd have a go."

Crispin gagged on his half-chewed food.

But it was amazing how after several glasses of Wendy's sloe gin, Crispin was finding it hard to recall the image of Frank and his probing finger. He was finding it hard to remember who Frank Fowle was at all.

"Pudding?" asked Wendy as she cleared the plates away.

"Do we have to describe it? And does it involve feeding Milly and Rosie?" Sylvester asked, nodding at the two dolls who were sitting at the table with them.

"Only if you want to," said Wendy. "They had thuch fun when you were here the other day…"

Sylvester assured her he was quite happy to eat pudding himself and while she was in the kitchen, he scooped up the two dolls and dropped them behind the sofa.

"Bye-bye, Silly and Dozy," he said as he dusted his hands together. Crispin looked at him in disapproval.

"Their eyes were following me," Sylvester said defensively. "If you'd been here at the Doll's Tea Party, you'd know what I mean. I'm probably scarred for life."

"Where are Milly and Rothie?" Wendy asked as she came in with an enormous Christmas pudding.

"Gone for a walk," said Sylvester quickly.

"I hope they'll come back thoon or there won't be any pudding left."

"Yes," agreed Sylvester, helping himself to another large spoonful.

"That was lovely," said Crispin, patting his stomach.

"Thank you," said Wendy, "but I'm getting a bit worried about Milly and Rothie. I think we ought to go out and look for them."

Sylvester looked out of the window at the frosty landscape and shivered.

Serves you right, mouthed Crispin.

"Serves what?" said Sylvester out loud.

"Ooh, you're playing that funny game again! Let me play! What do I have to do?"

"I know," said Sylvester, "let's open our presents. I'll show you my spy kit and if you like, you can wear a false moustache. Then if Silly… err, I mean Milly and Rosie aren't back, we'll have a game of hide and seek. I'm sure they'll turn up by then."

Wendy squealed with delight at her scarf, bobble hat and mittens. They were in her favourite shade of pink and Crispin had sewn some pockets on the scarf and the hat where she could store her sweets. There was a small, pink scarf for Trilby too and Wendy went into the kitchen to fetch him, to try it on. When she came back, she had the struggling cat under her arm, screeching in protest.

"Twilby ith behaving very, very badly." She frowned as she held him down while Crispin tied the scarf in a bow around his neck. Trilby thanked Crispin by sinking tiny, needle-like teeth in his hand.

"Oh, Twilby, you naughty kitty!"

The naughty kitty took full advantage of the mayhem and fled to the kitchen where he lapped up the remaining milk in his saucer, to try to get rid of the taste of Elf before disappearing through the cat flap.

"That was a surprisingly nice day," said Crispin, rubbing his distended stomach and swapping the heavy bag of presents to his other shoulder. They'd decided to take a detour to Nina's Toadstool so that Doggett could heal Crispin's bite wound before they returned home, and Sylvester had grabbed the opportunity to get a bonus dose of Christmas tingles.

"I'll make us a nice cup of coffee when we get in and then we can unwrap all our pressies," Sylvester said once the tingles had worn off and the sloppy grin had faded.

Crispin didn't fancy coffee at all. The messages his brain was sending to the rest of his body seemed to have been intercepted, and in the absence of sensible instructions, his feet were acting independently of each other. He also had the irresistible urge to giggle.

Too much sloe gin, he thought. A cup of strong coffee might be just the thing.

Sylvester's attempts to evade Wendy under the mistletoe had also been thwarted by the sloe gin which had displaced four moustaches in total. She'd finally seized the end of one that was still successfully sticking to his lip and with a flick of her wrist, she'd pulled it off. But the sloe gin had slowed Sylvester down and before he could react, she'd planted a kiss firmly on his cheek.

"I wonder if that's why they call it 'slow gin'," Sylvester mused remembering the indignity and wiping his cheek at the memory.

"Well, 'ello, me old China*..." said a cheery voice.

Peggy the Pram stepped out from behind a tree.

An enormous jolt of adrenalin banished all traces of sloe gin from Crispin's brain and it fired multiple messages to his feet telling them to run. Unfortunately, the messages didn't agree on which direction each foot was to go. He spun on the spot and tripped, dropping the bag and spilling presents over the ground. Peggy helped him pick them up.

"I 'ear you been givin' everyone scarves this year..."

Crispin gulped and nodded, his eyes nearly popping out.

---

* Cockney Rhyming Slang. China plate = Mate

"And other knitted stuff?" Peggy asked.

Crispin nodded again. He wanted to put his hands over his brows to protect them but his arms seemed to be paralysed.

"I'll be over to see you boys tomorrow. I've got a business proposition for you both."

"Both?" asked Crispin.

"Yeah. I'm interested in you supplying me with goods. 'Ow about 'alf a dozen scarves to begin with and as your young friend is about to get 'is winnin's from McTavish, I thought 'e might like to invest it in my business. Like a sleepin' partner."

And with that, Peggy was gone.

"Well, it could be worse," said Sylvester to Crispin who was still kneeling on the ground, "we might make our fortunes. And I think she's definitely forgotten about you sending her to the Shed of No Return…"

"Shhh!" said Crispin looking around in alarm. "She might hear you! And I assure you that if there are fortunes to be made, *we* won't be making them."

"But being a sleeping partner can't be too hard."

"When she says 'sleeping', she probably means something altogether more permanent than you have in mind…" said Crispin, getting to his feet. "Anyway, what did she mean when she said your 'winnings'?"

"Oh that," said Sylvester airily. "I placed a bet against it being a White Christmas with McTavish…"

"You placed a bet on Christmas?" Crispin was incensed.

"There's no need to sound so cross. Wendy placed a bet with McTavish too."

"That's not the point. It's Christmas. You can't go around betting on it. It's not right. And now, thanks to you and your gambling, we're unlikely to see the New Year."

The two Elves walked home in silence, each lost in his own thoughts and therefore unaware that Trilby was following at a safe distance with a pink scarf around his neck that he had been unable to remove.

He had revenge on his mind.

"I know," said Sylvester as they neared the Toadstool, "tomorrow, we'll put on disguises from my spy kit and Peggy'll never know it's us."

Crispin ran his fingers along his eyebrows. It had taken so long for them to grow back properly after one of Peggy and the Boys' previous visits. Putting on a false moustache would just give the Dragon more to aim at. Unless…

"I've got a better idea," said Crispin, "quickly, open the door, I've got a lot to do before morning. And I'm going to need coffee – lots of coffee – so you'd better fire up the Beast."

As Sylvester took his hands out of his pockets, the damp, false moustaches which had come off in the sloe gin, fell out on the ground but neither Elf spotted them, in their haste to get into the Toadstool.

The closer Trilby got to the Toadstool, the more he could smell the two evil Elves and he shivered in distaste. Quite how he was going to exact his revenge, he had no idea, but he was sure something would come to him. However, two things were worrying him. Firstly, he'd definitely heard the older Elf say something about a beast and he feared they'd got some sort of guard dog – or worse. Secondly, he'd found what looked like little bits of hairy, animal skin by the front door. It was as if something furry had been torn limb from limb and all that remained were scraps of its pelt.

Having second thoughts, Trilby backed away from the Toadstool, down the path towards the gate. Perhaps he'd come back in the daylight when things didn't look so scary. As he turned, his scarf caught on the gate catch, nearly garrotting him. That was the final indignation and Trilby saw red. As if it wasn't enough to have one of those monsters tie something around his neck that he couldn't get off, the *something* was pink and it would be the death of him. But not if he struck back first. Finally, he freed the scarf and crept back up the path. The older Elf had pulled the curtains in the living room, so he tiptoed around the back to the kitchen and waited in the shadows. When one of the Elves came into the Garden to put the rubbish in the bin, he would sneak into the Toadstool and… well he wasn't sure what he'd do then, but he was resourceful and patient and what's more, he had the element of surprise on his side. And he was sure by then he'd at least have control of two of his knocking knees.

It was going to be a long night. But Sylvester was up to it – especially if Crispin was doing all the hard work. Clicking and clacking came from the living room as Crispin knitted furiously. He'd explained to Sylvester that as well as the six scarves, he needed to make four balaclavas before Peggy came with her Boys in the morning.

"What's a balaclava?"

"It's a sort of large sock that goes over your head and has holes for your eyes."

"Oh, I see," said Sylvester, who didn't see at all why anyone would put a sock on their head, "but Peggy only asked for scarves."

"They're presents for Peggy and the Boys."

"Why don't you just make them scarves?"

"Because a Dragon can't breathe flames through a fire-retardant balaclava and Gargoyles aren't so scary if you can't see the faces they're pulling."

"Brilliant!" said Sylvester. "But why d'you have to make Peggy one? She doesn't breathe flames or make scary faces."

"Bribery."

He's so clever, thought Sylvester as he went into the kitchen, relieved he couldn't knit and therefore didn't have to spend the evening wiggling needles. He'd been desperate to have a go on the new machine and now, he had the perfect opportunity to play with it and to keep Crispin well-fuelled with coffee and pieces of the homemade fudge Wendy had given them for Christmas. He popped a piece in his mouth and chewed as he poured water into the "Beast" and tipped coffee into the chamber. Once he'd lit the coal in the tiny furnace, he stood back out of range of the intense heat and waited. He wondered whether Crispin might knit him a fire-retardant balaclava for when he made coffee.

Crispin had been right when he'd referred to the machine as a "Beast". It even sounded like an animal, with its hissing, spitting and growling. Sylvester suddenly realised the fudge he'd been eating had become rather chewy and had a distinctly bubble gum flavour. He took another square from the box and cut it in half. Trust Wendy to have combined bubble gum and fudge. She'd recently challenged him to a bubble blowing contest but once he'd seen the size of the bubbles she blew, he told her he was too grown-up for such baby stuff. He had a feeling it was harder than it looked. But now was a perfect time to try – away from prying eyes. He could practise and then when he'd perfected it, he'd nonchalantly blow a bubble the next time he saw Wendy. His first effort resulted in him spitting it halfway across the kitchen but after a few more attempts, he managed to blow small bubbles and with a flick of the tongue, took them back inside his mouth for further chewing and moulding. He crouched down behind the kitchen table, blowing bubbles and watching for signs the "Beast" had finished.

Steam whistled through various orifices until the vibrating appliance was enveloped in a cloak of mist. Sylvester started to blow an enormous bubble. He had a feeling this one was going to be a success and he went cross-eyed as he watched it grow and fill his vision. This one, he decided, would be as big as his head. There was a hiccup from the machine and a gurgling, just as he remembered he hadn't put anything under the coffee nozzle. The pink bubble bobbed and dipped in front of his nose, as he rushed out from behind the table, grabbed a mug and thrust it into the machine. Coffee was ejected so forcibly from the nozzle, it ricocheted out of the mug and flying upwards, it hit the bubble, rupturing it with a loud pop. A film of gooey gum smeared itself over the contours of his face in a pink, featureless mask. Sylvester staggered backwards blindly, arms flailing, knocking over the table and smashing everything in his path. He tried to scream but the sound and his breath were trapped inside the gum which inflated to another bubble and then inverted into Sylvester's mouth as he inhaled in panic.

Trilby cowered in the bushes. The sounds coming from the Elves' kitchen were like nothing he'd ever heard before. He couldn't imagine what type of animal was inside and he was reconsidering his position on taking revenge. Perhaps he could live with his dislike of the Elves without demanding a settling of scores. Yes, the more he thought about it, the more he was sure he could.

The noises grew in volume and tempo. What kind of animal could roar, hiss and squeak at the same time? There was an enormous thud, followed by the crash of breaking china and glass and one of the Elves began shouting. What was happening in the kitchen? Had the Beast turned on the Elves? Hope rose in Trilby's heart. He wanted – no, he needed – to see what was happening. He crept forward and leapt up onto the dustbin. He'd be safe outside, surely? With both front paws on the windowsill, he craned his neck to get a better look. The kitchen appeared to be full of fog, which was surprising because behind him, in the Garden, the night was clear. Suddenly out of the misty depths burst a terrifying sight and Trilby fell backwards off the dustbin onto the grass. It was a sight that would haunt his nightmares for some time to come. A terrifying monster had stared at him… Well, that wasn't strictly true because in order to stare, a monster has to have eyes and this monster had no eyes, in fact, no features at all. There was a lump where the nose should have been. Where you might expect a mouth, there was an oval, concave depression. There was just a head covered in bare, wrinkly, pink skin and to make matters worse – the monster clutched at what should have been its face as if trying to scratch it off.

Trilby lay on the grass, petrified with shock.

And then, the kitchen window opened.

Trilby had never run so fast in his life.

Crispin managed to make a hole in the bubble gum for Sylvester to breathe and painstakingly peeled the rest of the goo off his skin, although so much of it was stuck in his hair, Crispin suspected a trip to the barbers would be necessary. He doused the flames in the coffee machine's furnace and opened the window to let out the steam, although so much had been produced that droplets had condensed on the ceiling and were still dripping down like rain. He mopped up the puddle of coffee and swept up the broken crockery and glass, then made Sylvester a calming mug of hot chocolate before resuming his knitting.

Sylvester was too disturbed to sleep and he sat up watching the mesmerising motion of Crispin's knitting needles, sipping his hot chocolate.

"I've never seen anyone knit as fast as you," he remarked.

"That's because our lives depend upon it."

"Haven't you done enough yet? I'm getting quite tired," Sylvester said after a few hours. His eyes had started to droop.

"No, I haven't done enough until I have four balaclavas and the six scarves that Peggy wants by tomorrow – well actually by later today. But you go to bed. I've only got two balaclavas left to make."

By the time Peggy and the Boys arrived, Crispin had just finished the last balaclava.

"Well," she said cheerily, "we'll 'ave a nice cup o' Rosie Lee* and talk terms."

"Terms" seemed to involve Sylvester handing over his winnings and Crispin handing over his scarves with the promise of more orders.

"Threat" of more orders, thought Crispin wryly.

"Here," he said as cheerily as he could, "Merry Christmas," and he handed Peggy and the Boys their balaclavas.

"Perhaps you could try them on, so I could see if they fit? Please?" Crispin's voice had risen an octave with fear.

But he needn't have worried because the Gargoyles couldn't wait to try theirs on and after some help, the Dragon managed to get his over the

---

* Cockney Rhyming Slang. Rosie Lee = Tea

spines on his neck. Even Peggy removed her green cap and pulled hers over her head.

Crispin felt slightly safer as it would take the Dragon a while to get his balaclava off and so there'd be time to duck if he decided to throw flames about. And the Gargoyles looked quite benign with their balaclavas on. They even looked slightly cuddly. However, it didn't seem to matter what headgear Peggy was wearing, she still exuded menace, and she now brought the subject back to business.

There was no escape. Crispin handed over the scarves and looked at Sylvester who was hopping nervously from foot to foot.

"Um, there's a slight problem," he whispered.

"Go on," said Peggy threateningly, through the balaclava.

"Well, McTavish hasn't paid me yet."

"I see. Well, we'll take an IOU, won't we boys?"

But there was no reply because the Boys were looking intently out of the window.

"Time to go," said the Dragon, trying to pull the balaclava off. It remained bunched up over his eyes and he tripped over the coffee table, knocking the Gargoyles off balance. Peggy leapt to her feet and jumping over the Boys, she rushed into the kitchen. Crispin heard the back door open and slam shut. The Boys untangled themselves just as there was a loud knock at the door.

Now what? Crispin wondered.

It was Bartrum.

"Where's that swindling, cheating Leprechaun?" he demanded.

"That way!" the Elves said, pointing to the kitchen door which had just swung closed as the last of the Boys disappeared.

Bartrum thundered through the living room in hot pursuit.

A few minutes later, he returned, red-cheeked, wheezing and clutching his heart.

"They… got… away…" he finally managed to get out and collapsed on the sofa.

"Shall I fetch Doggett?" Crispin asked.

Bartrum shook his head. "Just… need… to get… my breath," he gasped.

Overall, it had been an excellent Christmas, reflected Crispin. True, the coffee machine had been removed from the Toadstool and had been destroyed, on health and safety grounds. Apparently, there was a high risk of explosion, as Mrs Bartrum had discovered the first time she'd used hers. But Doggett had been on hand to heal Mrs Bartrum's burns and she was apparently quite pleased that her kitchen would now be completely refitted. Bartrum was not so pleased. Like Sylvester, he too, had bought the machine from Peggy the Pram and he was keen to get his money back – or else. Peggy would be unlikely to return for some time and when she reappeared, if indeed, she ever did, Crispin hoped she'd have forgotten about her business proposal. She might have run off with Crispin's scarves but she hadn't got her hands on Sylvester's winnings, which McTavish delivered shortly after Peggy had fled.

Crispin had woken quite refreshed after a few hours' sleep and just as he had been wondering what to make for lunch, Wendy had arrived with Millie and Rosie and two enormous plates of sandwiches.

"I made turkey and jam," she said. "I hope you like them."

Don't take the biggest one... Crispin had mouthed as Sylvester reached out to the plate Wendy had placed on the table.

"Don't what?" Sylvester had enquired out loud, as he took the largest sandwich with turkey spilling out of it and crammed it in his mouth. He froze.

"There's jam in this sandwich!" he said aghast, his mouth still full of half-chewed food.

I told you they were turkey and jam, Wendy mouthed at him. "I think I'm getting the hang of thith game. Can we get your thpy kit out? I'd like to twy on a dithguithe..." she added out loud.

The Wooden Robin had been seen strutting about the Garden in his new purple socks, without having to stop to pull them up and people strolled past the Toadstool with colourful scarves wrapped around their necks. From time to time, if Crispin looked out of the window towards the begonias, a small, red bobble hat repeatedly shot skyward; each flight accompanied by a triumphant fanfare as it spun and landed back in the begonias to be retrieved and propelled upwards again.

Yes, all in all, it had been a fine Christmas.

Bellarella

"It's rubbing my neck," said Sylvester, tugging at his collar, "and I can't do this stupid tie up."

"Stop grumbling," said Crispin. "Let me do it." And within seconds, he'd deftly fashioned a bow at Sylvester's throat.

"Very smart," he said, brushing dust off the young Elf's dinner jacket.

Sylvester pushed his hand away irritably. "I feel like a dog with a collar. I can't believe Jubbly planned a formal ball and not a Mexican fiesta."

"He was going to, but then he spotted a rather glamorous ball gown in a catalogue, and he couldn't resist it."

Sylvester checked his reflection in the hall mirror. "Huh! I look just like Mr Willetts, Her Ladyship's butler."

"You'll enjoy it when you get there and all your mates will be dressed the same… Come on, cheer up, it'll be exciting."

"Will there be strippers?"

"No, of course not! It's a New Year's Eve ball, not a stag night."

"No strippers? Then, trust me. It won't be exciting." He paused. "Will the Fairies who live at the end of the Garden be there?"

The words "flirty" and "flighty" always popped into Crispin's mind when the Fairies who live at the end of the Garden were mentioned. "I expect so," he said apprehensively. But at least Sylvester had cheered up which was a relief as his grumbling had started to dampen Crispin's enthusiasm. And that was a shame, as he'd been looking forward to the ball, knowing that Jubbly had volunteered to organise it.

Bartrum had wanted Crispin to be in charge as usual, but his resolve had crumbled when Jubbly, with the dress catalogue clutched to his chest, had got down on his knees and begged.

Not that Crispin had been able to avoid all responsibility. Jubbly had asked him to come early, to meet and greet the guests at the entrance to the Gazebo, and Crispin had been more than happy to agree. He hadn't been quite so keen when he realised Frank Fowle would be at the door too, "in case of any trouble". But it was still preferable to organising refreshments, music and all the other things that Jubbly had agreed to arrange. Crispin had no idea what sort of trouble Frank was expecting, but at least he looked the part in his t-shirt, with "SECURITY" emblazoned across the front. Crispin noted that it actually said "SEUCRITY" but he doubted anyone would point this out or indeed even dare to stare at the Troll's chest for any length of time, to spot the error.

"Ah Crispin!" said Jubbly, flouncing towards the entrance, smoothing the tiers of tulle on his enormous ball gown skirt. "Well, what d'you think? Have I overdone it? The skirt's a bit on the large side," he said, raising the hem to show off layers of net petticoat, "but it's hoopless."

"Looks pretty *hopeless* to me," whispered Sylvester.

"Hoopless," Crispin whispered out of the corner of his mouth at Sylvester, "meaning it has no hoops."

"It doesn't have any hope either," Sylvester whispered back.

Jubbly's smile was beginning to slip.

"Erm," said Crispin. "It's… well, it's…

"Hoopless," said Sylvester, trying to help Crispin out.

"You don't like it, do you?" Jubbly's bottom lip began to tremble.

"Yes, it's… well, I'm just speechless," Crispin finally managed. "Yes, it's speech-defying."

"Speech-defying!" Jubbly's smile was back and his eyes glittered with excitement. He did a twirl, sending the skirt ballooning out as he spun. Halfway through the second twirl, he stopped abruptly and shouted, "No! Don't put those in there!" The Gnome who was about to place a large bouquet in the punch bowl froze and began to tremble as Jubbly strode menacingly towards him.

"Lots o' nervous tension 'ere tonight," remarked Frank. "People need to chill. Yeah, to chill," he added thoughtfully and pushed his finger up his nostril.

"No! No! This bowl is for punch," Jubbly shrieked, "something I'm going to do to you if you try to put those flowers in there again!"

Frank Fowle shook his head " 'E's gonna blow a gasket before midnight if 'e don't calm down."

A small delivery Pixie staggered towards Frank carrying a large crate of glasses.

"Where d'ya want these, mate?"

"Better see 'im over there," said Frank nodding his head at Jubbly.

"The bloke in green?"

"Nah!"

The Pixie peered short-sightedly into the Gazebo. The only person in there was Jubbly, furiously tweaking the flowers.

"*Not* the bloke in green?"

"Nah," said Frank, "it ain't green, it's chartreuse."

"Wossat then?" asked the Pixie.

"It's like green," said Frank.

"Aah!" said the Pixie and he lurched forward with the crate of clinking glasses.

"Can I be of assistance?" asked Crispin, grabbing the end of the crate that had tipped perilously close to the ground.

"Cheers, mate," said the Pixie letting go of the other end and leaving the crate to Crispin. He tipped his hat to Sylvester and Frank as he left, whistling.

"I've been trying to think what Jubbly reminds me of," said Sylvester to Frank, "and it's suddenly come to me. Standing there with his hands on his hips, he looks like a lettuce with handles."

Crispin was doing his best to meet and greet guests but Frank Fowle wasn't making it easy. He insisted on checking each ticket individually and searching all bags.

"What are you looking for?" Crispin asked in exasperation.

"You never know," said Frank tapping the side of his nose with one finger and then sliding it up the adjacent nostril.

Crispin wandered off to get a sausage roll while Frank inspected a Gnome's enormous handbag. He could see it was going to take a while before Frank got to the bottom of what looked more like a suitcase. On his return, the Troll had allowed the Gnome and her bag in, but was now standing with arms crossed, blocking the way of the most beautiful being Crispin had ever seen.

"Stop dribbling," said Sylvester, who'd suddenly appeared next to him. He pushed Crispin's lower jaw up to meet the top one. "It's not a cool look."

"Stop it," said Crispin crossly but he couldn't take his eyes off the vision in the brilliant white dress. Her golden curls were held back by a colourful butterfly which periodically took off and fluttered delicately around her head to alight on her shoulder or arm, then to resume its position holding back her blonde locks.

"Looks like she needs help," said Sylvester, nudging Crispin. "What're you waiting for?"

Crispin strode forward importantly.

"What's the problem, Frank?"

"This young person, *claims* she's an Angel."

"Well, that certainly seems likely," said Crispin looking from the dainty white shoes up to the glowing halo. "Is there a problem with that?"

"No, but she doesn't have a ticket. No ticket, no ball."

"But I don't want to go to the ball, sir, I simply want to speak to someone," said the angelic being.

"That's what they all say," said Frank.

"Who?" asked the Angel.

"Anyone who wants to gate-crash."

"But I don't want to come in, I'd just like a word with McTavish. Please, if you could bring him here, I could see him and I wouldn't need to bother you anymore."

"Sorry. Can't do that. Rules is rules," said Frank stubbornly.

"What rules are they?" asked Crispin, finally finding his tongue.

Frank glared at him.

"Would you mind if I dealt with this, Frank? There are lots of people with tickets who are waiting to come in."

" 'Ear, 'ear," said someone in the rapidly growing queue.

"On yer own 'ead be it," declared Frank, turning to the Fairy who was next in line.

"About time too," she said tartly, snapping open her clutch bag and pushing it under Frank's nose.

"If you'll follow me," Crispin said, leading the Angel into the Gazebo. It wasn't far to the room at the back where McTavish was playing poker, but Crispin was stalling for time and he led her in the opposite direction.

"I'm Crispin," he said and paused, waiting for her to introduce herself. She merely smiled.

"And you are?" Crispin prompted.

"I'm pleased to meet you," she said.

"And I'm pleased to meet you too… but you are…?"

"I'm still pleased to meet you," she said. "This is a lovely ball. I wish I'd been invited."

"You can stay," said Crispin, staring into her blue eyes. "Please," he added.

She blushed slightly. "I need to find McTavish. His sisters and I have come a long way and his house is locked. He usually leaves the key under the flowerpot but it's not there. We're all really tired."

"Of course, of course," said Crispin.

"You, sly old dog, Crispin," said Jubbly when he spotted Crispin and the Angel. "I didn't know you were bringing someone. And someone so beautiful." He smiled at her. "And you are?"

"Very pleased to meet you," she said.

“Likewise,” said Jubbly, winking at Crispin.

“You wouldn’t happen to know where McTavish is, would you?” she asked.

“Yes,” said Jubbly, he’s out there,” indicating a door at the back of the Gazebo. Crispin now had no excuse to delay taking her directly to the room, so he made full use of the press of dancing bodies to take as long as possible while he enjoyed the company of the beautiful Angel at his side. The feel of her downy wing brushing his hand was giving him shivers of delight that made Doggett’s tingles appear like the merest itch.

“Perhaps we could have one dance before we find McTavish?” Crispin asked hopefully.

“I’m really sorry,” she said, as he’d known she would, “but I can’t help thinking of the others. They’re waiting for me…”

“Of course, I understand,” said Crispin. She was, after all, an Angel, and an Angel wouldn’t leave people outside a locked house in the dark while she danced with a stranger. But he was disappointed all the same.

The cards hadn’t been kind to McTavish and he’d been losing heavily, so he wasn’t exactly welcoming when the Angel disturbed him.

“Here,” he said, handing her a key, “let yourself in. I’ll be home later. Don’t wait up.”

Crispin had watched from the door and was astonished that McTavish hadn’t greeted her or asked how her journey had been.

"Thank you," she said with a smile that made Crispin's knees tremble. But McTavish had already turned back to his cards.

"So, what happened?" Sylvester asked when Crispin finally got home.

"Nothing."

"But the Angel. Don't tell me you let her get away."

Crispin sighed. That's exactly what he'd done. He'd escorted her to the entrance but Frank had distracted him and she'd slipped away.

"What's the rush?" Frank had asked as Crispin had pushed past him but it was too late, she'd been about to disappear into the woods.

"Please!" he'd called. "Please don't go! At least tell me your name…"

A sound like tinkling bells drifted out of the woods towards Crispin. Unfortunately, Gusty Bob had been drinking fizzy lemonade and chose that exact moment to vent off some of the fizz.

"Nooo!" yelled Crispin but it was too late. All he knew about the exquisite Angel was that her name began with "B" and that she'd lost a feather from one of her wings. He stooped to pick it up and stroked it against his cheek.

"For goodness sake, stop moping and go and look for her," said Sylvester. "So what if you don't know her name? She's staying with McTavish and if you can't remember what she looks like, which is highly unlikely, you can always match her up to that feather. Oooh! It's just like Cinderella."

"Don't be so ridiculous,"

"Have you got a better idea, Prince Charming?"

"This had better not take long," grunted McTavish the next morning over a mug of black coffee. "I'm feeling a bit under the weather." He puffed at a fat cigar and coughed.

"It's about your sister," said Crispin politely.

"Which one?"

"The one you gave the key to, last night."

"I don't remember giving a key to my sister last night. What's her name?"

"Well, that's just it, I don't know. All I know is that it begins with 'B'."

"They all begin with B. Bess! Come and sort this out!" he yelled, wincing at the sound of his own voice. "Now see what you've made me do." He scowled at Crispin.

A tall Angel glided into the room.

"Yes, dear?"

"Deal with this. I'm going to bed…"

"Yes, dear," said Bess looking enquiringly at Crispin. "Can I help you?"

"I met one of your sisters last night and I wanted to… well, I wanted to… say hello…"

"Beryl and I are the only two here," she said. "The others left about an hour ago."

"And it wasn't Bess or Beryl?" asked Sylvester.

Crispin shook his head sadly.

"So, what *was* her name?"

Crispin shrugged.

"It doesn't matter now. All McTavish's sisters, except Bess and Beryl, have gone."

He sighed and stroked the feather in his palm.

"My Cinderella," he whispered.

Not far from the Ornamental Bridge, Bella, the Angel, sat, staring at the tiny stream which trickled into the lake. A colourful butterfly tried vainly to pull the golden curls off her face and finally, giving up, it fluttered into the air and alighted on her outstretched finger.

"He was so handsome, Mr Lambert," she said to the butterfly, "and so kind and gentle. And I'll never see him again."

A tear slid down her cheek.

The butterfly rose into the air and hovered near her ear, dipping and bobbing.

"Yes, Mr Lambert," Bella said to the butterfly, "I *have* asked Uncle McTavish if he knows Crispin but he's been in such a bad mood since he lost at cards, he said he's never heard of him and anyway, he can't be expected to know every Tom, Dick and Harry in the Garden." She shook her head forlornly.

"I don't want any Tom, Dick or Harry. I just want Crispin."

Mr Lambert heaved a butterfly sigh. He'd never seen his Bella so distraught. But if she'd set her heart on Crispin, then he'd see what he could do.

In the meantime, he wondered what were the chances of interesting her in a Tom, Dick or a Harry instead…?

The Stag Omen

Being short and dumpy had its advantages. It meant that Cook had a low centre of gravity which had helped her to remain upright on more than one occasion. And it served her well now. She pirouetted 360 degrees with the grace of a ballerina and more impressively, she managed to prevent any of the jam tarts she was holding from succumbing to centrifugal force and spinning off her tray.

"Mr Willetts!" she shrieked. "Have you gone mad?"

"Sorry! I'm so sorry!" He gasped for breath, having just run from upstairs all the way down to the kitchen.

Cook slammed the tray of jam tarts on the table, turned and glared at the butler. With a steely look in her eye and hands on her hips, she was formidable indeed.

"It's that dratted Gardener!" he said between gasps. "Her Ladyship's giving him another one of them mysterious parcels…"

"How d'you know?" Cook's curiosity was aroused.

"He's with Her Ladyship now. And Roger told me when he picked her up from the station, she had a large, strange-shaped parcel. He carried it in from the car to the library for her. And then Mr Po Lin arrived."

"So, what're you doing in the kitchen? Why aren't you upstairs listening at the door or whatever it is you normally do?"

"He never opens parcels in the house. So, I thought I'd follow him and find out what it is. But I need to cut through the kitchen—"

"Look, here he comes," said Cook squashing her nose against the windowpane.

Mr Willetts scooped up three jam tarts, piled one on top of the other and quickly crammed them in his mouth. It wasn't often that Cook took her eyes off the food in the kitchen. He immediately regretted his impulsiveness when the scalding, hot jam touched the roof of his mouth.

"Disgusting," commented Cook. "Look, it's all done up in brown paper. We all know about parcels done up in brown paper, don't we?"

She wiped the condensation from the windowpane with her sleeve, then pressed her nose to it again.

"And it's got legs. I wonder if it's a table… What d'you think, Mr Willetts?"

"Mffff. Mffff." Mr Willetts opened his mouth and fanned the contents wondering which would be worse; the second-degree burns he was currently experiencing or Cook's wrath if she discovered he'd eaten three tarts without permission.

"What did you say?" asked Cook.

"Mffff. Mffff," said Mr Willetts again, aware that

steam might be escaping through his nostrils and ears.

Cook turned around.

"I don't believe it!" she yelled. "Three of my jam tarts are missing!"

"Mffff?" said Mr Willetts, backing away from Cook.

"That dreadful boy! I don't know how he does it! I'm going to have a word with that father of his. You mark my words! The nerve! He thinks he can come in here and help himself, pinching my tarts, pinching my muffins and pinching my buns!"

"Mffff," said Mr Willetts in what he hoped Cook would interpret as outrage on her behalf. His eyes were watering and he wondered if the inside of his head was melting.

"If you're going to follow Mr Po Lin, I'm coming too!" declared Cook. "I'm going to tell him what a shifty, sneaking, snivelling excuse of a boy his son is…" She paused. "Are you all right, Mr Willetts? You're looking awfully flushed…"

There was nothing for it. He swallowed his scalding mouthful.

"Mr Willetts, are you having a heart attack?"

"No," he said as calmly as he could.

"Then why are you clutching your chest?"

"Just suffering some minor digestive discomfort," he said as the jam slipped down, searing the inside of his oesophagus and finally bringing the contents of his stomach to a gentle simmer. He gratefully drank the glass of water she offered him.

"It's probably stress," she said, "brought on by a severely annoying Gardener and son."

Mr Willetts nodded weakly.

"Well, I don't know about you but I've had enough." She thumped the palm of her hand with the rolling pin.

"I'm going to find that Po Lin Jnr and if he's got jam tart crumbs about his person, I'm going to give him and his father a piece of my mind! Are you coming, Mr Willetts?"

The butler wiped his mouth quickly with his sleeve and followed Cook into the Garden.

In the garage, Po Lin Jnr ducked behind the Morris Minor and watched his father walk through the Kitchen Garden with a large parcel under his arm. The boy continued to watch until his father had nearly disappeared, then, just as he was about to stand up, Mr Willetts and Cook came out of the kitchen. He ducked down again and watched as they set off in the same direction as his father. Cook was armed with a rolling pin and Po Lin Jnr had no doubt she would use it.

The only parts of Roger, the chauffeur, that were visible, were his boots which protruded from beneath the rear of the car, tapping the air in time to the rock'n'roll beat that was blaring from the radio.

Po Lin Jnr crept away. With any luck, he'd make it into the kitchen and get back again with a handful of raisins or the cooking chocolate, if he could find it, before Roger requested a spanner.

Bartrum's son, Wilmslow, and his friend, Euclid, were strolling through the Kitchen Garden when they spotted Po Lin Jnr stealing into the kitchen. "Strolling" was what they told themselves they were doing but as both the young Gnomes had been banned from going anywhere near the house, they were, in fact, scurrying from one piece of cover to the next. This was the first time they'd dared to invade the Kitchen Garden although other than Big Po, they had no idea who they might encounter there. From behind the water butt, they watched Po Lin Jnr, recognising the same furtive behaviour they were exhibiting and knew he was up to no good. The constant swivelling of his head to search for observers and the casual way he poked the kitchen door with one finger, as if to satisfy himself it was indeed a solid object, were all giveaways. Apparently, the door was solid – and unlocked – and the Gardener's son slipped into the kitchen, with one backwards glance to make sure he was unobserved. Seconds later, he emerged with a pile of jam tarts balanced on one hand. He closed the door and with one last glance left and right, he wandered off with his mouth bulging.

"Well, if he's allowed free food, perhaps we should go and get some," whispered Wilmslow.

"Are you sure?" Euclid's courage was failing. It was one thing to trespass in a Garden but quite another to go into the big house and face... well, he wasn't even sure what they might face.

"Of course, I'm sure," said Wilmslow confidently and then he played his trump card. "There are jam tarts in there..."

Sneaking from one hiding place to another, they finally reached the kitchen and after a brief disagreement about whether they should proceed, Wilmslow suggested they simply give the door an exploratory nudge to see if it was still open. Four, tiny Gnome hands pushed the glossy wood. Having no experience of opening human-sized doors, they applied more force than was necessary and they lurched into the kitchen, landing on all fours on the mat.

"Now what?" asked a wide-eyed and open-mouthed Euclid.

"Jam tarts," replied Wilmslow.

"But how?" Euclid scanned the distance between the tiled floor and the dizzying heights of the jam tarts on the cooling rack.

"Like this," said Wilmslow. He pulled out the bottom drawer and stepped onto the tea towels with which it was filled. From this elevated position, he pulled open the next drawer up, and climbed into that. He carried on making his drawer-staircase until he reached the worktop.

"C'mon," he shouted.

But Euclid's courage had failed even with the tempting aroma of the jam tarts wafting from above.

"Um…" he said desperately, but before he could come up with a good reason why he shouldn't climb the drawers, something soft, sticky and sweet-scented landed on his head.

"Butterfingers!" shouted Wilmslow, throwing another tart down.

Shrieks from above were accompanied by more jam tart missiles which rained down on Euclid. He slipped and slid on jam and squashed pastry crumbs, as he dashed about, picking up any intact tarts.

"Cook! What on earth is going on in there?" An imperious woman's voice came from somewhere not too far away.

Heavy footsteps could be heard approaching the kitchen and both Gnomes froze.

Wilmslow bounded down the makeshift, drawer-staircase and slithered across the messy floor after the rapidly disappearing form of Euclid.

"Who… d'you think… that was?" Euclid asked between gasps for breath.

"Dunno," said Wilmslow, "but it was a close shave, she nearly caught us…"

They'd kept as much to the undergrowth as they could until they'd arrived in the woods, covered in jam, twigs and mud. Euclid's armful of jam tarts had been compressed into a sticky, shapeless lump that was smeared all over his jacket and trousers.

He broke a piece off and offered it to Wilmslow. "Want some?"

"Nah. I'm not hungry."

"Me neither." Euclid dropped what remained of the squashed jam tarts and wiped his hands on his trousers. "My mum's gonna ground me forever."

"Mine too," said Wilmslow gloomily.

"In the unlikely event we're ever allowed out again, let's never, ever go up to the house."

Wilmslow nodded emphatically.

"Cook! Cook! What's going o…?"

Her Ladyship's hands flew to her mouth.

"Cook, this is a disgrace!"

She surveyed the kitchen from the doorway, taking in the greasy, jammy mess on the floor, the open drawers and contents spilling over the top and the crumbs and chaos on the worktop. Smiling, she closed the door and made her way back upstairs. This was going to prove to be most diverting and she couldn't wait to see how Cook was going to explain the state of her beloved kitchen. Kitchen inspection hadn't been as entertaining as this since… well, since ever.

"Which way?" asked Cook, as they reached a fork in the path. Mr Willetts peered about and then shrugged.

Tall rhododendron bushes rose on either side of them, hiding the rest of the Garden.

"I hate this place." Cook shuddered. "It's dirty, disgusting, full of creepy crawlies and it feels like we're being watched." She turned around in a circle, head moving back and forth, scanning the rhododendron bushes for the owners of the eyes she fancied were peeking at her through the foliage. She thumped the palm of her hand in what she hoped was a menacing way with the rolling pin.

"Oh, good grief!" said Mr Willetts. "It's beginning to rain."

"That's it!" shrieked Cook. "I've had enough! Take me back to civilisation. I'll deal with that snivelling excuse for a boy the next time he takes a shortcut through the kitchen. Now, take me home!"

Mr Willetts had also had enough of the Garden. It was far bigger than it looked from the windows of the Old Priory and much scarier. Whether Mr Po Lin had deliberately given them the slip or not, he had no idea, but he was keen to get back to the house as soon as possible and definitely before he lost his bearings completely.

"This way, Cook," he said, with more confidence than he actually felt.

Cook had been right about one thing. She and Mr Willetts had been observed from the rhododendrons – but not by dozens of pairs of eyes, as she'd supposed.

Mr Po Lin had slipped behind the bushes where the path forked and waited until Cook and Mr Willetts passed. He was sure that once they realised he'd disappeared, they'd give up and go back to the house. The rain had proved to be a deciding factor and Mr Po Lin was very relieved to see them hesitate at the fork in the path and then retrace their steps.

They'll have to try much harder if they want to outwit me, Mr Po Lin thought gleefully.

Avoiding the path, he set off through the woods. He'd unwrap the new Garden Ornament that was tucked under his arm, in privacy, then he'd place it in position – and he had the perfect location in mind.

If Cook had overestimated the number of observing eyes, Mr Po Lin had underestimated them. It hadn't occurred to him that he wasn't alone.

"What d'you reckon is in the parcel?" asked Doggett, from behind a large fern.

"It's some kind of four-legged animal," said Crispin, screwing up his eyes to see more clearly.

"It's got a very large head. Perhaps it's an elephant…"

"No, the legs are too skinny. What about a horse?"

"No, the head's too big."

"I know," said Crispin, "how about a stag? Its head might appear to be large because of the antlers…"

"Oooh!" wailed Doggett. "It's an omen!"

Crispin looked at him in alarm. "We're not doing the whole Plague Thing again, are we? As far as I know, there's never been a plague of deer…"

"No, it's one of them omens that Nina keeps talking about."

"What omens?"

"The sort of omens that say I ought to be asking her to marry me."

"Oh, those kinds of omens."

There was silence for a few moments, then Crispin asked, "Well, don't you want to get married?"

"I'm not sure. I never really thought about it. But I'm not happy about being dictated to by a bag."

There was a sharp intake of breath, as Crispin looked around, wondering if Nina might suddenly appear. "Don't let Nina hear you call her that!"

"Not Nina!"

"Then?"

"Teabag," said Doggett. "Nina says it's all in the tea leaves."

"But you can't read tea leaves in a teabag."

"*You* can't and *I* can't, but apparently Nina can and they're full of wedding omens."

"Oh, I see. But how is the new Garden Ornament an omen?"

"Stag night. The night before the wedding that I haven't popped the question for."

"Oh. So, what're you going to do?"

"You can't go against the omens, you know. I

tried ignoring them but those teabags just don't give up. And now there's the stag to keep reminding me. I'll just have to propose, I suppose…"

Mr Po Lin found a clearing and began carefully unwrapping the new Garden Ornament. He started at the legs and worked his way up to the head which was encased in metres of bubble wrap, to prevent breakage. At least Mr Po Lin hoped it had prevented breakage. He held his breath as he took the last piece of bubble wrap off to reveal the horn. Yes, it was still intact and how wonderful it was. One single, spiral horn set in the middle of the unicorn's forehead.

Absolutely magnificent.

The Wedding Carriage

"What d'you mean it's not a stag?" asked Doggett incredulously. "We saw Big Po unwrap it."

"We didn't stay to see him take all the packaging off. You said you wanted to go home to pop the question. Would it have made a difference if you'd known it was a unicorn?" asked Crispin.

"Would it have made a difference to what?" asked Nina, suddenly appearing from nowhere.

"Nothing, dear," said Doggett.

"Did you say 'unicorn'?" asked Nina.

Crispin nodded.

"It's an omen," she said.

"It is?" asked Doggett.

"Definitely. It's every girl's dream to arrive at her wedding in a carriage drawn by a white unicorn. It is a white one, isn't it?"

"Yes."

"You see, I knew it! A white unicorn, how wonderful! I must tell Wendy, she'll be so excited. She's my bridesmaid, you know," she said to Crispin.

"Yes, I know," said Crispin who'd heard about little else the previous day when Wendy had turned up at his Toadstool with an armful of bridal magazines and had insisted he sit with her and go through them to choose a bridesmaid dress.

Nina almost skipped out of the room on her way to the Wendy House.

"Well, I might have been wrong about it being a stag but it looks like the omen was telling me to propose," said Doggett with relief. "Have you met him yet?"

"Who?"

"The unicorn."

"Oh, you mean Stanley. Yes, I met him yesterday at Garden Inspection. Big Po placed him in that clearing in the woods, you know the one where the Fairies hang out."

"What am I going to do?" asked Doggett. "How can I ask a complete stranger if he'll pull a rather large bride and even larger bridesmaid about in a wedding carriage?"

"He seemed quite nice…" said Crispin.

"Yes, but it's a big ask, isn't it?"

"Well, as I see it, you don't have a lot of choice."

"No," agreed Doggett gloomily, "but if you'll come with me, I'm sure that between the two of us, we could persuade him."

"Well…"

"Please!" said Doggett putting his arm around Crispin's shoulders.

"Ow! Oooh! Mmm!" said Crispin. "Oh all right. When is the wedding, by the way?"

"Yes, when is it?" asked Nina, appearing from nowhere.

"I thought you were going to see your bridesmaid, dear," said Doggett.

"Later," said Nina. "So, when's the wedding?"

"How about Midsummer's Day?"

Nina flew at him and covered his face with kisses.

Crispin whispered, "I'll come back later…" and crept out. It didn't do to get in the way of true love or even to be in the same room.

"Ow! Oooh! Mmm!" said Nina as Crispin closed the door.

"Stanley P. Weissmeister," said the unicorn when Crispin introduced Doggett, "at your service, sir."

"Pleased to meet you," said Doggett.

"Well, what can I do for you gentle Gnomes?"

Doggett's eyes bulged with the effort of ordering his thoughts. He gulped and began, "It was the teabags, you see. I didn't know it but they were telling me – well they were *omenising* me – and it wasn't until Nina – she's my intended – except at the time she wasn't because I hadn't realised what the teabags were saying – well, I did but I didn't believe them. And when she told me, well I wasn't sure but then we saw the stag although of course, it wasn't. It was you. And apparently, that's also an omen. But I don't really like to ask, especially now with you being so slender. You see Nina and Wendy are slightly large. No, I lie. They're both normal-sized large and you might not be able to move them *and* a carriage and now Nina's asked her sister, so that'll be three people – three large people – in the carriage—"

"Sit down, dear chap, you seem quite overwrought,"

said Stanley producing a hip flask from nowhere. "A cup of rosehip tea," he said unscrewing the top and handing it to Doggett, "is fortifying in a crisis and full of vitamin C. Take your time, my good chap."

By the time Crispin had clarified Doggett's request and explained about the teabags, Doggett had drained the hip flask and Stanley had agreed to pull the wedding carriage.

"I'm stronger than I look, old chap, and one couldn't stand in the way of an omen, could one?"

Doggett gratefully agreed that one couldn't, and then invited Stanley to the reception and the stag night.

"So, when can I take sight of the wedding carriage?" asked Stanley.

"Well," said Doggett, "I'll let you know when we've built one…"

"So, the carriage doesn't actually exist?" asked Crispin with an air of foreboding, as they walked back to Nina's Toadstool.

"Only in Nina's imagination," admitted Doggett.

"What are you going to do?"

"Build it, of course."

"Out of what?"

"No idea. I'll ask Nina."

"Suppose she says pumpkin or crystal or something impossible?"

"Well, we'll just have to worry about that if it happens—"

"We? You mean as in you and me?"

"Well, you know how dreadful I am at making things…"

"What makes you think I'm any better?"

"Look at all those lovely things you made at Christmas…"

"But they were all knitted. I can't knit a carriage," said Crispin with a laugh.

"Why not? I bet you could if you tried…"

"No," said Crispin, "definitely not. I vowed I'd never pick up another pair of knitting needles after staying up all night making balaclavas for Peggy and her Boys.

"But how are we going to make Nina a carriage?"

"I don't know," said Crispin, "but knitting isn't an option—"

"Knitting isn't an option for what?" asked Nina, appearing from nowhere.

"Nothing, dear—"

"Don't you 'Nothing, dear' me, Doggett! What is knitting not an option for?"

"A carriage."

"A carriage!" she said rapturously, clasping her sausage fingers together. "Oh, yes, yes! I can see it now—"

"No!" squeaked Crispin. "No, really…"

"Tea," said Nina. "What we need is a nice cup of tea."

Crispin knew what was coming and if he had dared, he'd have groaned.

"I knew it," said Nina, pointing to the dripping teabag she was holding up. "Look just there, it's a unicorn and it's pulling a beautiful, knitted carriage..."

Crispin knew there was no point challenging the omen in the teabag. His time would be better spent looking for his needles and a knitting pattern.

The unicorn-drawn, knitted carriage had captured everyone's imagination and there had been no end of offers of help. Bartrum had given Doggett four large wheels and Klaus had some lengths of wood, out of which he was making a frame. The design bore more than a passing resemblance to a Wild West covered wagon that might have been more at home on a prairie. However, in this instance, the wooden base would be draped in knitted panels as well as the hooped struts. Jubbly had said that if Nina was certain she didn't want him as a bridesmaid, he'd be happy to dress up in livery and drive the coach. Although he made it clear he'd be willing to assume the duties of bridesmaid at short notice should Nina change her mind. But the bride-to-be expressed her preference to have Jubbly in livery rather than in pink satin. Little did she know that Jubbly's idea of livery actually involved pink satin.

Nina ordered enough white wool to knit a cavalcade of carriages and checked daily to see whether it had arrived. Crispin was beginning to panic. Not only was he running out of time but each day that he delayed starting the project, meant the teabags came up with something else he needed to include. Finally, one morning, the knock on Crispin's door wasn't Nina, it was the delivery Pixie.

"Parcel for Crispin…"

"Thank you, that's me."

"Fifty balls of tartan wool," the Pixie read off the list on his clipboard, "sign 'ere."

"What?" screeched Crispin. "Tartan?" He pressed his palms to his temples. "I ordered white!"

"All right, keep yer wig on, it was just my little joke. Lighten up, will yer. You've 'eard of jokes, 'ave you? Let me explain, it's a joke because there's no such thing as tartan wool. Mind you, there should be. I reckon there's a market for it. Any old how, your wool's all 'ere, present and correct. Sign 'ere. Fifty balls of brown wool."

"Heh, heh!" he added as he sauntered down the path.

"Please don't be brown," Crispin muttered as he tore at the packaging.

The wool was white. Crispin nearly collapsed with relief.

He put a chair in his garden. It was going to be a long process and he might as well enjoy the sunshine while he knitted.

"What're you doing?" asked Sylvester when he arrived home.

"Knitting." Crispin's needles were clacking together furiously, and he yanked at the ball of wool.

"Can I do some?"

Crispin knew better than to refuse. It would be faster if he cast on a few stitches and showed him what to do. He was certain that within minutes, Sylvester would lose interest and he could carry on without interruption.

But surprisingly, Sylvester wasn't too bad at knitting and since the strip he was making was fairly narrow, it grew quite quickly.

"What're you doing?" Wilmslow was peering over the garden gate at Crispin and Sylvester.

"Knitting."

"Can I do some?"

Crispin sighed. He cast on a few stitches and Sylvester showed him how to knit.

"Hey, Wilmslow, what're you doing?" It was Euclid.

"Knitting."

"Can I do some…?"

By mid-afternoon, Crispin's garden was filled with the click-clack of knitting needles, the occasional swear word, requests for more wool and dozens of faces with determined expressions and tongues poking out.

Doggett had tried to join in but Crispin had begged him to stop when it became clear that despite his eagerness to help, sparks kept leaping from his hands and igniting the wool.

"I can wear gloves…"

Crispin was adamant and eventually, Doggett had been persuaded to keep well away from the wool.

"Go and check Klaus' wooden frame," Crispin suggested, "but don't touch it – please."

Doggett had returned later with trays of drinks and plates piled high with sandwiches for the knitters and reported that Klaus had finished the carriage frame. "It's going to be amazing," he said happily.

"Amazing" wasn't the word Crispin would have used but his mental search for a more appropriate word, such as "disastrous" or "woeful" was interrupted by one of the knitters.

"'Ere! Mind where you're treading!" said Frank Fowle.

"What on earth are you doing, Euclid?" Crispin asked.

"Skipping."

"Yeah, 'e's skipping all over my feet," said Frank, jabbing at Euclid with a knitting needle.

"D'you think it might be better to put the knitting down if you want to skip. Or even better, stop skipping?" suggested Crispin.

"Will it still work if I'm not holding it?" asked Euclid.

"Will what work?" Crispin put his knitting down

and moved between Frank and the skipping Euclid. Frank's hands were bunched menacingly.

"The knitting," said Euclid. "The pattern says 'skip' but the knitting's not getting any longer."

Crispin picked up the pattern and scanned the instructions.

"Where?"

"There," said Euclid, pointing to the page.

"Ah, I see. It actually says 'skp', not 'skip', that means slip, knit, pass slipped stitch over…"

Euclid looked horrified.

"Can't I just carry on skipping?"

A Wild Stag Night

The following morning, Crispin checked his drawings of the wedding carriage and laid all the pieces of knitting that had been completed the previous day, on the living room floor, making a note of what still needed to be done. There was a depressingly large number of panels still to be knitted. Despite the lack of knitting experience, yesterday's helpers had done remarkably well. A few pieces were so full of dropped stitches they'd have to be re-knitted and Frank Fowles' piece of knitting was grimy and needed a good wash but the rest was satisfactory. Crispin was concentrating so hard on how to tackle the remainder of the task, he didn't hear Sylvester come into the living room, eating a bowl of cereal.

"Come on, Crispin. You'll be late."

"What for?"

"Bartrum's called a meeting. Don't tell me you've forgotten."

"Oh no!" Crispin turned back to the woollen pieces on the floor. "It'll never be ready in time," he wailed.

Doggett was waiting for them outside the Toadstool.

"Only seven more sleeps 'til the big day," he said, "and you know what today is?"

"Bartrum's meeting," said Crispin gloomily.

"And…?" asked Doggett.

"Is it your birthday?"

"No! Don't tell me you've forgotten! It's my stag night. You're my Best Elf," he said to Crispin anxiously, you're supposed to have organised a really memorable night. You have, haven't you?"

"Oh yes!" said Crispin with his fingers crossed behind his back. "Yes, a really memorable night." He wondered how furious Nina would be if her carriage wasn't quite finished. Missing Bartrum's meeting definitely wasn't an option. And as Doggett's Best Elf, he was responsible for organising a night of mayhem and madness. There was nothing for it, he'd just have to knit all night – every night for seven more sleeps – or in his case, seven more lack-of-sleeps.

"Are you all right, Crispin? You're looking really pale," said Sylvester.

"Of course, I'm pale, I'm a white Marble Elf!" Crispin snapped.

"All right, there's no need to get snippy…"

I will not panic, I will not… thought Crispin, as his knees gave way.

Doggett and Sylvester hauled Crispin to his feet and helped him to the meeting.

"D'you think he's taken on too much?" Doggett whispered to Sylvester.

"He's panicking the knitting might not be done in time. But don't worry, lots of people are coming over today to help. I'll have a word with Jubbly and see if he can sort out the stag night. Would you be very upset if you had a Mexican do?" asked Sylvester, who'd already spotted the top of a sombrero poking up above the sea of heads and guessed Jubbly's persona for the day.

"A Mexican stag night would be just perfect, amigo!"

There was something about being in his garden that always soothed Crispin and the fact that he was surrounded by a crowd of volunteers, was cheering him up no end. He was particularly grateful to see that yesterday's knitters had returned with friends and were enthusiastically showing them what to do. And he was extremely relieved to see that Euclid wasn't amongst them. The skipping fiasco had resulted in so many dropped stitches in the young Gnome's knitting that Crispin was thinking about using it anyway and passing it off as lace. But things had got rather heated whilst Euclid had been skipping. He'd tripped over Frank's large, hairy feet and had dived headfirst into the Troll's lap, knocking the knitting from his hands. There had been an instant of silence before someone shouted, "Uh oh! Duck everyone! The Troll's gonna blow!"

Crispin had grabbed Euclid from Frank's lap, tucked him under one arm and raced to the garden gate. He'd put him down, thanked him for his time and suggested he skip home before Frank had managed to extricate himself from the wool and struggle to his feet. Doggett had rushed forward and pressed a cup of tea in the Troll's enormous hand and Nina had appeared from nowhere with a chocolate muffin of such proportions that Frank had immediately forgotten about his grievance with the skipping Euclid.

Difficult incident averted.

And all was peaceful now. Well, not exactly peaceful, with so many voices chattering, and twice as many needles clacking together at various speeds, but at least all was harmonious. And the pile of knitted panels was growing.

Crispin checked his watch. He'd have to stop knitting soon and try to arrange something for Doggett's stag night.

If only he knew what.

He checked his watch again. Yes, he'd have to stop soon.

But not just yet.

There was a limit to what a Gnome could do on his own, even if he was a party organiser extraordinaire. Jubbly hadn't expected the stag night arrangements to be so difficult. He had music, drink and party poppers, as well as ideas to make such a celebration go with a swing. He'd even acquired a lamp post and handcuffs with which they'd secure Doggett – once they'd relieved him of his trousers – since his research had shown that this was obligatory. However, he'd expected people to give him a hand. It had been Sylvester who'd asked Jubbly to arrange the party at short notice and it would have been nice if he'd helped. It was very disappointing. He'd put up some of the lights in the Gazebo but if he was going to be ready in time, he needed assistance.

As he made his way to Crispin's Toadstool, in search of Sylvester, it occurred to him he hadn't passed anyone since he'd left the Gazebo except that strange, young Gnome, Euclid, who appeared to be hopping up and down. As he approached Crispin's Toadstool, he could hear voices – lots of voices, just like the sort of chatter and laughter found at a party. Jubbly started to run. Had he got the venue wrong?

"What's going on?" he demanded, trying to catch his breath.

Almost everyone who lived in the Garden, was now in Crispin's garden – knitting.

"We're just doing some last-minute stuff for the wedding carriage before the stag do," explained Sylvester.

"Listen up, everybody," Jubbly shouted above the hubbub, "the stag party starts in half an hour and I need a few volunteers to help me put up the rest of the lights…"

While he waited for several people to finish their rows, he picked up a pair of needles and started knitting. Half an hour later, he realised that people had finished the particular row that had been so important, and many more besides, but they were still reluctant to leave their woolly pieces. Strangely, the pressing need to party had waned in Jubbly's mind as he was lulled by the tapping of needles and the cheery chatter.

It wasn't until Crispin passed around lanterns so that people could carry on in the failing light, that Jubbly remembered what he'd come for.

"C'mon people," he begged, "there's a party going on in the Gazebo, or there will be, as soon as someone arrives."

More people expressed the need to "just finish this row", before they could possibly consider a party and Jubbly sat down again. He'd been a bit worried that he wouldn't be able to remember where he was in the knitting pattern and he could understand their concerns.

"Did you have a lovely time, dear?" asked Nina when Doggett finally got home in the early hours. "How did you get your trousers back?"

"Hmm?" asked Doggett, who was too tired to reply.

"And how did you get out of the handcuffs?"

"Hmm," said Doggett as he curled up in bed and thought back over the evening. Miraculously, all the pieces of the knitting were finished and Crispin had promised that the carriage would be ready by the end of the following day – well, actually, today, since it was past midnight.

Very much past midnight.

"You certainly know how to hold a party, old thing!" said Stanley when he bumped into Jubbly much later that day.

"Oh well, you know how it is…" said Jubbly bashfully. "I've had a lot of practice, over the years."

"I must admit, I thought the decoy lamp post was simply genius, dear boy! Simply genius!

"Probably best we keep what really happened to ourselves," said Jubbly, tapping the side of his nose. "The bride-to-be might be a bit… er, put out, if she knew what actually happened, you know how women are…"

"Mum's the word, dear boy."

Yes, it's best we keep it to ourselves, thought Jubbly as he made his way home. Nina might not be too happy to know her intended hadn't spent a night of riotous merrymaking to celebrate his final days of bachelorhood, as was customary. The stag night had not taken place at the Gazebo as she'd assumed, neither had it involved large quantities of alcohol or dubious jokes. And unless someone told her, she would never suspect it had involved copious cups of tea, plates and plates of biscuits and plenty of knitting.

Wedding Preparations

Crispin was dreaming about teabags. They'd been making all sorts of improbable demands for the wedding and now, they were dancing around the Maypole, with Nina, her mother and her grandmother, while Crispin was trying to escape from the treacle pit, into which he was rapidly sinking.

"Are you all right?" It was Sylvester, banging on Crispin's bedroom door. "You keep screaming."

Crispin sat up, he was covered in sweat but thoroughly relieved to have escaped the teabags, the treacle and three generations of Nina's family.

"Yes, I'm fine… It was just a nightmare, sorry to have woken you."

Crispin could hear Sylvester grumbling that sunrise was a thoroughly uncivilised time of day, as he shuffled back to bed. The subject of sunrise had come up quite often since Nina had informed everyone that the wedding, which was to take place in three days' time, would begin at dawn and the celebrations were set to go on well into the night, as decreed by the teabags. This would allow the bride and groom time to enjoy every hour of the longest day of the year.

And it was probably just as well because if the teabags suggested many more things, they'd need several days to get through them all. As Best Elf, it was Crispin's job to see that everything the teabags wanted, Nina got. And now that Nina's mother and grandmother had arrived, the list of essential items for the wedding was growing exponentially. Nina's mother, Queenie, was insistent that her daughter should have a day to remember. Well, thought Crispin, if Nina doesn't remember her day, he definitely would. It would be imprinted on his memory.

Crispin sat up in bed. He was too afraid to go back to sleep although he had to admit, real life was just as fraught as his nightmares at the moment. The more so, since Nina's mum and gran had arrived.

"They look like Russian dolls," Sylvester had observed.

"Shh!" Crispin had elbowed him in the ribs. He could tell it wouldn't do to upset Queenie. She shared that same dogged determination with her daughter. And combined with the obsessive "mother of the bride" viewpoint, she would be formidable indeed. Not that Granny was any less scary, with her gimlet eyes and rather startling set of dentures that seemed to have a life of their own.

But Crispin had to admit that Nina, Queenie and Granny did look just like Russian dolls – dumpy, brightly dressed women in three distinct sizes. And it didn't take much imagination to visualise a "Granny" doll nesting inside a "Queenie" doll, inside a "Nina" doll.

Crispin wondered if Doggett and Nina were planning to have children. If the next generation grew large enough to contain all the other dolls… Crispin tried – and failed – to imagine the size of Nina's offspring.

"D'you think the women in Nina's family start out as giants and then shrink as they get older?" Sylvester asked.

But when Lulu, Nina's younger sister arrived a few hours later, she disproved Sylvester's theory by being slightly smaller and slimmer than Nina although very, very much louder. And that wouldn't have been so bad, thought Crispin, if she hadn't taken an immediate shine to him and followed him around for the rest of the day, assaulting his eardrums with her thunderous voice and shrill laughter.

"As the Chief Bridesmaid, I expect to spend a lot of time with the Best Elf," she'd told Crispin and batted her eyelashes. His heart had sunk. Not only would he have to put up with her noise, but he also knew there would be trouble when Wendy learned that Lulu had appointed herself Chief Bridesmaid.

There was still an hour to sunrise but Crispin decided to get up. He wasn't going to get back to sleep now and he might as well take advantage of the quiet while the rest of the Garden slept to go over his pre-wedding list. It had been his fault that it had grown so long, so rapidly. In an attempt to limit Nina's suggestions, he'd recommended she consult a wedding website, expecting her to select *one* of the ideas on how to organise the perfect day. But a consultation with the teabags had resulted in *all* the ideas from the website being on her wish list. And then Queenie had arrived… He sighed and flicked through the many pages of what had started out as Nina's Wish List but had evolved into Queenie's Demand List.

Crispin ran his finger down the items on the first page. He ticked off the unicorn-drawn, wedding carriage that was now beautifully decorated with knitted panels and awning. *Tick.*

Wedding buffet. Frank Fowle had agreed to cook a hog roast at the reception. Nina had wanted a sophisticated sit-down meal, just like Bartrum's dinner party but Crispin had tried to persuade her otherwise, explaining that Frank had merely heated and served the meal the French Chef had made and that his culinary skills were definitely not up to a stylish three-course dinner. Crispin's advice fell on deaf ears and Nina had asked Frank anyway.

"I can do you burgers in buns," he'd offered helpfully, "but I don't know what half them things were we had at that meal. And I've no idea where you can buy lobster beaks." Nina had finally been persuaded that hog roasts were in fact, the height of fashion. *Tick.*

Aeroplane flypast. Well, that was completely out of the question. *Large cross.*

Everlasting flame. Nina wanted an archer to shoot a burning arrow into an enormous container of inflammable stuff. But Crispin was certain Bartrum would have something to say about that, if indeed they could find an archer brave enough – or stupid enough, to try. Crispin was going to have his work cut out preventing Doggett from starting fires. It had been a dry spring and when he got excited, he produced more sparks than usual. *Large cross and note to himself to ensure fire blankets and buckets of water were available in case Doggett ignited something.*

Three-tier wedding cake. Mrs Bartrum had made a magnificent creation covered in millions of hundreds and thousands. Sylvester had told him that Wilmslow had found them in the kitchen of Her Ladyship's house, but Crispin didn't believe it. Garden Ornaments didn't just wander into the Old Priory's kitchen willy nilly and Wilmslow's story was much too far-fetched, involving ladders, drawers, jam tarts and a broom-waving cook. Anyway, however Mrs Bartrum had acquired the jar of hundreds and thousands, the cake was now finished and more importantly; Nina thought it was breathtaking. *Large tick.*

Flowers. Wendy was in charge of flowers and would start to arrange the bouquets and buttonholes the day before the wedding, so there was nothing Crispin could do but trust that Wendy would get it right. *Small Tick.*

Photographs.

"I've found a photographer, so you can cross it off the list," Doggett had said a few days ago.

"Who've you got?" asked Crispin who'd been having trouble finding anyone.

"You remember that delivery Pixie who brought Nina's wool? Well, he told me his brother knows his way around a camera."

Alarm bells rang in Crispin's head.

"Are you sure that delivery Pixie is trustworthy? Have you seen any of his brother's photos?" Crispin had asked anxiously, well aware that if anything went wrong, Nina would blame him.

"He's got a camera and he's not doing anything on the day. What could possibly go wrong?"

Crispin was tempted to buy a camera and take a crash course in photography, just in case. But there was no time. He'd just have to trust that Spanners, the delivery Pixie's brother, did actually know his way around a camera and more importantly, could take photos with it. *Small tick.*

White Doves. A white Owl to deliver the wedding rings in its beak. McTavish had booked Doves and an Owl from a friend of his who ran a bird agency and they were due to arrive the night before the wedding so they could rehearse. *Tick.*

Candyfloss machine. Wendy said she could probably make something similar to candyfloss although she hadn't been specific and Crispin couldn't think of anything similar to candyfloss, except cotton wool.

Question Mark and note to ask Wendy exactly what she was going to make.

A circus with a big top. Large cross.

An ice rink. Very large cross.

Maypole. This had proved rather difficult but eventually, a Maypole had been found and erected in a clearing in the woods. *Large tick.*

Pre-wedding dancing lessons for all Garden Ornaments who didn't know how to dance around a Maypole. This had puzzled Crispin who assumed it was just a question of grabbing a ribbon and skipping round and round the Maypole until the ribbon was so short you had to stop, then you reversed direction and unwound. Nina and Wendy assured him this was not the case and that it might be best to be on the safe side and make pre-wedding dancing lessons compulsory. Crispin had asked if any of the Garden Ornaments knew how to dance around a Maypole and if they'd be willing to teach everyone else. Thankfully, several of the Fairies who live at the end of the Garden agreed to instruct all those whose education was lacking in the finer arts of country dancing. There would be a lesson for everyone after breakfast and Nina had a list of all Garden Ornaments in case anyone should forget to turn up or should be misguided enough to believe that what they'd planned to do was more important than dancing correctly at her wedding. Nothing and no one would be allowed to jeopardise the smooth running of the Maypole dancing. *Tick.*

Flash mob. Thankfully, the Fairies had loved the idea of a singing, dancing "spontaneous" performance and had assured Crispin they would organise the most exciting flash mob the Garden had ever seen. As he'd never seen a flash mob and wasn't quite sure what one was, he was more than happy to leave it to them. *Tick.*

Photo booth. The delivery Pixie said that his brother, Spanners, would bring a photo booth with him but Crispin was reluctant to place a tick next to the item. He wasn't sure that Spanners would turn up at all. *Question mark.*

Skydiving display. No, definitely not. *Very large cross.*

Masked ball. Jubbly had been very pleased to be asked to organise this, so it was one less thing that Crispin had to worry about. *Large tick.*

Jousting tournament. Crispin wasn't sure what jousting was and wondered whether it would be something that Jubbly would be interested in organising. Jubbly had said definitely not because he was afraid of horses and he didn't hold with people whacking each other with large sticks. That had been enough for Crispin. *Two large crosses.*

By the time Crispin had got to the end of the list, the sun had risen and Sylvester had come into the kitchen yawning.

"You'd better have some breakfast," said Crispin, "we've got dancing lessons shortly."

Sylvester was still grumbling after two bowls of porridge and four slices of toast.

"You're going to be sick. That'll really give you something to moan about," said Crispin removing the toaster before Sylvester could insert any more slices of bread.

Crispin was pleased to see every single Garden Ornament on Nina's list had arrived at the Maypole in the clearing five minutes before the lesson was due to begin. From Bartrum to the Hermit – from Stanley, with four legs, to Arnold the Snail, with none. And each one had been ticked off the list. Sylvester continued to complain under his breath and Queenie had told him that if he didn't turn his frown upside down, she'd turn him upside down, because nothing and no one were going to ruin her little girl's wedding, especially a sulky Elf.

The Fairies were the last to arrive and Crispin stepped forward to suggest that if they needed a few more minutes to get dressed, he was sure everyone wouldn't mind waiting. He added he was worried about them catching a chill, dressed only in their underwear. Sylvester's frown was now definitely upside down, his jaw had dropped and his eyes were bulging. Doggett was blushing and a salvo of sparks fired into the air from his skin. Nina glowered, looking from scantily-clad Fairies to her incandescent intended, who was now gently smoking.

"Music!" shouted one of the Fairies as she

jumped up onto a small rock, so everyone could see the demonstration.

The grass around Doggett's feet began to smoulder.

"Right," said the Fairy, "we'll start with some warm-up exercises. Firstly, we'll touch our toes…"

She bent double and placed her palms on the rock.

"I had no idea skipping around a Maypole could be so painful," Sylvester whispered to Crispin as he bent forward and grabbed the pointy end of his boots.

There was a lot of grunting and wheezing as arms reached down to feet. A few Garden Ornaments managed to get close but most were struggling to touch their knees.

"The trouble… is… my arms aren't… long enough…" grunted Bartrum.

"If he had arms long enough to go over his stomach and reach his toes, his knuckles would scrape the ground when he stood up," whispered Sylvester.

"Shh!" said Crispin and elbowed him.

"Stop the silliness at the back," bellowed the Fairy as Sylvester toppled into the Gnome next to him and the domino effect flattened the rest of the row.

"I think that's enough warming up," said the Fairy when everyone had picked themselves up and Wendy had stopped giggling.

"Right, I'll demonstrate on the pole and then you can each have a go," said the Fairy.

"Well, that was much more fun than I'd expected," said Sylvester as he and Crispin went back to the Toadstool. "Apart from the bruises when you pushed me over, of course. It's a shame Nina stopped the lesson so soon."

"Mm," muttered Crispin. He knew he was in trouble, not only for causing the domino falling fracas but also for booking the Fairies to give a pole dancing lesson. Well, how was he to know that dancing with a pole could come in so many diverse forms, one of which was absolutely not the sort that was usually performed around a Maypole and especially not at a wedding?

"I wish you hadn't offered to give the pole-dancing Fairy the kiss of life," said Crispin.

"I was only trying to help and how was I to know everyone would push me out the way to get to her first?"

"But she hadn't fallen at that point. She didn't need the kiss of life, although by that time, it looked like Doggett did. He'd been quite overcome by smoke. If you'd left the Fairy alone, she'd have been fine."

"Well, I've never seen anyone upside down, halfway up a pole before. She wasn't wearing a safety harness."

"She wasn't wearing much of anything," said Crispin gloomily.

"I was only trying to do the decent thing," said Sylvester.

"If you'd been trying to do the decent thing, you'd have looked away."

"What! And have missed all the fun!"

"You didn't find it much fun when Granny grabbed you."

"No, that's true. She's really scary when she gets cross."

"Lucky for you she only told you off. The way her teeth were snapping, I thought she was going to eat you – well, until they fell out anyway. I hope they turn up before the big day or the wedding photos are going to be ghastly. That is if Spanners turns up to take any."

When Crispin arrived home, he made himself a large cup of tea to calm his nerves. As he ran his finger down the list, a dreadful thought occurred to him. The Fairies were going to organise the flash mob and if it was as X-rated as their Maypole dancing, Doggett might spontaneously combust. And as for Nina… Crispin groaned. In three days' time, it would be the longest day of the year and the longest day of his life. If indeed, he survived until then. Queenie had asked for a wedding update this afternoon to find out how many ticks were on the list. Crispin feared there were going to be far too many crosses for her liking.

"What's for lunch, Crispin?" asked Sylvester.

"Hmm?"

"Lunch. I'm starving. What've we got?"

"Whatever you can find. I haven't got time for lunch."

"I shall be glad when this wedding is over," grumbled Sylvester.

"If I live that long, so shall I…"

Sylvester opened the larder, slid tins across the shelves and restacked them in towering heaps.

"Have we got any baked beans? I fancy beans on toast. We must have beans somewhere…"

"You're searching in what was the fruit section," said Crispin, "but it looks like you've done a good job of muddling all the tins up, so the beans could be anywhere."

A large pile of tins toppled onto the floor.

"Sylvester, please! I can't concentrate if you make so much noise."

"Well, I'll stop if you'll find the beans for me. What're you doing anyway? P'raps I can help you, then you can make lunch."

Crispin groaned. He didn't have time to stop, on the other hand, he couldn't concentrate while Sylvester was disturbing him.

"I'm making a timetable from the items on the list so everyone will know where they're supposed to be at any given time. The only trouble is, there aren't enough hours in a day – even the longest day of the year – if everything is done according to Queenie's instructions. People need to be in two places at one time. It's just impossible."

"You need a break," said Sylvester looking over Crispin's shoulder at the list, "make yourself some beans on toast and have a rest. You'll think faster if you have something to eat. Beans are brain food."

"You're thinking of fish," said Crispin.

"Beans are the vegetarian brain food option."

Sylvester's probably right, thought Crispin, I ought to eat something and a short break might do me good.

"Can I have four slices, please?" asked Sylvester.

Crispin rummaged in the larder.

"I knew exactly where everything was before you messed up my storage system. You're banned from all kitchen cupboards in future."

"Oh dear," said Sylvester without much feeling.

Crispin reorganised the tins in the larder, stacking them neatly by type and in date order. How was he so easily manipulated? If he survived the wedding, there were going to be changes in his life. He was fed up being everybody's doormat.

Even More Wedding Preparations

"Shh!" said Sylvester frowning at Crispin's wedding timetable. "I can't concentrate with you bashing all those tins together. But I can see what you mean about these timings. Stanley'll have to be up before he goes to bed to have the carriage ready for the ceremony. Unless…"

"Unless what?"

"Unless you use Pie Skology."

"What's that?"

Sylvester tapped the side of his nose.

"I'll tell you all about it once I've had beans on toast…"

"That's brilliant!" said Crispin. "Now let me get this straight. You say something to get people to change their minds so they do the things you wanted them to do in the first place? Like mind games?"

"Mmmwf," said Sylvester, nodding.

Another slice?"

"Mmmwf."

"Wipe your chin. You're dribbling bean juice."

It was likely that the dirty, lunch plates would still be piled up in the sink when Crispin returned later, but he would forgive Sylvester almost anything if his Pie Skology plan worked. It had better work because he'd already printed out all the timetables with his new timings and it was too late to change anything now. Not that Nina or her family would necessarily agree and if they didn't like his amendments, they'd expect him to keep to the original impossible plan and to redo the timetables but if Sylvester's Pie Skology worked, everyone would have a great day and Crispin would still be alive at midnight on the day of the wedding.

"Well, aren't you going to Nina's to show her your timetable?" Sylvester asked.

"Ummm… I thought I might wait until later… or possibly tomorrow." His nerve was failing at the thought of the Russian dolls – Nina, her mother and grandmother.

"The early bird catches the worm, so strike while the worm is hot," Sylvester said.

"But… but…" Nina was almost speechless when Crispin proposed that the ceremony started well after sunrise.

Queenie stood with hands on hips and Grannie gnashed her gums but Crispin stood his ground.

"Well, it was just a suggestion but I suppose you're right. I was a bit worried that Stanley might not be able to see where he was going but I'll tell everyone to stand well back from the path, in case he runs anyone down in the darkness."

"But if people stand well back, they won't be able to see my little girl in her wonderful carriage…"

“That’s true,” said Crispin. “No, I suppose they won’t be able to see much in the darkness…”

“Oh, I hadn’t thought of it being completely dark,” said Nina. “It would be a shame if no one could see me, wouldn’t it?”

Queenie and Granny nodded.

“Yes, everyone needs to see my little girl,” said Queenie. Granny muttered something toothlessly, which Crispin took as agreement. Surprised and delighted by this minor triumph, he carried on.

“Well, how about this for a plan? You and Doggett watch the sunrise together, perhaps from the Alpine Garden. We could delay the ceremony until it’s light and then we’d all be able to see you when you arrive in your carriage.”

“Good idea,” said Queenie.

Crispin couldn’t believe it had worked. Using Pie Skology, he’d done the equivalent of moving a mountain. And now the bride and groom would share a romantic sunrise, preparing for their wedding and everyone else would get an extra hour of sleep.

Now for the Maypole dancing…

“And, I wanted to propose that perhaps we didn’t insist everyone danced around the Maypole.”

Queenie’s hands were back on her hips, a scowl on her face.

“I just didn’t want people to wear themselves out around the Maypole and then not have time to dress for the masked ball in the evening. And of course, if people are tired in the evening, they might not dance and a ball where no one dances might not be considered a total success…"

"Hmm, Crispin has a point, Mum. Perhaps it might be a good idea if just a few people took part."

"If you think so, dear. But please keep those dreadful Fairies away from the Maypole."

Crispin couldn't believe it. He'd struck while the worm was hot and turned an impossible day into one that just might be enjoyable – and possible – after all.

How did Sylvester know about the use of Pie Skology to get people to do something they hadn't previously wanted to do? And more importantly, how often had he used it on Crispin? He had the distinct feeling it had been used on him more than once.

When the wedding was over, things were definitely going to change.

"Crispin, wait for me!" It was Lulu. And she was running down the path after him.

He sighed and gritted his teeth as her shouts assaulted his eardrums.

Try as he might, Crispin's Pie Skology wasn't potent enough to convince Lulu not to accompany him while he delivered the timetables to those Garden Ornaments who had key roles in the wedding. Crispin's first stop was the clearing, to give Stanley the good news that he had extra time in bed and he wondered if the unicorn would be able to lend him any cotton wool to stuff in his ears before Lulu's piercing tones ruptured them. The unicorn was indeed delighted he had more time to get himself in harness on the wedding day and handed Crispin a large handful of cotton wool.

"What's wrong with your ears?" Lulu asked.

"Umm…" said Crispin, who'd tried to stuff the cotton wool in his ears without Lulu seeing. "Umm…"

"He has an allergy," said Stanley quickly.

"Oh, what's he allergic to?" asked Lulu.

"Well, it's a bit complicated," said Stanley.

"But with that in his ears, he won't be able to hear me," said Lulu. "Shall I speak up?"

"No!" said Stanley and Crispin together.

The next stop was McTavish's house. Crispin's heart was heavy, remembering the last time he'd been here, looking for the beautiful Angel he'd met at the New Year's Ball. He hadn't been able to get her out of his mind but McTavish's sisters hadn't returned to stay with him and the Cherub was very vague about their whereabouts or even their existence.

"I can't be expected to remember every Tom, Dick or Harry," he'd grumbled the last time Crispin had broached the subject of his sisters. And Crispin had given up. If McTavish didn't know where his sisters were or even *who* his sisters were, Crispin was unlikely ever to see Bella, the lovely Angel, again. If the feather that had fallen from her wing hadn't still been on his bedside table, he might be tempted to wonder if he'd imagined her.

McTavish was at the door, in his dressing-gown, a cigar in one hand and a glass of brown liquid in the other. A raw egg yolk bobbed up and down in the brown sludge, as the Cherub became agitated.

"Yes, yes, I told you it was all under control. A dozen Swans and an Owl."

"No!" said Crispin in alarm. "A dozen white Doves and an Owl."

"Doves, Swans. Whatever," said McTavish. The egg yolk surfaced on top of the drink like a rising sun and then sank again into the depths.

"But they must be Doves," insisted Crispin.

"Yes, Doves," said Lulu, picking up on the hysterical note in Crispin's voice and adding her support.

"Stop shouting," shouted McTavish.

"Please," said Crispin, "I just need to know. Did you order Doves or Swans?"

"Doves or Swans?" insisted Lulu.

"Yes!" said McTavish and with that, he slammed the door.

Lulu tucked her hand under Crispin's arm and led him down the path.

"Never mind," she boomed, "I'm sure it'll be all right."

Crispin tried to pull away from Lulu's vice-like grip but she held him close. Anyway, he had more important things to worry about and he determined to return when the bird handler arrived later, and ask him. Opening a basket full of Doves would result in a beautiful spectacle, as they fluttered upwards and flew into the sky. But the consequence of cramming a dozen Swans into that same basket and then releasing them, might well be more excitement than Nina had anticipated.

Crispin gave out a strangled sound.

"Never mind, Crispin, I'm here," Lulu bellowed and she wrapped her arm around his shoulders and hugged.

Upstairs in one of the bedrooms in McTavish's house, Mr Lambert dipped and bobbed excitedly by Bella's ear.

"Mr Lambert," she said with mock severity, "I can't make out a word you're saying." She held out her finger for the butterfly to settle on.

"There," she said, "now start again. Holding him close to her ear, she listened intently as he whispered.

"Are you sure?"

Mr Lambert nodded.

"Where?" she asked jumping up in excitement. Mr Lambert lost his footing and dropped off her finger.

"Are you sure?" she asked again.

He rose into the air and hovered in front of her face, nodding.

"But McTavish said he'd gone away." She held out her finger for the butterfly and listened to his reply.

"Yes, I suppose you're right, my uncle did say he'd never heard of Crispin, so he can't be a Garden Ornament. But perhaps he's come back for a visit. Perhaps he's here for the wedding!" She clapped her hands together in delight, narrowly avoiding crushing the butterfly.

"Oh, I'm sorry, Mr Lambert, I'm just so excited at the thought of seeing Crispin again. Where is he now?"

Mr Lambert alighted on her shoulder.

"Really? He's in the woods. You're sure he's coming this way? Well, what're we waiting for? We need to unpack and find my hairbrush."

Mr Lambert kept out of the way while Bella sorted through her case and brushed her hair.

"How'd I look?" she asked, patting her glossy, golden curls. "Is my halo straight?"

If Mr Lambert had owned a pair of hands, he'd have clapped them together in delight. He flew to her head and settled on her fringe, pulling it back off her forehead with his feet.

"I've grown up since I was here before, and this time, Mr Lambert, I'm going to be an Angel of the world. I'll be cool, calm and I'll impress him with my charm, not like at the ball when I might have seemed a bit… well… a bit inexperienced."

Mr Lambert let go of her fringe and fluttered in front of her.

"Yes, you're right, dear Mr Lambert, I'd better go downstairs or he'll have been and gone."

She rushed to the door, hotly pursued by Mr Lambert who quickly checked the halo hadn't slipped and grabbed her fringe with his feet, pulling it out of her eyes.

Bella could hear her uncle at the door speaking to someone. He was getting cross. Nothing new there. McTavish spent most of his time at home, in a bad temper.

"Doves or Swans?" said a female voice. A very loud female voice. And then the door slammed and McTavish stomped back to the kitchen.

"Oh, Mr Lambert, that doesn't sound like Crispin at all. Are you sure you saw him?"

She dashed back upstairs and looked out of the window. The owner of the loud voice was now walking down the path with her arm around Crispin.

"Oh no! He's found someone else."

Bella and Mr Lambert watched in horror as the couple walked off into the woods together.

"I'm too late, Mr Lambert. I don't think I can bear it."

She sobbed into her hands.

With much wing-flapping, Mr Lambert managed

to lift a hankie and carry it to her. Once she'd taken it and buried her face in it, he flew out of the open window after the unfaithful Elf.

"Where are we going now, Crispin?" asked Lulu.

"Umm…" Crispin wasn't sure his eardrums could stand much more. "Home?" he said.

"But you've got other things on your list. Don't you have to give out more timetables?"

"Umm…"

"Come on, we can do them together."

"Umm…" If only he could think of some Pie Skology to persuade Lulu she wanted to do something else.

I'm going to get Sylvester to teach me all he knows about Pie Skology, thought Crispin, and after the wedding is over…

"Well, I suppose we could take a timetable to Bartrum," he said knowing he actually ought to find Wendy. But the thought of her reaction when she heard of Lulu's promotion to chief bridesmaid was daunting indeed.

"Cwithpin! Hello, Cwithpin! Wait for me!" Wendy galloped out of the woods, carrying a basket containing some daisies.

Oh well, thought Crispin, the two bridesmaids have to meet sooner or later. If only it wasn't now.

"Lulu, Wendy. Wendy, Lulu."

"Ah," said Lulu, "my second-in-command. Nice to meet you."

"Thecond-in-command?"

"Yes, I'm Nina's chief bridesmaid."

Crispin winced and waited for the explosion – or at least the tears.

But surprisingly, Wendy wasn't too bothered about her demotion to second bridesmaid.

"Have you theen any flowerth?"

"Flowers?" asked Crispin.

"Yeth flowerth."

"Well, I haven't really been looking but there must be loads in the flower beds."

"Yeth, I expect there are begoniath, if Guthty Bob hathnt killed them off but I wanted larger flowerth."

"Please tell me they're not for the bride's bouquet…" said Crispin with a terrible feeling of foreboding.

"Yeth. I met Jubbly earlier and he told me the fairieth had been picking flowerth to weave into their hair for the wedding and they haven't left any."

"But you ordered some from the florist, right?" asked Crispin although he felt certain he already knew the answer.

"Of courthe not. We live in a garden. Gardenth are full of flowerth… Well, usually. Anyway, you've got a fluffy thing in your ear."

"It's cotton wool," said Crispin.

"He's got an allergy," said Lulu helpfully.

"What're you allergic to?" Wendy asked.

"It's complicated," said Lulu.

"Not flowerth, I hope."

"If only there were flowers to be allergic to," murmured Crispin.

"Shall I thpeak up?"

"No! I'm fine, thanks. By the way, did you manage to find out how to make candyfloss?"

"Oh yeth, but I need to find wire cutterth."

"For candyfloss?"

"Yeth. I've already got a whithk, plathtic bin bag and wooden thpoon. Oh and sugar."

"Mrs Bartrum may have some wire cutters. She did a metalwork course last year," said Crispin, "but are you sure it's candyfloss you're making? You know, fluffy, pink stuff made of sugar?"

"Yeth, of courthe."

"It's just that you don't often hear of people cooking with wire cutters…"

"You don't cook with them, thilly. They're for cutting off the end of the whithk…"

"Right," said Crispin slowly, making a mental note to cross candyfloss off his list. He was so deep in thought that it took him a few seconds to realise he was under attack.

If Crispin's ears hadn't been full of cotton wool, he might have heard Mr Lambert's war cry or the frantic beating of wings and he might have ducked. But, as it was, other than a momentary glimpse of a furious butterfly with proboscis extended, Crispin was aware of nothing until the moment of impact. Mr Lambert had launched himself like a dart, at the spot between Crispin's eyes and scored a bull's eye.

"Ow!" yelped Crispin.

Mr Lambert bounced off the Elf's forehead and gathering his wits, he rallied himself for another attack. Crispin would regret the day he'd broken Bella's heart – Mr Lambert would personally see to it.

Crispin swatted madly at the lepidopteran air-to-ground missile.

"What'th the matter, Cwithpin?"

"Aargh! Stop it!" shouted Crispin, as his assailant seized a clump of hair and tugged.

"Cwithpin! Cwithpin! Oh, get off you beatht!" Wendy screamed and swung her basket at the butterfly, catching Crispin on the chin with a glancing blow. Mr Lambert was much faster than Crispin and he dodged the basket with ease, taking advantage of the confusion caused by Lulu and Wendy. They were both trying to comfort the injured Elf, who was clutching his jaw.

"Oh, Cwithpin, I'm tho thorry!"

Mr Lambert circled above their heads and diving again, he swooped past Crispin's head and grabbed another tuft of hair. The ease with which the hair detached itself from the Elf's head took Mr Lambert by surprise and he flew backwards tumbling over and over, a large lump of cotton wool tangling his feet.

"Regroup!" squeaked Mr Lambert as he rose out of range of the swinging basket and hovered above. It wasn't clear who he was urging into formation, as he was a lone assailant but he began to realise that if he merely flew towards the Elf, the two females did their best to defend Crispin, which consistently resulted in more damage to the Elf.

The furious, basket-waving little girl was swinging wildly and as well as a glancing blow to the Elf's chin, she managed to score a direct hit to the side of his head which had almost felled him. The loud, large female Gnome had assumed the pose of a karate fighter.

"Hi-yah!" she'd yelled as her hand sliced so close to Mr Lambert when he'd darted towards Crispin, he'd almost spiralled out of control but as the hand continued on its trajectory, it made contact with the tender part of the back of the Elf's neck.

Mr Lambert's first attack had been more successful than he could possibly have imagined.

"Retire!" he squeaked and flew off with a decided list to the left.

"You idiot! You've killed Cwithpin!

"Me? You kept whacking him with your basket. I took out that killer insect with my bare hands before it got Crispin—"

"No, you didn't. I thaw it fly off."

"No, it didn't."

"And anyway, you hit Cwithpin—"

"So did you…"

"Ladies, please," said Crispin, staggering to his feet, "perhaps we ought to get out of here while the going is good."

"Here, Cwithpin, let me help you—" Wendy took an arm.

"No! Let me help you," said Lulu grabbing the other arm.

"Ow!" screamed Crispin as his minders "helped" him home.

One More Sleep

Sylvester upended a bowl of cornflakes over the sleeping Crispin. "Well, thank goodness that woke you up at last," he said picking a rather large cornflake off Crispin's shoulder and popping it in his mouth. "Don't scowl at me like that – you ought to be thanking me for waking you. I've looked at your diary for today and you're already behind."

Reality suddenly caught up with Crispin and he dashed for the shower. As well as removing all traces of the milk and cornflakes Sylvester had tipped over him, the water jets cleared Crispin's head and he began to remember all the things that hadn't been done yesterday and that would now join the extensive list of things to be done today.

Sylvester hovered uncertainly as Crispin grabbed a piece of dry toast for breakfast. He obviously felt rather guilty about his messy wake-up call but didn't know how to make amends.

"Wendy and Lulu delivered the rest of the programmes yesterday after they brought you home," he said helpfully. "And Wendy said not to worry because she'd definitely find some flowers for the bouquet today, so you weren't to panic and Lulu said she'd be over this morning to help you with everything else…"

"What!" shrieked Crispin, leaping up. "So she could be here any minute?"

Crispin hopped down the garden path pulling on a boot. He stopped at the gate and inspected the boot he was trying to put on.

"Sylvester!" he yelled as he hopped back up the path. "Where's my other boot?"

Sylvester stood at the door with Crispin's boot, his wedding list, a colander in case he came under aerial attack by hostile insects, an umbrella in case it rained, a pack of mustard sandwiches and two pairs of bicycle clips. It seemed he'd applied a lot of thought to how he was going to make it up to Crispin for his earlier misdemeanour. And if he was lucky, Crispin wouldn't insist he did the laundry this week too. He didn't fancy picking cornflakes out of Crispin's sheets.

He held one pair of bicycle clips and the boot out to Crispin. "I've got the tandem out," Sylvester said as he fixed the other pair of clips round his legs and dropping the items in the wicker basket, he leapt onto the front saddle. "C'mon!" he said. "Let's go!" as Crispin held the gate open and jumped on to the rear saddle.

"Aargh!" yelled Crispin, as Sylvester sharply applied the brakes. "I've told you before not to brake so hard. I nearly sailed over your head. Why've you stopped?"

"I don't know where you want to go first."

"To the Fairies at the end of the Garden, by any path that doesn't go near Nina's Toadstool…"

"When I said 'any path that doesn't go near Nina's Toadstool', I didn't have *that* sort of route in mind," said Crispin picking twigs out of his hair. "And promise me we won't go home that way. We might not be so lucky freeing the tandem from that boggy patch a second time."

"It'd be too hard to go home that way. It's all uphill. I can't imagine what that shopping trolley was doing there, though…"

"No. I don't know how you missed it. Well done. It'd have made a nasty dent in the bike… or us."

Sylvester glowed with pride. At least Crispin assumed he was glowing with pride. It was hard to tell with all the stinging nettle welts and dock leaf juice that streaked his face.

"Have you got any more of that dock leaf juice?" Sylvester asked.

From the perch, in what he thought of as the forest canopy, but was actually a bough in the apple tree in the woods, Boggy, the zealous Eco-Gnome was able to see through a gap in the trees into the Fairies' clearing. It was fascinating viewing, with glimpses of tiny figures spontaneously bursting into song and dance. It was certainly different from the last time Boggy had been there in the middle of some terrible gangland battle. He looked back to the Fairies and wondered if he'd made a mistake and this was somewhere completely different. He knew it wasn't though, because the last time he'd been here, he'd escaped with the clothes he stood up in and nothing more. Miraculously, the gang members hadn't found the shopping trolley that he'd hidden in the undergrowth, nor the primus stove, hot water bottle or sleeping bag that were still in the tree. The Garden might seem very different but it was definitely the same place. He'd had to evict a small, black cat with a pink ribbon around its neck from the sleeping bag and sustained several puncture wounds and a deep scratch for his troubles but otherwise, everything else was as he'd left it.

After his previous experiences in this Garden, he began to wonder at the wisdom of returning but he hadn't had much luck spreading his message elsewhere and he had nothing to lose and everything to gain – especially if he saved the world.

He'd just made the bough as comfortable as he could and was planning his campaign when he heard a commotion from below. Someone was screaming "Stop! Stop!" and another voice, equally loud and panic-stricken was yelling "How? How?"

Boggy watched two figures on a tandem bicycle hurtle into the clearing beneath his apple tree. Their mud-covered legs were held out sideways, away from the pedals which were spinning so fast, they were a mere blur.

"Aargh!" they both yelled, as their course took them through the middle of a large patch of stinging nettles which Boggy thought might have slowed them down, but there was no appreciable decrease in speed as the bicycle raced towards the shopping trolley parked under the apple tree. The rear passenger spotted the obstacle first and clutched at the driver in panic.

During his solitary Eco-Gnome nights in trees, Boggy had often wondered whether sound bent around corners and now he saw, or rather heard, the phenomenon first hand.

The driver's words, "Hold tight!" came at him head-on, then as the handlebars were swung to the left, "Hold tight!" seemed to hit him sideways, finally tailing off as the sound caught up with itself.

Boggy watched in fascination as the fearless riders ground to a halt some way off and leapt from their saddles. They grabbed handfuls of leaves and rubbed them over their faces and arms.

Camouflage! thought Boggy with a thrill of excitement. This was indeed the cutting edge of Eco-warfare. He could learn a lot from experts such as these.

"Madam, will you please stop screaming!" Crispin said. His eardrums were rather fragile since the previous day which had been spent with Lulu.

The Fairy stopped shrieking and peered at the two muddy, twiggy, puffy-faced Elves.

Crispin took the checklist from the bicycle's wicker basket and turned to the relevant page.

"What're you doing?" asked the Fairy suspiciously.

"I'm just checking the flash mob is under control."

"Of course, it's under control. We've been rehearsing for weeks. What's it to you?"

"I'm the Best Elf and I need to make sure everything's going to be perfect tomorrow."

"Well of course it's going to be perfect tomorrow. We don't need you poking your nose in."

"All right!" said Sylvester, "he's only doing his job. Don't give him such a hard time."

The Fairy peered at Sylvester.

"Hah!" she said triumphantly. "I thought you looked familiar. Don't think all that green stuff on your face will stop me recognising you! You were the one who caused all that fuss at the pole dancing lesson."

"It wasn't my fault. I was only trying to help…"

"Help like yours, we can do without."

"Well, anyway, Madam," said Crispin politely, "if I can just check on the costumes for tomorrow…"

"Hah! So that's your game!"

"What game?" asked Crispin. "There's no game. I just need to check the costumes."

"I'm not letting you anywhere near my girls."

"But I need to know they'll be dressed appropriately."

"So you say! Now, be off with you!" The irate Fairy seized the umbrella from the wicker basket and started menacing the Elves.

"Well, we'll just have to keep our fingers crossed the Fairies are dressed, I suppose," said Crispin as he and Sylvester rode off.

"Where now?" Sylvester called over his shoulder.

"To the Gazebo. I need to check Spanners has delivered the photo booth."

To Crispin's surprise, not only was Spanners at the Gazebo with his camera but he'd also brought the photo booth as promised.

"You're here," said Crispin in wonder.

"Yes, weren't you expecting me?"

"No, err, yes…" said Crispin. "That is yes but, well, no…"

"Rightio," said Spanners, "if it's okay, I'm going to have a chat with the bride and groom and make sure I cover the whole event as they'd like. Is that okay?"

"Oh yes!" said Crispin. "Yes, please."

"Now, I just need the plug socket so I can test out the photo booth and then I'll go and find the lucky couple."

"Plug socket?"

Spanners held up the plug from the photo booth. "Yes, I'll just plug it in and make sure everything's working."

"Aaargh!" said Crispin.

"I think what he's trying to say, is that we don't have a plug socket outside the Gazebo," said Sylvester.

"Well, we have two options," said Spanners. "Either we move the photo booth or we set up the cycle generator."

"Cycle generator?" asked Crispin.

"We can generate enough electricity to run the photo booth," said Spanners.

"We?" asked Crispin.

"You just need a volunteer to cycle while the photo booth is in operation," said Spanners.

"Sylvester?" asked Crispin.

"No way, I've had enough cycling for one day. I've got so many bruises on my shins from those pedals I'll be lucky if I can still walk by tomorrow."

"Well, can you think of anyone who might be willing?"

"No one's going to want to spend their time cycling rather than enjoying themselves at the wedding," said Crispin. "I suppose I'll have to do it myself."

"Hmm," said Sylvester thoughtfully. "Not necessarily. Just leave it to me. Now, where're we off to next?"

"I've got a bad feeling about this," said Crispin, checking his watch again. "Where is everybody? And suppose the Bird-Gnome doesn't come? What if McTavish ordered the wrong birds?"

"Stop panicking," said Sylvester. "We're half an hour early."

Crispin paced up and down the Sunken Garden.

He'd positioned the lectern from which Bartrum would conduct the ceremony and he'd set out the chairs for the guests. A large area had been strewn with rose petals ready for the bride and groom. Nina was afraid that if Doggett got too excited, he might set fire to a chair so it was agreed the couple would remain standing. Several buckets of water and several fire blankets were at hand in case, despite his best efforts, the groom went up in flames or set fire to Nina's dress.

Crispin moved the lectern slightly to the left, then moved it back to its original position.

"It's all perfect," said Sylvester. "Stop fiddling with things."

"Don't sit there!" screeched Crispin as Sylvester started to sink onto one of the chairs in the front row. "You're filthy."

Sylvester leapt to attention. "Don't shout! And anyway, you're just as dirty, so stop touching things."

Crispin looked down at his muddy legs and groaned. "D'you think we've got time to go home and shower?"

Before Sylvester could reply, Lulu appeared.

"Oh, you poor darling!" She rushed at Crispin and hugged him tightly. "What happened? You look dreadful!"

"Mwmff," said Crispin.

"Lulu! Put him down, he's filthy," shouted Queenie. "I hope you're not planning to turn up tomorrow looking like that!" she added, wagging her finger at the Elves.

Crispin sucked air into his crushed lungs, grateful that he hadn't had time to shower and change. At least now he was off-limits to Lulu – until tomorrow, anyway. But first, he had to survive the wedding rehearsal.

When Wendy arrived, she was rather vague about the bouquet and buttonholes although she assured Crispin he wasn't to worry. "It will all be fine," she said. Crispin decided to call by the Wendy House on his way home from the rehearsal to check. If he had to comb the Garden for flowers overnight, so be it. Better that, than the bride finding she had a daisy chain on her big day.

The Wooden Robin hadn't been invited to the rehearsal but he turned up anyway. He didn't have a role despite his best efforts to volunteer. In the end, to reward his persistence, Nina had said he could be the Wedding Robin although she hadn't been specific about what this entailed. It had been enough for the Wooden Robin that he had a wedding job title and he hopped excitedly from foot to foot.

"If that wooden creature doesn't stop tripping me up, I'm going to tread on him," said Queenie grabbing the back of the chair to steady herself.

"Wooden Robin, I wonder if you could check the, umm, the wind chimes. Yes, the wedding wind chimes," said Crispin. "It's most important they err, chime. And perhaps while you're there, you could check the, err, wind."

The Wooden Robin hopped excitedly out of the Sunken Garden just as McTavish arrived with his friend, the Bird-Gnome, and two large cages – one full of Doves and the other containing a single white Owl.

Bartrum had been the last to arrive and had immediately taken over although Crispin could see Queenie and Granny were beginning to get rather cross at being ordered about. But Bartrum did seem to know what he was doing and the rehearsal was going well, with everyone in position and no one missing their cues.

Crispin laid a fire blanket on the ground for the bridal couple to stand on as Doggett was beginning to char the grass around his feet.

"Now," said Bartrum, "we need to rehearse the giving of rings. Who has the rings?"

Everyone turned expectantly to Crispin.

"I haven't got them" he spluttered, blood draining from his face.

Doggett patted his pockets. "I don't think I've got them," he said. "Are you sure you haven't got them, Crispin?"

"No! You haven't given them to me yet."

"Don't panic everyone," said Nina fishing in her handbag. "You don't think I'd trust anyone with the rings, do you? And there'd be no point giving them to Doggett. He'd have short-circuited himself with two rings in his pocket."

"Well, this is the part where the Owl flies in with both rings in her beak, so Crispin, if you'd carry the rings to the yew tree and give them to the Bird-Gnome, we can proceed," said Bartrum.

Crispin was happy to hand them over to the Bird-Gnome to place in the Owl's beak. He didn't trust the bird. At first sight, it appeared to be asleep but when it blinked, Crispin was struck by the vicious look in its eyes.

Don't be so fanciful, he told himself, it's just a bird. It's probably upset at being woken during the day.

He realised something was wrong as he walked back to Doggett and Nina. The Owl was behind him but he could see the rest of the wedding party's surprised expressions and hear the powerful flap of wings.

"Stop him!" cried Nina. "He's got our rings!"

"It's a her, not a him. And stop shouting, you'll frighten her!" shouted the Bird-Gnome. "Come on girl, come back, look, I've got a lovely mouse for you… Mavis! Come back, Mavis!"

But with a single backwards glance, in which Crispin was convinced Mavis was grinning, she flew off.

Nina was screaming. Queenie and Granny were trying to console her and Doggett was showering the grass with sparks as he ran back and forth, looking upwards. The Sunken Garden was in uproar.

"Cwithpin! Do thomething!" screamed Wendy.

Crispin sighed.

Everyone turned to look at him expectantly. He was the Best Elf and it was up to him to rescue the situation. But his mind had gone blank.

Sylvester sidled up to him and out of the corner of his mouth whispered, "Use Pie Skology."

"How?"

"Like this," Sylvester whispered. "Now, listen up everyone, Crispin has an important announcement," he said loudly.

"I have?" asked Crispin in horror.

Granny's gimlet eyes bored into him. "Yes, you have. You were going to say something like 'Are we going to let a little thing like some missing rings spoil our wedding day?' weren't you?"

Crispin nodded. He wasn't sure whether this particular Pie Skology might just backfire but he was completely out of ideas.

A few people looked at him uncertainly, a few shook their heads. "Yes?" suggested Doggett looking hesitantly at Nina.

"No!" said Sylvester. "Crispin says we are definitely not going to let the loss of some rings spoil the day. It's going to be the very best day of all our lives!"

"Hear, hear!" said Bartrum, banging his gavel on the lectern.

"Who needs rings?" shouted Lulu.

"Well…" said Nina uncertainly.

"It's going to be the best day of our lives, rings or no rings," shouted Sylvester. "According to Crispin, anyway."

"Three cheers for the Best Elf!" said Doggett.

Crispin wondered if he was going to faint.

Bartrum called an emergency meeting and explained to all the Garden Ornaments what had happened during the wedding rehearsal.

"A perfidious bird of prey has purloined the wedding rings…"

"What?" whispered the Wooden Robin.

"A naughty Owl stole the rings while you were checking the wind chimes," whispered Crispin.

"Outrageous," squeaked the Wooden Robin, "what is the world coming to?"

"Well volunteered," said Bartrum.

"Eh?" squeaked the Wooden Robin. "Who's volunteered? Why's everyone looking at me?"

"Wooden Robin, you are the perfect person for the job," said Bartrum.

"I am?"

The Wooden Robin's delight at being the "perfect person for the job" soon turned to dismay when he realised what he was expected to do.

"But I can't fly," he'd explained when Bartrum had told him he was going to deliver two substitute rings to the bride and groom in place of the Owl.

"Not a problem," said Bartrum and he instructed Klaus to install a zip wire from the top of the tall oak tree to the lectern in the Sunken Garden and to provide the Wooden Robin with a harness.

"Where are the brakes?" squeaked the Wooden Robin. He looked nervously up to the top of the oak. "And how am I going to get up there?"

"You'll be hoisted up. Don't worry. All you've got to do is keep the rings in your beak and then hand them to me when you get down here," said Bartrum.

"Couldn't I just be in charge of the wind chimes?"

But Bartrum had turned away.

"Now, I expect every Garden Ornament to keep a watchful eye out for the real rings and for the treacherous thief. I am putting up a reward for the return of the rings and the apprehension of the perpetrator of the crime."

The Elves were nearly home when Crispin remembered he'd forgotten to check on Wendy's bouquet and buttonholes and that the cage of Doves had been left in the Sunken Garden after the Owl fiasco.

"Don't worry, I'll sort out the Doves. You go and see Wendy," said Sylvester.

"Thank you, Sylvester. You've been a real help today," said Crispin as he turned off to the Wendy House.

"Oh, Cwithpin! How lovely to thee you. Ith Thylvethter with you?"

"No, he's sorting out the Doves for me but I just wanted to check you found enough flowers for the bouquet and buttonholes."

"Well," said Wendy nervously, "actually, I didn't. Thothe fairieth have taken all the flowerth, but I've improvithed."

Crispin began to panic. A bouquet of stinging nettles would definitely not be good news.

"I made thith," said Wendy, leading him into her living room.

"Ooh, Wendy!" said Crispin. "It's beautiful!"

The bride's bouquet would have been a sorry sight indeed if it had simply consisted of flowers and ribbons. The Fairies had certainly stripped the Garden if these were the only blooms Wendy had been able to find. But the lack of floral content was eclipsed by the colourful and sparkling array of sweets that were incorporated into the bouquet. Jewel-like boiled sweets, foil-wrapped toffees, pastel peach twists of cough candy coated in sugar were tastefully arranged amongst the flowers and long tendrils of red and black liquorice coiled round the lengths of pink ribbon.

"I hope it'th all right…" said Wendy hesitantly.

"It's wonderful, Wendy. You're so clever."

Wendy beamed.

"Unfortunately, there weren't any more flowerth for the bridethmaidth or the button holeth, tho I made thethe. I hope they're all right."

She gently raised a cloth to reveal two posies and dozens of buttonholes made of colourful lollipops. Each buttonhole lollipop had several leaves attached as if it were a flower and the posies were spherical arrangements of lollipops, decorated with bows and lengths of gently coiling ribbon.

"They're really lovely," said Crispin. "I can't tell you how pleased I am…"

Wendy blushed.

"Well, tho long ath you don't hug me. You're very, very dirty and quite thmelly." She wrinkled her nose.

It was time for Crispin to go home and have a long, hot soak in the bath. There was nothing more he could do tonight and the longest day was only a few hours away.

The Wedding Dawn

Crispin was having a nightmare about teabags. Giant teabags. They flew overhead, swooping out of the sky with wickedly sharp talons extended down as if they were going to seize him. One of the teabags carried two golden rings in its beak which it seemed to be showing off as it swooped ever closer to his head.

"Go away!" Crispin batted the air, fending off the enormous, menacing teabags. He screamed and ducked as one particularly threatening one dropped out of the sky, its unblinking eyes fixed on him.

"Arrgh!" Crispin sat up in bed with sweat dripping down his face. Relief flooded through him as he realised he'd been dreaming and the giant teabags had gone. He checked the clock. It was 3.15 am on the day of the wedding and this time tomorrow, it would all be over. Would he survive the day? That remained to be seen…

One thing was sure, there were going to be changes in his life. The stress of the last few weeks had been too much. For a start, in future, he would buy loose tea leaves. He never wanted to look another teabag in the face. And he'd take control of his life. He was fed up being told what to do all the time. Perhaps he'd take a holiday. Bartrum only granted permission to leave the Garden in exceptional circumstances and Crispin was certain that reluctance to do everyone's bidding – including Bartrum's – wouldn't qualify. *The only way I'm ever going to be able to live my life in peace*, thought Crispin, *is if I run away.*

That was it! Why hadn't he thought of it before? He'd run away. His mind began to whir feverishly with plans and possibilities. As soon as he could get away from the wedding, he'd leave the Garden and by the time anyone wanted him to do something, he'd be gone. He stuffed a few things in a rucksack and hid it in the wardrobe ready for his escape.

He hummed a tune as he left his bedroom and walked through the living room to the kitchen.

"Shut up, can't you?" said Sylvester crossly. "Some people are trying to sleep."

"Well, why're you on the sofa and not in your bedroom?"

"There's no room."

"What d'you mean there's no room? Who's in there?"

"Doves."

"But their basket isn't that large. Surely there's room for you as well." Crispin paused. "Please tell me they're still in their basket…"

"Umm. Not exactly."

"You mean you've got twelve Doves loose in your room?"

"Not exactly. One escaped through the window…"

"Oh, honestly!"

"I felt sorry for them being cooped up. I made a space for them to sit on the chest of drawers and I expected them to go to sleep but they just kept flying around the room and I couldn't get them back in the basket."

"Well, if you want your breakfast, you'd better go and round them up."

Sylvester's cajoling soon turned to swearing as the squawking and flapping became more frenzied.

Crispin took pity on him. After all, he'd been trying to be kind. "Shall I bring you some breadcrumbs? Perhaps you can lure them down with some food," he shouted.

"No! Don't come in!"

"All right. Suit yourself."

There was a crash, followed by the splintering of wood and enraged screeching.

"Don't peck!" Sylvester shouted. "Ow! Ow! Ow!"

There was the sound of a basket being slammed shut and a loud sigh of relief.

"What's going on in there? Have you got them all?" Crispin called.

Sylvester's door opened a fraction. "Well, I've got eleven of them. The other one's in the Garden. We might be able to get him later."

"Your breakfast is ready," said Crispin.

"Right, I'll be out in a minute."

The door closed.

How odd, thought Crispin, he can't usually wait to get to his breakfast. It's almost as if he's hiding something…

"Are you hiding something?"

"Err, no…"

"Well come on out or I'm coming in."

Sylvester sighed and opened the door slightly.

"It's probably best you don't come in or even look in here today," he said, "it's a bit of a mess. Those Doves don't seem to be house-trained."

It was still dark when Crispin and Sylvester left the Toadstool, dressed in their finest clothes. The escapee Dove had been remarkably easy to catch when lured with breadcrumbs, and they'd hastily pushed him into the basket with the other birds.

"Where are we going first?" asked Sylvester.

Crispin consulted his timetable. "We'll check Stanley's all right."

Stanley *was* all right. In fact, he was more than all right, he was magnificent. He'd brushed his white coat until it gleamed and polished his spiral horn until it shone like silver. The bells he'd attached to the knitted harness jingled merrily as he stamped and shook his head, eager to set off.

Jubbly arrived, resplendent in shocking pink satin and silver livery and a jaunty cap with a feather.

"I hope you're not thinking of using that whip, old chap," said Stanley when he saw him.

"It's just for show. One needs to look the part, you know. Is everything ready? Are the Doves in the carriage?"

Sylvester nodded.

"I hope you cleaned the basket out this morning, said Jubbly. "They're messy creatures."

"No need," said Sylvester, "their basket is quite clean. Trust me on that."

"Right," said Crispin, checking his watch. "It's nearly time for Jubbly and Stanley to pick up the bride. Park at the bottom of the Alpine Garden and wait for her there. You'll then pick up the bridesmaids and drive around the Garden. Sylvester and I will meet you at the Sunken Garden with Doggett."

The bells jingled as Stanley strained against the harness.

"Giddy up!" shouted Jubbly, waving the whip in one pink-gloved hand and flicking the reins with the other. The wheels slowly began to turn as the knitted carriage creaked, trembled and then began to move forward.

"We're off!" shouted Jubbly and he waved his hat at the Elves as the carriage rolled by.

"One unicorn-drawn, knitted wedding carriage," said Crispin and with satisfaction, he placed a large tick on the first item on his list.

He'd barely had time to sigh with relief when the carriage, which had disappeared into the pre-dawn gloom ground to a halt and both Jubbly and Stanley began shouting.

"Use the brakes, old chap!" Stanley yelled angrily. "If I stop, the carriage has to stop."

"No one showed me where the brakes are," replied Jubbly, equally angrily.

Crispin ran towards the carriage. What had happened? Had the wheel fallen off?

"Why have you stopped?"

"Bally idiot ran out into the middle of the path and stood there, pointing a bow and arrow at me," said Stanley.

"Just like a highway robber," said Jubbly, "he was terrifying."

"Who?" asked Crispin.

"A Gnome dressed in camouflage gear," said Stanley.

"Did he say anything?" asked Crispin.

"He made a sort of 'Eeeeee' sound, like air coming out of a punctured tyre."

"D'you know what he wanted?" asked Crispin.

"No. He just stood in the middle of the road holding a bow and arrow. I lowered my head, shoved my horn up his nose and said, '*That's* not a weapon, *this* is a weapon.' "

"You should have seen his face," said Jubbly excitedly. "It turned as green as his outfit. Then he dropped some bits of paper and ran off into the woods."

Sylvester picked up one of the sheets of paper. "It says 'Save our Planet, Rethink, Reduce, Reuse, Recycle, Renew. The world will be destroyed by carbon footprints. Beware. Stamp out carbon footprints before it's too late.' What does that all mean?"

"I've no idea," said Crispin, "we'll worry about that later. C'mon, we need to get to the Alpine Garden. No, don't drop it, Sylvester! Pick them all up. We can't have litter blowing around the Garden during the wedding."

Sylvester retrieved all the bits of paper and stuffed them in his pocket.

Boggy peeped out nervously, from behind the holly bush, panting with the exertion of having run through tangled undergrowth. He'd had an amazing escape. That terrifying white beast had threatened him and nearly impaled him with some sort of sharp implement like a thermic lance. And he'd nearly run Boggy over.

It had all been such a surprise. Boggy had been crossing the path when he heard the rather pleasant jingling of bells. Pausing in the middle of the road to see what was making such a lovely sound, he didn't see the enormous, ghostly thing materialise out of the gloom until it was almost upon him.

He'd only read about carbon footprints and how dangerous they were but he had a feeling that the white beast pulling the pink creature on top of the moving monstrosity might well be the sort of thing that made carbon footprints. Exactly how a footprint could be so hazardous, Boggy had no idea. After all, it was merely what was left behind after something had been somewhere and it was hard to imagine how a footprint could possibly be threatening, but you couldn't argue with science, could you? Anyway, the whole incident had given him quite a turn and he'd almost dropped his bow and arrow. In fact, he *had* dropped his information leaflets but he didn't dare go back and look for them. It was a shame he had no idea how to shoot an arrow from his bow or he'd have given that snooty, white beast a shock. Perhaps he ought to think about getting a different sort of weapon although he couldn't imagine what. Perhaps one of those sharp, spiral thermic lances? But somehow, a bow seemed the weapon of choice for an eco-warrior.

Boggy peeped out from behind the holly bush again to see if anyone had followed him but there was no one there. The voices he'd heard earlier were now silent and the jingling of bells was becoming fainter.

The sunrise had been spectacular. Not that Crispin had noticed. He'd been too preoccupied with his list.

The sky was still tinged with pink and orange when Nina and Doggett arrived, hand in hand at the bottom of the Alpine Garden. Nina was beaming and Doggett was flashing and sparking.

"You look beautiful, Nina," said Crispin.

Nina beamed more broadly, if that was possible.

And she certainly did look spectacular in a white satin and tulle, off the shoulder gown, with lacing at the back.

Crispin helped her into the carriage and placed another tick on his list.

"I hope this dove basket is clean. I don't want to release a load of filthy Doves. And you know how messy they can be…" said Nina.

"Trust me," said Sylvester, if there's any mess anywhere, it's not in the basket."

"Right," said Crispin, checking his watch, "it's time to leave. Jubbly, you need to go to the Wendy House and pick up Wendy, Lulu and the bouquets. Make sure you go all around the Garden, so everyone gets a good look at the bride and her party and then meet us at the Sunken Garden. Doggett, Sylvester and I will pick up the buttonholes and make sure Queenie and Granny get there on time."

"Giddy up!" shouted Jubbly, waving his whip.

"D'you think Nina knows she looks like a meringue?" Sylvester whispered to Crispin.

The Wedding Ceremony

This is like herding ants, thought Crispin. Although he was pleased that everyone who should have been at the ceremony before the bride arrived, was there in the Sunken Garden. Bartrum had acquired a black gown which he thought lent him an air of gravitas and he strode about, like a black crow, checking all the details. Queenie and Granny, dressed in matching dusty pink suits and large, lacy hats marched back and forth, checking the details that Bartrum had already checked. They followed the ribbon into the begonias, making certain it was still attached to Gusty Bob's leg and ensuring he was in tune and hadn't nodded off. Granny's gummy grin, as she straightened his straw boater and bow tie so unnerved him, he let out a blast of trumpet involuntary, which made her jump and guaranteed she didn't venture into the begonias again.

The Wooden Robin had been hoisted into the oak tree, wearing his safety harness and a blindfold.

"You won't be able to see what you're doing with that over your eyes," Crispin pointed out.

"Good," squeaked the Wooden Robin.

Both socks had slipped straight off the end of his dangling feet as he was winched up.

"Don't worry, I'll keep them for you," Crispin shouted up at him. "Make sure you take that blindfold off when you're up there or you won't see the signal to come down with the rings…"

A faint, strangled sound drifted down from somewhere amongst the oak branches.

"You *do* have the rings, don't you?" Crispin yelled.

An even fainter and more strangled sound floated down.

Crispin hoped it was a "Yes".

The rings were in fact curtain rings which would be used during the ceremony. Doggett would buy new golden rings at the first opportunity after the wedding, as it looked very unlikely the stolen ones would be found, despite the offer of a reward.

Sylvester was giving out lollipop buttonholes to guests as they arrived and showed them to their seats.

So far, so good, thought Crispin, hardly daring to believe what he was seeing. He checked his watch. Sylvester had shown all the guests to their seats. Those with buttonholes in their jackets had been given one of Wendy's lollipop creations to slip into it and several guests were surreptitiously licking theirs. Black-gowned Bartrum was waiting at the lectern, looking sternly at anyone who spoke in tones above a whisper. Queenie and Granny were waiting at the entrance for Nina, ready to lead her down the aisle and give her away. Doggett was pacing about on the rose petals and Crispin suggested that perhaps he could keep still and concentrate on not sparking because the carefully strewn rose petals were beginning to look like the accidental spillage of a bag of pink potato crisps. The Wooden Robin was still on his perch in the tall oak with the blindfold on. Crispin had suggested, pleaded and then insisted he remove it, to no avail.

"Can't I come down and look after the wind chimes?" he called. "Please!"

"You can look after them when you've delivered the rings," Crispin shouted back. "Now please take that blindfold off. You won't be able to see where you're going."

"Good…"

Crispin checked his watch again. Where was the bride? He wondered with dread if the highway robber had appeared again.

Despite Bartrum glaring sternly at the guests, the volume of the chatter in the Sunken Garden was slowly rising and Crispin began to panic. Bartrum banged his gavel and for a second, everyone stopped speaking. In the silence, Crispin thought he could hear the merest hint of jingling bells. Or was he imagining it? No, there was definitely a tinkling sound and the rumble of wheels.

"She's here!" someone at the back shouted excitedly.

"Music! Music! Cue the Toad!" Queenie yelled as she elbowed everyone out of the way in her haste to meet the carriage. Granny followed in Queenie's wake, like a dinghy attached to a ship.

Somebody pulled the ribbon which was tied to

Gusty Bob's leg and music reverberated through the Sunken Garden, just as Nina appeared, flanked by Queenie and Granny. They moved slowly down the aisle followed by the bridesmaids, Wendy and Lulu, with their lollipop posies. Wendy was also carrying a small basket, in which Trilby sat, decorated with pink ribbons. Doggett was so excited, he was almost incandescent by the time the bridal party reached the lectern and Crispin was beginning to wonder if he ought to cool him down with a bucket of water but wasn't sure what Nina might do if he drenched the groom.

To Crispin's relief, the ceremony progressed without Doggett going up in flames although he now began to worry that the Wooden Robin would miss his cue and not deliver the rings.

Doggett had finished making his vows and Nina was halfway through hers but the Wooden Robin still had his blindfold on and even worse, he seemed to be facing the wrong direction. With a series of hand gestures, Crispin signalled to Sylvester to pull the rope which had been used to hoist the Wooden Robin into the oak tree.

"Who has the rings?" asked Bartrum.

Sylvester sidled over to the rope and gave it a vigorous tug.

"Aaargh!" screamed the Wooden Robin as he lost balance and fell off the perch. He slid backwards down the zip wire, gathering speed as he plunged through the treetops towards the lectern. Approaching the Sunken Garden, where the gradient of the zip wire started to decrease, he began to decelerate and if he'd been facing forwards, he might have opened his wings to slow himself down. Instead, his wings were pinned to his side and he slammed into the lectern with a dull thud. He began choking. Crispin rushed forward, picked him up and slapped him on the back. When the Wooden Robin had finished coughing, he took the blindfold off, blinked in the sunlight and a large tear trickled down his beak.

"I've swallowed the rings," he said, clutching his throat.

There was a sharp intake of breath and all eyes swivelled expectantly to Crispin. In the ensuing silence, while the Best Elf considered his options and found that in fact, he didn't have any, Arnold the Snail slithered, unheard and unseen, up the aisle on a glutinous layer of slime.

"Ahem," he said politely. "Ahem, I believe you may be needing these."

Arnold's eyes were situated on the top of eyestalks which he waggled from side to side like antennae as he looked from Crispin to the bridal couple. Around each eyestalk was a golden wedding ring like a fairground game of hoopla.

Arnold lowered his eyestalks as if closely observing the ground and the rings slipped off, spun gently and then settled, one slightly overlapping the other in a pool of snail slime.

"Who do I have to see regarding the reward?" he asked, exuding a large glop of mucous which oozed out from beneath his body and enveloped the rings. Crispin grabbed them with finger and thumb, holding them at arm's length. He shook them gently to try to remove the glutinous goo with the help of gravity and then heaved as the silvery rope of viscous slime clung tenaciously. There was nothing for it, he'd have to sacrifice his neatly starched handkerchief.

"That's so romantic," said Nina, as Crispin handed Bartrum the two clean rings. "I'd never have thought of having the rings delivered by snail. It's so much more elegant than an Owl. Crispin, you're an absolute marvel."

Queenie gave Crispin the thumbs-up sign to show her approval and Granny grinned gummily.

"Ahem," said Arnold politely, "there's still the small matter of the reward..."

Married at Last

Crispin hadn't had time to change the item "white Owl to deliver the rings" on his wedding to-do list to "Arnold the Snail to deliver the rings", and then to give it a large tick because the ceremony had resumed almost immediately after the Wooden Robin had been taken under Granny's wing – literally. She'd scooped him up, tucked him under her arm and marched back to her seat.

"Help!" screamed the Wooden Robin, craning his neck away from Granny's gnashing jaws. "She's going to eat me!"

He began to relax, however, once she'd sat down, placed him on her lap and began to stroke his head.

Bartrum put the rings on his book which he was just about to hold out to offer them to Doggett, so he could place one of them on Nina's finger, when Arnold began to shriek, "Save me! Save me!"

Sylvester had escorted Arnold to the side of the Sunken Garden being careful not to step in the mucoid trail the Snail left behind. He'd politely offered Arnold a lollipop buttonhole which had been refused because of the lack of a place to insert it and he'd ensured that Arnold was as comfortable as one can be sitting in a puddle of slime. Then, thoughtfully, he'd placed a few of the leaflets he'd earlier stuffed in his pocket over the gooiest part of the slime trail in case anyone stepped in it. He was just about to go back to his seat when he realised that Arnold's eyestalks which had been retracted while he slithered along, were now both taut and erect – and pointing at the sky. It could almost have been said that his eyes were protruding so far, they were eye stalks – on stalks. Then Sylvester became aware of a shadow passing overhead.

It was Mavis, the white Owl, circling over Arnold.

"Where are those rings, you thieving mollusc?" she shrieked and dived towards him. Arnold moved surprisingly rapidly for a creature with no legs – or perhaps he slipped on his own slime – but in no time at all, he was trying to squeeze between Sylvester's legs.

The Elf's legs weren't long enough to accommodate Arnold and he found himself lifted and carried along on top of his shell.

"Shoo!" shouted Sylvester, waving his arms at Mavis who was directly above, poised for another attack.

"Mavis! Mavis! You get back here!" The Bird-Gnome had rushed down the steps of the Sunken Garden two at a time and was standing in the aisle, shading his eyes with his hand as he tried to outstare Mavis.

"Ahem!" Bartrum cleared his throat loudly.

"Pardon the intrusion," said the Bird-Gnome. "Don't mind me. Carry on with whatever you're doing…" He turned his attention back to Mavis.

"This is your last warning, my girl. Don't make me call for reinforcements…"

Mavis slowly circled, obviously considering her options. Without warning, she swooped, skimming Sylvester's head and then with powerful beats of her wings, she climbed up into the sky.

The Bird-Gnome shook his fist. "You asked for it," he yelled and pulling a whistle from his pocket, he gave three short, sharp blasts. Five Magpies flew from behind the tall oak and assembled themselves into flying formation. "This way, lads," the leader squawked and the others followed as one unit. Mavis doubled back over the Sunken Garden, trying to shake off her pursuers but the Magpie squad veered expertly, drawing ever closer to her tail. Nose diving towards the guests, she swerved to the left, obviously hoping to take cover in the woods but the Magpies had anticipated her manoeuvre and swooped down to head her off. The Owl ascended rapidly and followed by the Magpies, they skimmed the tall oak and disappeared.

"Ooh, Crispin! A flypast! I knew you wouldn't let me down," said Nina. "You really are the very *best* Best Elf."

"He's just wonderful!" bellowed Lulu.

Once Bartrum was satisfied the Bird-Gnome had gone and the flypast was over, he carried on with the service and finally, Doggett and Nina were Gnome and wife. There was a rapturous round of applause.

The Vengeful Butterfly

During the commotion caused by the arrival of Mavis the Owl, several guests arrived unseen – and very late. McTavish hadn't returned home until the early hours after a few games of cards with his friends and so he'd insisted on sleeping until well after sunrise. It had taken several cups of strong coffee to get him feeling himself, which meant that he, Bess, Beryl and Bella had arrived at the ceremony after it had started. They'd slipped in at the back and luckily, no one noticed their lack of punctuality. From her seat, Bella couldn't see what was happening at the front although she'd spotted Crispin as she crept in and of course, she'd heard Lulu's approval of the "*best* Best Elf".

Her heart was breaking.

Mr Lambert alone had seen the glistening tears trickle down Bella's cheeks and he vibrated with anger. Once the ceremony was finished, and Doggett and Nina were finally Gnome and wife, McTavish had insisted he couldn't go on without a cigar and more coffee. Beryl, Bess and Bella had returned home with him but Mr Lambert had remained. He'd flown into the bushes and watched, looking for an opportunity to make the smug Elf sorry. But Crispin was surrounded by people, including those two creatures who'd defended him before and Mr Lambert knew when he was outnumbered. He needed to be shrewd. He was too weak to mount an attack on his own. Dare he grab a bee around the middle and fly at Crispin with the business end pointed at him? He decided he didn't. Could he perhaps find some sort of weapon to use as a battering ram? He would scour the woods for a sharp stick or suitable stone. Flying over the clearing where the Maypole had been erected, he saw a shiny, white pebble which he thought would be perfect. As he landed, he noticed there were two pebbles. He probably wouldn't have been able to hold two separate stones, so he was thrilled when he clasped one pebble, rose into the air and discovered that the second stone seemed to be attached to the first. But they were much heavier than he'd anticipated, and he struggled to rise into the air. He was, however, quite determined, and with super-lepidopteran effort, he flew upwards, clutching the pebbles and made his way back to the Sunken Garden. After a few beats of his wings, he realised that what he was carrying was heavier than just two pebbles. He couldn't see because he was afraid with the extra weight, that if he looked down, he might plummet to earth so he looked forward in the direction of flight and flapped his wings vigorously. But he had the distinct impression that he was carrying some sort of geological formation which involved lots of pebbles joined together in such a way that they periodically clashed together.

Spanners rushed back and forth, moulding the group of people into a tasteful arrangement.

"Rightio, I want the bride, groom, bridesmaids and Best Elf. Everyone else, please could you step out of the picture… including you, Queenie and Granny… please… okay, I'll do one more of you two and then perhaps you'd step aside… *please.*" He finally managed to prise the bride's mother and her mother from the bride's side although they were poised at the edge of the photo, ready to rush in again at the first opportunity.

Mr Lambert made it back to the Sunken Garden with his guided missile although he was nearly exhausted by the time he arrived. But the memory of Bella's tears drove him on and once he'd spotted Crispin posing next to that large hussy, he found renewed strength to fly the distance towards the Elf's smug face. Crispin had hurt Mr Lambert's beloved Bella and now *he* was going to feel pain.

The first person to spot Mr Lambert was Wendy, who shrieked, "Watch out, Cwithpin! Incoming inthect, and it hath teeth!"

Spanners unclipped his camera from the tripod and pointed it at Mr Lambert. "Sorry, folks, I'll be back with you in a second. I've never seen a butterfly with such a large grin and I've got to photograph it while I've got the chance." He checked the digital screen on the back of the camera and nodded in approval. "I've definitely got some award-winning shots here."

Mr Lambert's muscles were going into spasm and he knew he wouldn't be able to maintain his grip on the weapon much longer, so he flew as fast as he could at Crispin's head, quite prepared to sacrifice himself as he was dashed against the self-satisfied face of his nemesis.

"Ow!" shrieked Crispin as Mr Lambert flew into his forehead with all the strength he could muster, slamming his weapon home.

"I'll get him, leave him to me!" bellowed Lulu, swatting the butterfly with her lollipop posy. But she needed have bothered because the violent sound waves from her ear-splitting shout had forcibly driven Mr Lambert backwards. He tumbled over and over, spiralling into a perilous spin and dropped to the ground. Luckily, no one noticed his nose dive as they were all crowding around Crispin, who had teeth marks on his forehead and Granny, who was gleefully holding her lost dentures aloft.

By the time Mr Lambert had recovered sufficiently to move out of the way of stampeding feet, Granny had cleaned her dentures off in the fire bucket and was demonstrating to everyone how they worked.

Spanners continued taking photographs and assured Crispin he would use some photo-editing software to remove the angry bite mark on his forehead. He lined Nina, Queenie and Granny up in height order, ascending and then descending and got some good close-ups of Granny displaying her newly-found teeth. When he was satisfied he'd photographed everyone, he left to download his shots and promised to come back the following day with a laptop to display them.

Mr Lambert, in the meantime, had rested and after drinking nectar from some flowers that Wendy and the Fairies hadn't spotted, he regained enough strength to fly back to Bella – a desperately disappointed butterfly.

The Eternal Flame

To Crispin's embarrassment, Nina took every opportunity to praise him for his organisation of the wedding, and even worse, Queenie and Granny were now following suit after the recovery of the dentures. It seemed every time he turned around, Granny was there with the Wooden Robin tucked under her arm, grinning maniacally at him displaying her unnervingly mobile teeth. Their alarming range of movements meant they appeared to be permanently falling out and Crispin's eyes were drawn to them, to see what sort of manoeuvre they would perform next. He managed to give her the slip during the hog roast, even though it meant he was trapped next to Lulu at the table. Lulu had swapped her name card with that of Wendy so she could sit next to the Best Elf, and Wendy didn't complain because it meant she was sitting next to Sylvester.

Crispin checked his watch and thought longingly of the rucksack he'd hidden in the wardrobe that morning. Had it merely been that morning? It seemed like days ago. But at least so far, the wedding had gone well. In fact, it had gone better than well. The meal had been delicious and very soon, it would be time for Crispin to announce the speeches.

Nina signalled that it was indeed time and Crispin stood up and tapped his wine glass with a spoon until the hubbub died. "I'd like to call upon the bridegroom to—"

One of the Fairies stood up and started to sing a plaintive little song and Crispin was about to tap the wine glass again when two others stood up and started singing. Suddenly, two more rose, joined in with the song and then began to jive. The tempo picked up and another group of Fairies stood up and joined in.

With relief, Crispin realised the flash mob had started performing and with even more relief, he saw that the Fairies were fully dressed. A few seats along, Nina had her sausage-pack hands clasped together in delight and from time to time she pointed out something to Doggett, Queenie or Granny. Her eyes were shining and Crispin was genuinely pleased she was enjoying her day. Everyone was now clapping in time to the music as the Fairies performed their finale and then melted away back to their seats. The audience cheered and whistled and Crispin mentally ticked "Flash Dance" off his list. It was too early to congratulate himself just yet but Crispin was very pleased with how the day was going. Not only had he hit all his targets so far but he'd also hit a few he hadn't even aimed at. Ticking off the flash mob item reminded him that Nina had requested an Eternal Flame and he wondered whether, at this late hour, something could be arranged. Of course, no one would be able to shoot a flaming arrow because no one in the Garden had an arrow to set fire to – much less a bow to shoot it from. But he might be able to set up a bonfire. He'd noticed Big Po had put some dead wood in the incinerator a few days ago and he was sure that it would burn quite merrily for a while. It wouldn't be eternal but that was probably a good thing anyway. Who wanted smoke drifting over the Garden from now to eternity?

Crispin found Sylvester and asked if he could put some paper in the incinerator so that it would catch fire easily and then he had a word with Doggett, who would definitely be able to provide a spark.

"Speech! Speech!" the guests chanted and Crispin obliged with a short piece he'd agonised over for several evenings. Doggett set fire to his speech and had to ad-lib but he managed to thank all the guests and to flatter Nina, Queenie and Granny, so everyone was happy. After several toasts and the cutting of Mrs Bartrum's wonderfully colourful cake, it was time for the Maypole dancing. With arms crossed over her chest to show she meant business, Queenie hovered near the dancers, turning away any Fairies who asked to join in. Granny looked equally determined that the innocent country dancing around the Maypole was not going to be sullied by any flighty Fairy folk, despite not being able to cross her arms because the Wooden Robin was tucked under one arm and in her other hand, she held an enormous plastic bag full of pink stuff. Her loose-fitting dentures now fit snugly inside her mouth, glued in place with some of Wendy's candyfloss, whose adhesive strength could be favourably compared to that of super-strength glue. Luckily for Crispin, Lulu had eaten quite a lot of the candyfloss before anyone had noticed its bonding qualities and she'd been quiet for some time while she worried the pink goo in her mouth with her tongue and tried to dislodge it. Crispin took the opportunity to slip away from her and to rest his eardrums and his arm, which she kept grabbing.

And then before Crispin knew it, the first part of the special day was over and everyone was heading home to put on their costumes for the masked ball.

"Tights?" said Sylvester, aghast. "I'm not wearing tights!"

"Fine," said Crispin wearily. He'd been dreading this moment since the costumes had arrived a few days ago. "Well, you'll just have to go bare-legged then."

"I'll have trousers on… won't I?"

"Breeches," said Crispin, "and they finish at your knees. So, it's up to you if you wear the tights or not."

"Huh!" Sylvester grabbed the box containing the costume, stomped to his bedroom and opened the door.

"Ugh!" he said. "I'd forgotten about the Doves." He slammed the door and made for the bathroom. The bathroom door slammed.

Crispin went into his bedroom. He wasn't happy about wearing the costume either but the thought that soon, he could wear exactly what he liked soothed him. He checked the rucksack in the wardrobe and added a few more pairs of socks and pants, Bella's feather and a small framed photograph of Sylvester.

Despite his earlier misgivings about the costume, Crispin was quite impressed with his reflection in the hall mirror. He looked every inch the eighteenth-century Elf.

"Aargh!" shouted Sylvester from the bathroom. Something hit the wall and there was the tinkle of glass. "Whoops."

"What are you doing in there?" shouted Crispin.

"These tights are too small."

"Well, they're the same size as mine and they fit. Come out so I can see."

A scowling Sylvester emerged from the bathroom. He had the lace-ruffled shirt and long coat on, as well as the breeches and from his hands, dangled what looked like two long, deflated balloons.

"They definitely don't fit."

Crispin looked at his legs. "You realise the tights go on first and then the breeches go on top, don't you?"

"Huh!" Sylvester slammed the bathroom door again. A lot of grunting and grumbling followed before he emerged fully dressed with his tights under his breeches.

"I look ridiculous!"

"Put this on," Crispin said, handing him an elaborate purple and gold mask, "and no one will know it's you."

Crispin helped tie the mask's ribbons at the back of Sylvester's head and then fitted his own mask. As they put on their full-length cloaks in the hall, Crispin noticed Sylvester turning this way and that, admiring his reflection in the mirror and he had to admit that Sylvester looked very dashing.

"Will everyone be wearing eighteenth-century clothes like us?" Sylvester asked.

"I think so although I expect Jubbly will do something a bit different because… well, because he's Jubbly. Why d'you ask?"

"I was trying to imagine what everyone will look like."

"Anyone in particular? Such as the Fairies?"

"Don't be so stupid!" said Sylvester crossly.

"Then why are you blushing?"

"Well, because… because you've made me dress up in this ridiculous costume, that's why. Anyway, how d'you know I'm blushing? I've got a mask on."

"There's steam coming out of your ears." Crispin checked his watch. "Right, I think it's time to go. Nina won't be happy if we're late for the group photographs."

"We're going to be photographed dressed like this?" Sylvester asked, aghast.

"No one will know it's you, behind that mask."

"No, but they might think you're me and that would be awful."

"Charming!"

It was taking much longer than normal to get to the clearing where the Maypole had been erected.

"Sylvester, you're going to put your fingers through those tights if you don't stop pulling them up. Leave them alone. They're fine."

"They don't feel fine. They keep going wrinkly round my ankles. Now I know how the Wooden Robin feels when his socks keep slipping down." Sylvester stopped again and pulled the tights up. "I wonder what the Wooden Robin's costume is like..." and at the thought of him wearing tights, both Elves began to laugh. They were both still chuckling when they arrived at the clearing.

Spanners was busy trying to organise the guests ready to take some group shots. The elaborate costumes were clearly giving him a headache, with the large wigs, masks and headdresses adorned with feathers, obstructing people at the rear. Jubbly in particular was proving quite a problem. The skirt of his eighteenth-century dress was draped over a frame that protruded on either side of him as if he had enormous hips. A gigantic plume rose above his huge, pink wig, blocking everyone behind him.

Spanners suggested he sit on the ground so he was less of an obstruction.

"Not in this dress!" Jubbly said emphatically. "Nor

in these shoes." He poked a foot out below the voluminous folds of his skirt, showing a shoe with such a platform sole, it was hard to imagine how he could walk in them. Spanners nodded sympathetically. It was obvious that anyone wearing shoes such as that and who was then stupid enough to sit on the ground, would need some sort of lifting device to raise them again.

"I could get a few of the chaps to help you up. It's just that you're blocking out so many people…"

"Blocking out people?" Sylvester whispered to Crispin. "He's eclipsing the sun."

"Shh!" said Crispin sternly.

Finally, Spanners managed some sort of arrangement and by moving people around, he was fairly confident he'd managed to capture everyone's photo. He announced he'd finished and that the guests could make their way to the Gazebo for the masked ball.

Doggett stepped forward and holding up his hands for silence, he asked everyone to wait where they were because he had a little surprise for Nina, who squealed with delight. There was a lot of whispering and conjecture as he and Crispin left the group and disappeared into the woods, towards the Shed of No Return.

Boggy couldn't believe his eyes. This Garden was the craziest place he'd ever visited. Ahead of him in a large clearing was a group of people dressed in clothes, the likes of which he'd never seen before. If only he could find the two eco-warriors he'd seen on the tandem, he'd have had more courage, but he was fairly certain they'd been campaigning because he'd stumbled across the Sunken Garden and it was obvious a meeting had taken place. Why else would all the chairs have been set out like that? And he was fairly certain the eco-warriors had been warning people about the threat of carbon footprints because they'd obviously been giving out *his* leaflets. He'd found them stuck to the ground in a long line. Proof positive that the eco-warriors had wanted the message to remain there for all to see. It was regrettable that many of the leaflets were face down but many more were the right way up, displaying the carbon footprint warnings.

However, there was no sign of his comrades, so he'd have to draw on his inner strength and carry on the campaign on his own. It wasn't often you found a ready-made audience, even if they were a bunch of weirdos, and Boggy would kick himself if he missed this opportunity to spread the word.

A few seconds later, Boggy was kicking himself for stepping out of the cover of the undergrowth into full view of the strangely-dressed people.

It had all started in such a promising fashion when the large, masked female dressed in white had squealed with delight and declared how wonderful it was to see him. Boggy had never had such a warm reception and he cleared his throat, ready to address the crowd. The white female held up her hands for silence and as everyone turned to him expectantly, someone shouted, "Hey, it's the highway robber!"

With most faces hidden behind masks, Boggy couldn't tell who'd spoken, but judging by the number of heads that turned to the right, he was fairly sure he'd pinpointed the speaker. It was a flamboyantly dressed lady, with impossibly wide hips who spoke in a very deep, husky Mexican accent. He also had the strangest feeling of déjà vu, as if he'd heard the voice before. She minced determinedly towards him, and if he hadn't known better, Boggy would have thought she was brandishing her fan as if it were a weapon. He was wondering whether he ought to take evasive action when the lady's progress was impeded by some obstacle on the ground and she swallow-dived into the grass. There was a lot of confusion as people raced forwards to try to raise her to her feet. Two burly Gnomes tried to get their hands under her shoulders to hoist her up but the side extensions on her skirt were hampering their attempts. The lady, whose voice had deepened considerably, was obviously quite distressed and issued orders from her prostrate position. "Ow! Watch it, you're treading on my wig," she yelled, pulling a pink ringlet from under one of her would-be rescuer's boots. "Stop interfering with my panniers," she shouted, and everyone jumped backwards with their hands in the air as if to prove their innocence.

"I never touched 'im. If anyone groped 'im, it wasn't me," said one of the burly Gnomes. The other burly Gnome added, "It's hard to know where any of his bits are under all that flouncy stuff," poking the skirt's side extensions.

"I told you not to touch the panniers, you'll dent them," shrieked the lady gruffly.

"Oh!" said the first burly Gnome with obvious relief. "You said 'panniers', I thought you said… Oh, never mind…" His cheeks reddened.

"What's a pannier?" a shrill voice asked.

"This." The burly Gnome pointed a large finger at the skirt's side extensions.

"I told you to leave the panniers alone," screeched the lady.

Finally, she was helped to her feet, by which time, Boggy was totally confused and had been completely forgotten, except by the lady in white.

"So, where's it going to be?" she asked Boggy.

"What?"

"The Eternal Flame, of course."

"Umm…" *What on earth was she talking about?* But she looked so eager, Boggy didn't feel he could let her down. "Umm…" he said again and then he had it. It must be a clue, like in a crossword. The "Eternal Flame" could only be one thing – the sun. Or could it? He crossed his fingers and hoped it was. "Umm… Over there?" he suggested uncertainly, pointing at the reddening sun which was beginning to sink behind the treetops.

It appeared he was right because the lady in white clasped her rather large hands to her very large bosom and looked rapturously at him.

"Wonderful!" she said and then shouting for everyone's attention, she pointed out where they needed to look.

How lovely, thought Boggy for people to be so appreciative of the sunset. As soon as the spectacle was over, Boggy would inform them all about the dangers of carbon footprints and people such as these who were obviously in tune with nature, would listen and join his cause. He felt a special camaraderie with these people, even if their dress sense was rather dubious.

He suddenly became aware that his eyes were on the sunset while everyone else's eyes were on him.

"Well?" said the lady in white, tapping her foot. "Could you do it now, please, we've got a ball to attend."

"Umm…"

"Come on, don't be shy," she said. "Now, do you need a match?"

"A match?"

"Yes, for the arrow."

"Arrow?"

"Yes. Look, you may have all night but we've got to get going and Doggett and Crispin are waiting."

"Doggett and Crispin?"

"If you repeat anything else that I say, I may be forced to take action. And trust me, it will hurt. Now, if you aren't going to shoot a flaming arrow, pass the bow over, so someone else can. Do I have any volunteers?" she shouted to the crowd.

There suddenly seemed to be quite a lot more distance between her and the others. Boggy wished that there was much more space between him and the lady in white, but she had a firm grip on his shoulder.

"Umm..."

As the sun disappeared behind the trees, the lady in white's patience ran out.

"Take an arrow out of that quiver, put it in the bow and shoot. Got it? Good. Because if you don't, I may be forced to snap that bow in two and make you eat it."

There was no mistaking the determination in her voice.

The bow was slung over his body, more to keep his jacket done up, because the buttons had come off than anything else but he took it off and with shaking hands withdrew an arrow from his quiver.

"Even I know an arrow goes in the other way round," she said scathingly, "and doesn't it need to be alight? And don't say 'Umm'."

"Err, I don't think so."

"Will it light up automatically when the arrow hits it?"

"Yes," said Boggy. He had no idea what was going on but he knew if he didn't fire an arrow... well, he didn't want to think about it and it seemed sensible to agree with anything the lady said.

Aiming towards the sunset, he let an arrow fly. It twanged into a tree trunk at the edge of the clearing.

"Just getting my sights," he squeaked when he realised that the lady in white wasn't satisfied.

With trembling fingers, he removed the remaining arrow from the quiver, placed it in the bow, drew back the string, aimed high and closed his eyes.

"Oooh!" said the crowd and Boggy opened his eyes in time to see the arrow soar over the treetops.

There was a pause and someone whispered, "I think he's missed..." Then suddenly, there was a terrific whoosh from behind. Everyone swung around and there, in the opposite direction, near the Shed of No Return, was a blazing fire.

The crowd cheered and several of those close enough patted Boggy on the back and demanded to know how he'd done it.

At the first opportunity, Boggy crept away. He'd worry about the danger of carbon footprints tomorrow. Right now, he longed to be anywhere but this Garden. He packed his shopping trolley and set off. As far as he was concerned, carbon feet could stamp their footprints over every one of the crazy inhabitants of this crazy place and he wouldn't be bothered.

"This is brilliant," said Doggett gleefully. "We haven't got an archer with a flaming arrow but I know Nina's going to love it."

It had taken them longer to get to the incinerator near the Shed of No Return than expected because their progress had been hampered by the costumes. One of the buckles had fallen off Crispin's boot and he'd had to backtrack to find it, then Doggett announced his breeches were chafing his legs and finished the rest of the journey walking with bandy legs.

The incinerator was piled high with wood and bits of screwed up paper, as Sylvester had promised. There was also the smell of petrol, which wasn't too surprising as he'd told Crispin he'd put a drop of Big Po's lawnmower petrol on the fire because some of the wood was wet and he was afraid it wouldn't light.

"A drop? You're sure it was no more than a drop?" Crispin had queried.

"Oh, yes," Sylvester had replied although it had worried Crispin that he wouldn't make eye contact.

Just in case Sylvester's idea of a "drop" differed significantly from his, Crispin found a dry stick and holding it close to Doggett, he managed to light it with a random spark, then tossed it into the incinerator. This turned out to be a sensible precaution because as he'd suspected, Sylvester's idea of a "drop of petrol" turned out to be appreciably more than one would normally add to a bonfire. The fumes emanating from the incinerator ignited while the stick was still mid-air and the explosion blew Doggett and Crispin backwards into the bushes.

"Nina's going to love it!" said Doggett excitedly, not having realised how much danger he'd been in when he'd wandered close to the incinerator earlier.

"Let's go," said Crispin who couldn't imagine the trouble he'd be in with Nina if he returned her new husband in anything less than pristine condition. He brushed the leaves and twigs out of Doggett's wig.

By the time the bridegroom and his Best Elf had returned to the clearing, the fire in the incinerator was roaring furiously. Everyone was cheering and Nina thanked them for arranging such a wonderful surprise.

"Oh, Crispin, you're so clever! Where did you find that funny, little archer? He fired an arrow that way," she said pointing towards the sunset, "and he lit up the fire over there," she pointed in the opposite direction, at the inferno near the Shed of No Return. "It was so clever and he made it look like he didn't know what he was doing but—"

Before Nina could finish, there was another explosion from the incinerator and a ball of fire shot into the sky. It hung there glowing for a second or two before disintegrating in a blaze of colourful stars.

"Ooh! Aah!" gasped the crowd.

Crispin grabbed Sylvester by the lacy ruff. "Not so fast! I thought you only put a drop of petrol in the incinerator."

"I did!"

"Well, it nearly blew Doggett and me out of the Garden. And what did you put in there that's going up like fireworks?"

"No idea," said Sylvester sheepishly, "nothing to do with me."

"Ooh! Aah!" roared the crowd as another fusillade of stars lit up the darkening sky.

Crispin's Farewell

By the time the "firework" display had finished, the bonfire had died a little – either that, or it had melted the incinerator and anything that was still combustible had fallen out. Crispin certainly wasn't going to risk going to check. People started to drift away in small groups, chattering excitedly as they made their way to the masked ball. Crispin promised Lulu he'd see her inside the Gazebo once he'd completed a few more of his Best Elf duties. She was reluctant to leave his side but was finally persuaded to go, complaining that she wanted to dance and hoped he wouldn't be long because she didn't want to turn too many would-be partners away.

"If you want to dance with someone else," said Crispin, "go ahead, I don't mind."

"You're sure?"

"Definitely."

"Okay, well don't be too long. Missing you already," she yelled over her shoulder.

Crispin winced but at least his eardrums would have a brief opportunity to recover while he delayed going to the ball.

There wasn't a great deal more for him to do now and he couldn't believe the day was drawing to a close. Just a few more hours of trying to evade Lulu and he'd be free to go home, finish packing and disappear. Relief washed over him. But first, there was one thing he realised he'd forgotten and it would need addressing immediately.

Spanners' photo booth had been set up next to the Gazebo ready for the guests but Crispin had forgotten to ask anyone if they'd provide the power by cycling. Sylvester had said he'd arrange something but Crispin doubted he'd remembered and he was reluctant to enter the Gazebo and risk running into Lulu.

This is ridiculous, he thought crossly, *if I'm going to start a new life, I need to be a bit braver, I need to Elf up and tell Lulu I'm not interested.* It would be kinder not to lead her on and at least he'd leave the Garden with a clear conscience, although not necessarily with intact eardrums, when she expressed her dismay. There would also be Queenie and Granny, not to mention Nina, to placate, once they realised Crispin had rejected Lulu. It was daunting indeed, but it was necessary. Like drawing a line under a chapter in the book of his life, he thought, as he neared the photo booth. He was surprised to hear voices coming from inside it. There was squealing and giggling, followed by a flash, then louder squealing and giggling. The curtain was thrown back and four Fairies spilled out laughing uproariously, followed by Sylvester, whose smile dropped when he saw Crispin.

"Just testing out the photo booth. It all seems to be in working order," he said patting the machine.

One of the Fairies seized the strip of photos as it

emerged from the slot and the others gathered around, shrieking with laughter.

"Look, Syl," one of them called, "you're at the bottom. Aren't you cheeky?" This was followed by wild hilarity.

Crispin averted his eyes. He had a feeling that at least one of the photos involved cheeks – and not the now rosy ones on Sylvester's face.

"Sort your tights out," he whispered to Sylvester, whose costume was looking rather dishevelled.

"C'mon, Syl," called one of the Fairies as they set off for the ball. The smallest one turned back and winked at Crispin.

"Comin', Big Boy?" she asked.

Crispin sighed. What on earth was Sylvester getting himself into? And who'd keep him on the straight and narrow when Crispin had gone? For a second, he wondered if he was doing the right thing in leaving, and then it occurred to him that Sylvester did exactly as he pleased anyway and with his advanced skills in Pie Skology, it could be argued he was more suited to life on his own than Crispin. After all, Sylvester had persuaded someone to cycle all night and provide the power for the photo booth – and miss the ball. He seemed to be able to persuade people to do what he wanted.

Crispin hurried around the back of the photo booth to find out who was there and how Sylvester had persuaded him or her. He was surprised when he realised there was no bicycle, just a few bits of machinery with wires leading to a pair of legs. Euclid's legs. He was skipping and Crispin could see the needle on a meter pulsating at the far right of the dial.

"Hello, Crispin!" Euclid said excitedly.

"Euclid, are you all right?"

"Of course."

"Don't you think you ought to slow down or even stop while there's no one in the photo booth?"

"Oh no, I can't stop."

"You can't?"

"Oh no. I'm set for a world skipping record."

"A world record? Who told you tha…? Oh, don't tell me. Sylvester."

"Yes, that's right. I could be world skipping champ by midnight."

"You know, it may not be a world record – more of a Garden record," Crispin pointed out. *Oh well*, he thought, if Euclid decided to abandon his attempt and go to the ball, Crispin would just take over although he didn't fancy skipping. He'd rather have cycled.

"It's fine, thanks," said Euclid. "I love a challenge."

"Well, why don't you stop and take that cloak off, it looks like it's getting in your way."

"Good idea," said Euclid, undoing the clasp at his neck and flinging the cloak aside without stopping.

"And the mask?" suggested Crispin.

"Oh no, I'll leave that on. It is a masked ball, after all." He adjusted his colourful mask and carried on skipping.

"Right," said Crispin, "well, I'll leave you to it." Euclid seemed happy enough. "I'll bring you a jug of water," Crispin called as he left. The needle on the meter was almost fused to the extreme right of the dial as Euclid skipped on relentlessly, probably producing more electricity than the photo booth actually required. At the rate he was skipping, he could probably have powered the Old Priory.

As Crispin entered the Gazebo in search of a jug of water for Euclid, Frank Fowle was at the door, wearing the "Seucrity" tee-shirt he'd worn at the New Year's Ball. No one had had the courage to inform him of the error then, and obviously no one had acquired more courage in the meantime.

Crispin decided it didn't really matter, after all, no security was needed, just like there hadn't been any need for it at the New Year's Eve ball. Sadness suddenly washed over him. Of course, there was no need for security because everyone in the Garden got on so well and soon, he'd be far away from all his friends.

Oh well, if it means I get my life back, it will be worth it, he thought resolutely. Memories from the New Year's Ball brought one particular face back sharply to him and he closed his eyes and savoured it. Bella. But it was too painful to remember her and as he opened his eyes, the beautiful face melted away and was replaced by that of a masked Frank – just inches from his nose. He leapt backwards in fright.

"You all right, Crispin?"

"Just a bit tired, that's all." He hoped the tears which had overflowed from his eyes at the memory of Bella would be hidden by his mask.

"I'm not surprised," said Frank, pushing his finger up his nostril. "You've worked so hard to make everything go with a swing. It's the best wedding I've ever been to. Mind you, it's the *only* wedding I've ever been to. Still, everyone's saying what a wonderful job you did. Tsk, tsk," he looked down at his tee-shirt. "Oh dear," he said, "just look at that." He pointed to a greasy smear just below "Seucrity".

"It's all right," said Crispin. "I'm sure no one will notice."

"Good," said Frank, removing the finger from his nostril and spitting on it. He rubbed the saliva into the stain, increasing its circumference and spreading it into the letters. "Sausage roll I dropped at the New Year's Ball," he explained as he made the dirty spot even larger. "Never mind, after a few more wears, it'll be due for a wash. I expect it'll come out then."

"Er, yes," said Crispin.

"Anyway, I just wanted to say 'well done'," said the Troll, and with that, he slapped Crispin on the back, almost felling him.

It occurred to Crispin that this would be the last time he'd see Frank and despite what would undoubtedly be a bruise on his back from the congratulatory slap, he would have nothing to take with him to remind him of Frank, nor of his friends. One of the group shots Spanners had taken earlier would have been perfect but they wouldn't be ready until tomorrow and anyway, with all those amazing masks, you couldn't see anyone's face. He'd just have to make a conscious effort to remember everyone and store their faces in his memory.

Then, he had an idea. He turned back to Frank and pretended his eyes were a camera. He looked intently at the Troll, memorised his face and blinked to simulate the shutter. As he wove his way through the dancers towards the bar, he decided he'd take an imaginary photo of as many people as he could, and say his mental farewells. Luckily, most people had abandoned their masks and were dancing, so he was able to take lots of memory shots. His courage nearly failed him when he heard Lulu's voice above everyone else's and realised she was close by, but he was resigned to seeing her before the end of the evening and letting her down as gently as he could. He steeled himself.

Klaus was teaching Jubbly a Bavarian folk dance as Crispin reached them.

"Should you be hopping about like that in those platform shoes?" he asked Jubbly.

"I've got my flatties on now," he said, poking one ballet slipper out from beneath his skirts.

Crispin blinked and took a mental photo of them with linked arms, swinging round and round. Jubbly's pink ringlets flying out with centrifugal force.

"Goodbye," whispered Crispin beneath his breath.

Arnold the Snail was seated in an inflatable paddling pool to contain the slime. Bartrum had insisted the health and safety precautions had been taken to protect the dancers, who couldn't be expected to risk life and limb in mollusc mucous. Crispin thanked Arnold for rescuing the rings but there was no reply. His eyestalks were drooping and when Crispin bent down, he saw that the eyes on the tips were closed. *He's nodded off,* thought Crispin patting him fondly on the shell. *I hope someone keeps an eye on him. That slime's likely to overflow before the ball's over and he might drown.* And who, Crispin wondered, would clean up the mess tomorrow?

He poured a large jug of water for Euclid and carried on with his tour of secret goodbyes and memory photographs.

"I hope that's not gin, Crispin," said Bartrum putting an arm around his shoulders. "I really have to take my hat off to you, young Elf, you excelled today.

"Yes," added Mrs Bartrum, "it's been such a wonderful wedding, I can't wait for the next one."

She winked at Crispin. "Perhaps you and that loud bridesmaid?"

"Oh no," said Crispin, "definitely not."

"What a shame, I was so looking forward to another wedding."

"Perhaps it'll be young Wilmslow next," said Crispin nodding at the young Gnome who was sitting at his parents' table, glowering.

"Oh yes," said Mrs Bartrum brightly, "perhaps."

"I should be so lucky," grumbled Wilmslow. "I'm never going to meet anyone if I have to sit with my parents."

Bartrum sat down again and Crispin blinked, taking a mental photo of the family. Proud dad, prouder mum, and one sulky teenager between them.

"Goodbye," he whispered as he walked away.

"Crispin! Where have you been all evening? I've been looking for you everywhere," boomed Lulu.

Crispin gulped.

"We need to talk – privately," she yelled, taking his arm and steering him outside. Several people winked and nudged Crispin, giving him knowing looks.

"Before we talk, there's something I need to tell you," said Crispin. He felt quite pleased with himself for taking control although admittedly, he hadn't actually told her he didn't want to be with her – yet.

"No," she insisted, "let me speak first before I lose my nerve. I know how much you like me but it's only fair I tell you I don't think it'll ever work—"

"You don't?"

"No, you're a wonderful Elf and I hope we can be friends but, well, the truth is, I find you a bit, well… quiet. I know it's not your fault but I need someone with more, well… oomph. Of course, if you could find a bit of oomph, I could reconsider?"

"Oh, no!" said Crispin. "I'm definitely a hopeless case. I'm completely oomphless. You're better off without me and I'm sure you'll soon find someone with more oomph."

"Thank you, Crispin," she said and planted a noisy kiss on his cheek, "you really are a special Elf. I didn't think you'd take it as well as you have. Now, what did you want to tell me?"

"Umm…" Crispin crossed his fingers behind his back. "Umm, I just wanted to say how lovely you look today."

"Oh, Crispin," she sighed, "are you sure you can't find some more oomph? Perhaps there are evening classes you could go to…"

"No," he said emphatically. "I'm a lost cause. Anyway, you'd best get back inside, you'll miss all the fun. I've just got to give this water to Euclid and I'll come in too."

Lulu strode back into the Gazebo, leaving a very grateful Elf behind her. Crispin couldn't believe his luck although her criticism of his lack of oomph stung slightly but at least he was now free. But free for what?

"Oh, if only Bella were here," he said softly to the night. "How could I have let her slip from my grasp?"

Crispin had the strangest feeling that someone was watching him. He turned around to check, but he was definitely alone. Above his head, there was the barest whisper but when he looked up, dust blew into his eyes and by the time he'd blinked it away, there was nothing above him but the starry sky. As he wiped his face, he noticed there were tiny, sparkly bits over his cloak but he had no time to wonder about it, because people were pouring out of the Gazebo, led by the newly-married couple. A jingling of bells heralded Stanley pulling the knitted carriage through the trees. He drew up by the Gazebo and Jubbly opened the door.

"Bouquet! Bouquet!" the crowd shouted and the bridesmaids rushed into position behind Nina, who threw her bouquet made of flowers and sweets over her shoulder. Lulu and Wendy collided in mid-air, with the result that the bouquet hit the Wooden Robin, bowling him over. Lulu did a rugby tackle and got to the bouquet first, leaping to her feet and holding it triumphantly aloft. Crispin clicked his eyelids and took a memory photo of Lulu with the bouquet and Wendy picking up the shaken Wooden Robin. She helped him straighten his tights and smoothed his green bib, which had flipped over his head.

Nina hugged Crispin tightly. "Thank you so much,

Crispin, I'll never forget all the effort you put into making my day absolutely perfect."

"Yes, my Best Elf, you've gone above and beyond. I'm indebted to you," said Doggett, giving Crispin a dose of the tingles as he shook his hand. With a lump in his throat, Crispin clicked his eyelids, freezing their faces in his memory.

"Three cheers for Crispin," shouted Doggett and as the crowd roared their appreciation, Queenie hugged and kissed him thanking him for making her daughter's day perfect and Granny had tears in her eyes as she clung to him and kissed his cheek, leaving a pink, sticky candyfloss smear but at least her dentures stayed in her mouth.

Finally, when all goodbyes had been said, Nina climbed into the carriage, closely followed by Doggett, and with a flourish, Jubbly shut the door.

"Stop!" shouted Nina and the door flew open. "We nearly forgot," she said, dragging the Doves' basket to the door and raising the lid. One dozen white Doves who'd been cooped up all day, took to the air in an angry flurry, flapped frantically and flew off.

"Hooray!" yelled the crowd and once again, Jubbly shut the door. With a stamping of feet and jingling of bells, the knitted carriage pulled forward and the cheers grew louder.

Crispin decided to go home and finish packing. The ball would be ending in about half an hour but no one would miss him and he was desperately tired. As he walked, he replayed all the mental photos he'd taken during the ball. At least he'd had a chance to prepare himself, which was more than he'd allowed Sylvester, who knew nothing about his intended departure. He wondered if he ought to tell Sylvester when he got home – if he got home tonight. Crispin sighed. He definitely couldn't leave without saying goodbye to Sylvester. But suppose he didn't get home until after everyone was up tomorrow? Crispin had to steal out of the Garden without anyone seeing him or he'd surely be stopped.

Finally, he decided to write Sylvester a letter in case he didn't come home before Crispin left in the morning and it might be nice to leave a small photo of himself too. Would Euclid have stopped skipping? Crispin doubted it. There were still ten minutes to midnight and Euclid desperately wanted the Garden skipping record.

Crispin turned around and went back to the Gazebo. He slipped into the photo booth and smiled at the hidden camera.

"Yes, you can!" shouted Mr Lambert, trembling with fatigue and emotion. He fluttered his wings, sending a shower of silver dust swirling down onto Bella. Still, she hovered some way from the photo booth. Bella had gone straight home after the group shots in the clearing, slipping away unseen while everyone watched the fireworks. It was too painful to see the loud bridesmaid with Crispin and she couldn't bear the thought of them dancing together at the ball. Still dressed in her costume, she sat at home wishing things had been different. Wishing she'd not been so naïve at the New Year's Ball and wishing she was the one in Crispin's arms tonight.

Mr Lambert thought his heart would break too. She looked so lovely in her midnight blue dress with silver trim and filigree silver mask. She'd sprinkled him with silver dust and when he sat in her hair, he shimmered when his wings trembled. He couldn't believe that anyone would prefer that loud-mouthed bridesmaid to a beautiful Angel. Bella was perfection. He called Crispin all the dreadful names he could think of, made up a few new ones and imagined what he would do to him the next time he saw him. And then it occurred to him there was no time like the present. Bella's hair had fallen over her face while she cried, and she no longer needed him to hold her fringe back. He flew out of the window towards the ball to seek out the one who'd rejected his beautiful Bella. How fortunate that when he arrived, the Elf was standing on his own in front of the Gazebo. The loud hussy was walking away from him but the Elf made no attempt to follow. In fact, Mr Lambert was struck by his expression. He looked as sad and lovelorn as his Bella. Hovering above the Elf's head, he was just in time to hear Crispin's softly spoken love declaration for Bella. Could it be true? It certainly looked like it was. Overjoyed, he'd flown home at top speed, losing most of his silver dust on the way and he relayed the wonderful news to Bella.

"Are you sure, Mr Lambert?" she'd asked, her sad eyes full of hope. He'd nodded and urged her to dry her tears and go to the ball but by the time they'd arrived, the newlyweds had left and Crispin was nowhere to be found. Bella sat silently on a tree stump. She was past crying.

Mr Lambert was distraught. He couldn't believe his efforts had been in vain but the Elf definitely wasn't there. It was time to give up. He fluttered gently in front of her urging her to get up and follow him home, comforting her with talk of finding Crispin tomorrow.

Bella stood, a figure of dejection, but before she turned to make her way home, she gasped and pointed.

"Mr Lambert," she said excitedly, "I think that's him… Isn't it?… It is him, isn't it? He's going into the photo booth. Ooh, Mr Lambert, Mr Lambert, shall I follow?"

"Yes, yes!" squeaked Mr Lambert. "Quickly before he disappears again."

And she'd run to the photo booth but now, she hovered uncertainly outside.

"I'm not sure I can, Mr Lambert," she whispered.

"Yes, you can!" he shouted again and to his relief,

she gently drew back the curtain and slipped inside. There was a terrific flash, which seared Mr Lambert's eyeballs.

Crispin couldn't believe it. He'd arranged his features into what he thought was a friendly, yet wise sort of smile – the way he wanted Sylvester to remember him. He held his breath, ready for the automatic photographs to be taken, when suddenly, the curtain opened and Bella – his Bella – was beside him.

"I didn't think I'd ever see you again," he said, taking her in his arms.

"Nor I, you," she said holding him tightly.

The photo booth flashed four times but neither Elf nor Angel noticed; they were too busy staring into each other's eyes.

It was many hours before the couple emerged hand in hand from the photo booth. There had been so much to talk about. Mr Lambert had satisfied himself that all was well and had then flown home to bed. The tap, tap of Euclid's tiny feet had long finished and the Gazebo was in darkness. Only Frank Fowle hadn't made it home after the ball and he was snoring on his back outside the closed Gazebo door as if still providing "Seucrity".

Crispin and Bella walked with arms entwined to the Alpine Garden, where almost twenty-four hours ago, Doggett and Nina had shared a special prenuptial sunrise. And now another couple would watch the dawn break over the Garden.

Later, they would share breakfast and Crispin would unpack the rucksack waiting for him in the wardrobe. There was no one he'd rather spend the rest of his life with than Bella.

And nowhere other than the Garden, that he wanted to be.

About the Author

Dawn spent much of her childhood making up stories filled with romance, drama and excitement. She loved fairy tales, although if she cast herself as a character, she'd more likely have played the part of the Court Jester than the Princess. She didn't recognise it at the time, but she was searching for the emotional depth in the stories she read. It wasn't enough to be told the prince loved the princess, she wanted to know how he felt and to see him declare his love. She wanted to see the wedding. And so, she'd furnish her stories with those details.

Nowadays, she hopes to write books that will engage readers' passions. From poignant stories set during the First World War, to the zany antics of the inhabitants of the fictitious town of Basilwade; and from historical romances, to the fantasy adventures of a group of anthropomorphic animals led by a chicken with delusions of grandeur, she explores the richness and depth of human emotion.

A book by Dawn will offer laughter or tears – or anything in between. But if she touches your soul, she'll consider her job well done.

You can follow her here: https://dawnknox.com
Facebook:: www.facebook.com/DawnKnoxWriter
Twitter: https://twitter.com/SunriseCalls

Like to Read More Work Like This?

Then sign up to our mailing list and download our free collection of short stories, *Magnetism*. Sign up now to receive this free e-book and also to find out about all of our new publications and offers.

Sign up here:
http://eepurl.com/gbpdVz

Please Leave a Review

Reviews are so important to writers. Please take the time to review this book. A couple of lines is fine.

Reviews help the book to become more visible to buyers. Retailers will promote books with multiple reviews.

This in turn helps us to sell more books… And then we can afford to publish more books like this one.

Leaving a review is very easy.

Go to https://smarturl.it/dcz4fu, scroll down the left-hand side of the Amazon page and click on the "Write a customer review" button.

Other Writing by Dawn Knox

The Basilwade Chronicles

Published by Chapeltown

The Basilwade stories were originally published on the CaféLit website, where you can access short stories that go nicely with a cuppa. We even suggest a drink! Dawn Knox's stories contain characters and situations that may seem a little larger than life at first glance but we can soon see that everyone involved is very human. And don't we all recognise the quirkiness of village/small-town life?.

"It's been a long time since I spent so much of my time laughing while reading a book. Endlessly inventive, crackling jokes, no two characters alike. And every story ends, not with a cliffhanger or a hook into the next one, but the eager need to answer the question, 'NOW WHAT HAPPENS?'

If Basilwade doesn't actually exist somewhere, it thoroughly deserves to!" (*Amazon*)

Order from Amazon:

Paperback: ISBN 978-1-910542-49-1
eBook: ISBN 978-1-910542-47-7

Chapeltown Books

The Macaroon Chronicles

Published by Chapeltown

The Macaroon Chronicles is a romp through relationships amongst some anthropomorphic characters. It is one of those quirky books that awakes your sense of humour. Come and follow the fun.Take a tour of the exotic Isle of Macaroon with Eddie and his zany friends who will be pleased to show you the cheese mines, Meringue Mountains and the Custard River while they flee unscrupulous promoters, bandit badgers and low-flying seagulls.

"This book is a joyous romp through absurdity, where the characters are all animals, the scenery is mostly edible and the events propel the action at breakneck speed. It's not Animal Farm, but a more gentle look at the everyday emotions of a group of friends battling their way through life. Not to be missed." (*Amazon*)

Order from Amazon:

Paperback: ISBN 978-1-910542-60-6
eBook: ISBN 978-1-910542-61-3

Chapeltown Books

Extraordinary

Published by Bridge House

From the furthest reaches of the universe, to the inside of a cardboard box, assorted characters play deadly games with their victims while others play practical jokes on angels or dirty tricks on aliens. Some have good intentions, others are scoundrels and a few are truly evil – but all of them are EXTRAORDINARY.

"A wonderful collection of amazing stories. An enjoyable read."
(*Amazon*)

Order from Amazon:

Paperback: ISBN 978-1-907335-51-8
eBook: ISBN 978-1-907335-52-5

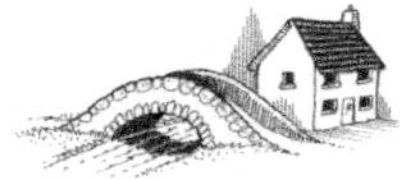

The Great War

Published by CreateSpace

One hundred short stories of ordinary men and women caught up in the extraordinary events of the Great War – a time of bloodshed, horror and heartache.

One hundred stories, each told in exactly one hundred words, written one hundred years after they might have taken place. Life between the years of 1914 and 1918 presented a challenge for those fighting on the Front, as well as for those who were left at home – regardless of where that home might have been. These stories are an attempt to glimpse into the world of everyday people who were dealing with tragedies and life-changing events on such a scale that it was unprecedented in human history.

"I love this little book; it's like snippets of our history told by someone who wanted to get the facts and feelings right for the time." (*Amazon*)

Order from Amazon:

Paperback: ISBN 978-1-532961-59-5
eBook: ASIN B01FFRN7FW

The Future Brokers

with Colin Payn

It's 2050 and George Williams considers himself a lucky man. It's a year since he – like millions of others – was forced out of his job by Artificial Intelligence. And a year since his near-fatal accident. But now, George's prospects are on the way up. With a state-of-the-art prosthetic arm and his sight restored, he's head-hunted to join a secret Government department – George cannot believe his luck.

He is right not to believe it. George's attraction to his beautiful boss, Serena, falters when he discovers her role in his sudden good fortune, and her intention to exploit the newly-acquired abilities he'd feared were the start of a mental breakdown. But, it turns out both George and Serena are being twitched by a greater puppet master and ultimately, they must decide whose side they're on – those who want to combat Climate-Armageddon or the powerful leaders of the human race.

"This book held my attention to the end and after the end. How will the world finish up? A great collaborative novel where you can't see the join!" (*Amazon*)

Order from Amazon:

Paperback: ISBN 979-8-723077-67-6
eBook: ASIN B08Z9QYH5F

Printed in Great Britain
by Amazon

79788450R00183